西方文学前沿

Frontiers of Western Literature

主　编　龙　云
副主编　周　春
编　者　刘馨茜　郑　澈　黄　敏
　　　　张　娟　刘齐平

南京大学出版社

图书在版编目(CIP)数据

西方文学前沿 = Frontiers of Western Literature：
英文 / 龙云主编. —— 南京：南京大学出版社，2022.3
ISBN 978-7-305-25120-7

Ⅰ. ①西… Ⅱ. ①龙… Ⅲ. ①外国文学－文学研究－
教材－英文 Ⅳ. ①I106

中国版本图书馆 CIP 数据核字(2021)第 235825 号

出版发行　南京大学出版社
社　　址　南京市汉口路22号　　　邮　编　210093
出 版 人　金鑫荣

书　　名　西方文学前沿
　　　　　Frontiers of Western Literature
主　编　　龙　云
责任编辑　裴维维　　　　　　　　编辑热线　025-83592123
照　　排　南京南琳图文制作有限公司
印　　刷　丹阳兴华印务有限公司
开　　本　787×1092　1/16　印张 13.5　字数 390 千
版　　次　2022 年 3 月第 1 版　2022 年 3 月第 1 次印刷
ISBN 978-7-305-25120-7
定　　价　43.00 元

网址：http://www.njupco.com
官方微博：http://weibo.com/njupco
官方微信号：njupress
销售咨询热线：(025) 83594756

✓ 课件申请
✓ 拓展资源

* 版权所有，侵权必究
* 凡购买南大版图书，如有印装质量问题，请与所购
　图书销售部门联系调换

前　言

为了更好推进新文科建设的创新发展，高校英语专业的文学课程改革势在必行。在夯实建设经典文学课程的基础上，高校还要思考如何来创新文学课程，从教学内容和教学模式上赋予文学课程新的生命力，使其真正"活"起来，走进学生的生活，从而更好地提升学生的思辨能力和研究能力。"西方文学前沿"课程的开设旨在帮助学生开拓学术视野，提升人文情怀，指导学生从传统经典中探索新视角，从现代经典中思考新问题。

一、使用对象

本教材是为提高高校英语专业学生文本阅读、文本赏析和文学研究能力而编写的课程教材。本教材适用于高校英语专业本科高年级文学类课程或者英语专业研究生文学选修课程，也适合对西方文学作品感兴趣的自学者使用。

二、编写原则和特点

本教材的编写坚持"前言视角、经典新解"的原则，所选的文章都是能够彰显作品流派、作家特色、多元主题、时代热点的代表性作品。课后问题在编排设计上力争能够指导学生透过文本表象来深入探讨作品的深刻内涵和时代意义，同时注重激发学生通过联系、比较来客观评判作品，具有启发性和思辨性相结合的特点。

三、教材构成

本教材包含十个单元，每个单元包括作家介绍、主题介绍、前沿论题、作品选段和问题理解五个部分。通过本书的学习，学生可以掌握不同时期、不同国家的作家生平、作品主题、思想内涵。本教材旨在培养学生在多重视角和语境下挖掘文本新内涵的研究能力，同时对于多样题材的西方文学经典的创作特色、源流和时代影响形成大致的了解。

教师和学习者可根据教学进度和兴趣特点对本教材的内容安排进行适当调整和有选择地使用。在本教材的编写过程中，参考了国内外出版的相关书籍，编者在此深表感谢。本教材第一单元由黄敏编写；第二单元由刘馨茜和张娟编写；第三单元由刘馨茜编写；第四、八、九单元由周春编写；第五、六单元由龙云编写；第七单元由郑澈编写；第十单元由刘齐平编写。张涵、张紫月、李文慧参与文字校对。由于编者水平有限，书中错误和不足之处在所难免，敬请大家不吝批评指正。

龙云
2022 年 1 月于北京

Contents

Unit 1   James Joyce: "Araby" ··· 1

Unit 2   Stendhal: *The Red and the Black* ······························· 11

Unit 3   Gustave Flaubert: *Madame Bovary* ····························· 21

Unit 4   Leo Tolstoy: *War and Peace* ······································ 33

Unit 5   Hermann Hesse: *Demian* ·· 56

Unit 6   Nevil Shute Norway: *A Town Like Alice* ······················· 78

Unit 7   John Robert Fowles: *The French Lieutenant's Woman* ······ 107

Unit 8   Alice Walker: *The Color Purple* ·································· 120

Unit 9   Toni Morrison: *Song of Solomon* ································ 143

Unit 10 Amy Tan: *The Kitchen God's Wife* ···························· 180

Unit 1

James Joyce: "Araby"

 James Joyce, one of the most celebrated authors in English literature, was born in February 1882 in Dublin, Ireland. The family was a traditional Irish one, a large family of 10 kids with Joyce as the eldest son. Joyce was sent to a boarding school for education. But when financial condition of the family worsened, he did not go back to school. Instead, he stayed at home and tried to teach himself. Later he went to a grammar school and did very well in his studies.

 Joyce's dissatisfaction with the Roman Catholic atmosphere began even before he entered college. Although he studied well and was favored by teachers and admired by fellow students, it was apparent that he was losing his Catholic faith. At University College Dublin, Joyce did not wait for the priests to lead him through his readings. He was particularly interested in the books that did not have a Catholic inclination. Joyce was also an active participant in the literary and historical activities on campus. He wrote articles and reviews, and published them in his college years.

 As a serious reader, Joyce persisted in writing and worked towards his ambition of becoming a writer. While taking up various jobs, Joyce wrote on his own and published a few stories in 1904 that later appeared in his short stories collection *Dubliners*. In the meantime, he decided to leave Ireland and persuaded his partner Nora Barnacle, who was to become his wife, to go with him.

 The years James Joyce spent on European continent were not immediately rewarding. Again, Joyce had to work at different places for a living. Despite all this, he was making a progress with his story writing. More short stories were formulated for *Dubliners* as Joyce obtained an aesthetic distance from his homeland, and started to think from various angles upon Irish culture and personality. A longer story, *A Portrait of the Artist as a Young Man*, was also written in these years by blending some of his early experiences and unpublished materials.

In 1909, Joyce had tried to visit Ireland, with an aim of seeking publication for his books. However, the visits brought him no good news. He left the country with frustration and dismay, and had never regained optimism from Ireland. In 1914, Joyce finally had his first book, *Dubliners*, published in serial form.

Joyce moved his family to Zurich during World War Ⅰ. He was able to attract the attention from Harriet Shaw Weaver, editor of the *Egoist* magazine, whose substantial grants supported him through his physical and financial troubles. *A Portrait of the Artist as a Young Man* at last saw print in 1916. It was during the war years that Joyce worked on his masterpiece *Ulysses*, with some episodes of the story published in American *Little Review*. When the war ended, Joyce went to Paris and stayed there for 20 years. *Ulysses* was published in 1922; and in 1939 his last book *Finnegans Wake* came out. The Second World War forced Joyce to return to Zurich, where he died in February 1941.

Dubliners, the book published in 1914, exemplified both traditional and modern elements in Joyce's career as a writer. For one thing, it demonstrates that Joyce followed the then popular, traditional narrative when he wrote his first stories. The highly-modernist experimentation with stream-of-consciousness and word play had not yet begun. For another, Joyce did choose the average, middle class personalities to present the insignificant and less-than-ordinary everyday life. This preference for triviality and vacancy of meaning that life offers is a common trait of modern texts. What's more, Joyce's adept treatment of the loneliness of individuals, the suppression of desires as well as the constant frustrations in life becomes eloquent and symbolic, not only of the people in Ireland who struggled for their Irish identity, but also of people in modern age who are trapped, lost and yet fighting a way through their helplessness.

Dubliners is a short stories collection that marked the early success of James Joyce. With a total of 15 stories, *Dubliners* depicted people, professions, and circumstances against the city Dublin. The stories show an interesting pattern as readers open the book to read from the first story "The Sisters" to the last one "The Dead." The book begins with the childhood episodes, moves through chapters in adolescence and young adulthood, and finally reaches more mature experiences of middle-aged men and women. The word "chronological" can, in some way, describe the progression of the story.

Yet, there is no central hero or heroine in *Dubliners*. Each story has its own protagonist. For example, "An encounter" tells two boys skipping classes for fun in the city but frightened away by a strange old man, a child molester. In "Eveline," the heroine wants to elope from her suffocating home but eventually fails to do so. The hero in "A Little Cloud" has dinner with his friends, and comes back feeling frustrated as he reflects on his past ambitions and present mundane life. In the longest, also the last story "The Dead," a couple goes to a Christmas party, meets friends and has a good time. But the end of the party brings back tender, sad memories of someone dead and gone.

"Araby" is the third story in the book and one of the most frequently anthologized short stories. The story is told by a young boy, whose name readers never get to know, but whose perception readers follow all through the story. The boy attends the Christian Brothers' School, becomes attracted to a girl in his neighborhood and promises to go to a bazaar Araby to bring her gifts. Much of the story is taken up by tedious, prolonged waiting time before the boy goes to the bazaar. When he finally goes to Araby, it is very late at night and the bazaar is almost empty. It is at this time and place that boy suddenly obtains some strange awakening.

Theme

One of the most important and most obvious themes in "Araby" is the frustration of young love. The boy, who is also the narrator "I," tells his crush on a young woman, Mangan's sister. His obsession with her becomes quite an impact on his life. The daily routine revolves around his wishes to see her. He peeps through the window every morning, and catches up with her on the way to school. Even the Saturday shopping is different as he muses on his love, imagining himself as a warrior. Then, a turning point comes when Mangan's sister talks to him, speaking of a certain bazaar Araby. The boy, in confused adoration, promises to go and bring her gifts.

The latter part of the story describes the boy's eagerness to go to Araby. He ignores schoolwork and is impatient on Saturday evening. When he does get the chance to go, he discovers himself on an almost empty train and arrives at a strange, desolate hall. Araby is closing. The boy listens to casual conversations of the vendors, and walks out of Araby feeling anguished and angry.

The reason for the boy's feeling at the end of the story is that he obtains an epiphany, a sudden awakening. He realizes that Mangan's sister has not meant anything serious when she talks to him, that he only tricks himself when he thinks that he is in love. The boy's blindness in his infatuation becomes a self-deceptive dream. He ignores his friends, his duties in school. He also fails to catch the girl's genuine intention. He builds upon his dream of Mangan's sister, and has fought to retain the dream as far as possible, until it breaks down and he feels humiliated and frustrated.

Cutting-edge Topic

"Araby" takes the theme of unfulfilled love and molds it in a modern context. A traditional type of rendering this very theme would be to recall one's first love with fondness and melancholy, as a part of the good old days. Yet Joyce presents none of this sentiment in the story. Instead, he breaks through the charm of love and finds love an illusion, which in a modern context, becomes an isolation.

The illusion has been suggested repeatedly in the story. To start with, love in "Araby" develops in a most unromantic setting. There were uninhabited houses and a dead priest, muddy lanes and dark dripping gardens, unlikely places for a romance. The naturalistic, cold note on which the neighborhood is presented carries a hint of unpleasantness for the reader. Joyce has done it on purpose, and he will see this unpleasantness runs through the story.

The next thing readers notice is the boy's feverish admiration of Mangan's sister, something bordering on idolatry. In addition to watching her movements, he thinks about her all the time, trembles, murmurs her name and makes quick promises. As to what has inflamed his passion, the story refuses to give an idea. So the reader's discomfort continues as a result of watching the boy isolating himself in a dreamy, fervent adoration.

The boy's obsession is broken in Araby, the bazaar he has wanted to go very much. But even before that, the frustrations the boy has gone through have given him some unnamed confusion as to why he has suffered so much for it. He remembers "with difficulty" why he has come. When the light goes out in the upper part of the hall, the boy is disillusioned. He feels ridiculed by his dream, and by himself.

The idea of isolation, or to use a modernist term, alienation, runs through "Araby." The houses and the lanes are not inspiring. The other characters seem to live in their own world as well. Mangan's sister, the girl the boy is in love with, speaks to him only once and does not give a thought to his promises. Even the vendors at the bazaar, those who are supposed to love having customers, do not appear interested in meeting the boy. Everyone is taken up with his own business, as the boy is consumed in his fantasy of love.

Joyce is relentless in presenting a city going downhill in the modern context. The minds of people in *Dubliners*, like the mind of the boy, are entrapped in something they long for but could not reach. In the meantime, their obsession alienates them from one another. "Araby" typifies this disconnectedness in an ordinary boy, in the boy's failure to concentrate on his duty at school, and in a family in which aunt and uncle have no real concern for the boy's feeling. It is a modern life in division and defeat. Such is the picture Joyce observed at the beginning of the 20th century.

Text

Araby

North Richmond Street, being blind, was a quiet street except at the hour when the Christian Brothers' School set the boys free. An uninhabited house of two storeys stood at the blind end, detached from its neighbours in a square ground. The other houses of the street, conscious of decent lives within them, gazed at one another with brown imperturbable faces.

The former tenant of our house, a priest, had died in the back drawing-room. Air, musty from having been long enclosed, hung in all the rooms, and the waste room behind the kitchen was littered with old useless papers. Among these I found a few paper-covered books, the pages of which were curled and damp: *The Abbot*, by Walter Scott, *The Devout Communicant*, and *The Memoirs of Vidocq*. I liked the last best because its leaves were yellow. The wild garden behind the house contained a central apple-tree and a few straggling bushes, under one of which I found the late tenant's rusty bicycle-pump. He had been a very charitable priest; in his will he had left all his money to institutions and the furniture of his house to his sister.

When the short days of winter came, dusk fell before we had well eaten our dinners. When we met in the street the houses had grown sombre. The space of sky above us was the colour of ever-changing violet and towards it the lamps of the street lifted their feeble lanterns. The cold air stung us and we played till our bodies glowed. Our shouts echoed in the silent street. The career of our play brought us through the dark muddy lanes behind the houses, where we ran the gauntlet of the rough tribes from the cottages, to the back doors of the dark dripping gardens where odours arose from the ashpits, to the dark odorous stables where a coachman smoothed and combed the horse or shook music from the buckled harness. When we returned to the street, light from the kitchen windows had filled the areas. If my uncle was seen turning the corner, we hid in the shadow until we had seen him safely housed. Or if Mangan's sister came out on the doorstep to call her brother in to his tea, we watched her from our shadow peer up and down the street. We waited to see whether she would remain or go in and, if she remained, we left our shadow and walked up to Mangan's steps resignedly. She was waiting for us, her figure defined by the light from the half-opened door. Her brother always teased her before he obeyed, and I stood by the railings looking at her. Her dress swung as she moved her body, and the soft rope of her hair tossed from side to side.

Every morning I lay on the floor in the front parlour watching her door. The blind was pulled down to within an inch of the sash so that I could not be seen. When she came out on the doorstep my heart leaped. I ran to the hall, seized my books and followed her. I kept her brown figure always in my eye and, when we came near the point at which our ways diverged, I quickened my pace and passed her. This happened morning after morning. I had never spoken to her, except for a few casual words, and yet her name was like a summons to all my foolish blood.

Her image accompanied me even in places the most hostile to romance. On Saturday evenings when my aunt went marketing I had to go to carry some of the parcels. We walked through the flaring streets, jostled by drunken men and bargaining women, amid the curses of labourers, the shrill litanies of shop-boys who stood on guard by the barrels of pigs' cheeks, the nasal chanting of street-singers, who sang a *come-all-you* about O'Donovan Rossa, or a ballad about the troubles in our native land. These noises converged in a single sensation of life for me: I imagined that I bore my chalice safely through a throng of foes. Her name sprang to my lips at moments in strange prayers and praises which I myself did not understand. My eyes were often full of tears (I could not tell why) and at times a flood from my heart seemed to pour itself out into my bosom. I thought little of the future. I did not know whether I would ever speak to her or not or, if I spoke to her, how I could tell her of my confused adoration. But my body was like a harp and her words and gestures were like fingers running upon the wires.

One evening I went into the back drawing-room in which the priest had died. It was a dark rainy evening and there was no sound in the house. Through one of the broken panes I heard the rain impinge upon the earth, the fine incessant needles of water playing in the sodden beds. Some distant lamp or lighted window gleamed below me. I was thankful that I could see so little. All my senses seemed to desire to veil themselves and, feeling that I was about to slip from them, I pressed the palms of my hands together until they trembled, murmuring: "*O love! O love!*" many times.

At last she spoke to me. When she addressed the first words to me I was so confused that I did not know what to answer. She asked me was I going to *Araby*. I forgot whether I answered yes or no. It would be a splendid bazaar; she said she would love to go.

"And why can't you?" I asked.

While she spoke, she turned a silver bracelet round and round her wrist. She could not go, she said, because there would be a retreat that week in her convent. Her brother and two other boys were fighting for their caps, and I was alone at the railings. She held one of the spikes, bowing her head towards me. The light from the lamp opposite our door caught the white curve of her neck, lit up her hair that rested there and, falling, lit up the hand upon the railing. It fell over one side of her dress and caught the white border of a petticoat, just visible as she stood at ease.

"It's well for you," she said.

"If I go," I said, "I will bring you something."

What innumerable follies laid waste my waking and sleeping thoughts after that evening! I wished to annihilate the tedious intervening days. I chafed against the work of school. At night in my bedroom and by day in the classroom her image came between me and the page I strove to read. The syllables of the word *Araby* were called to me through the silence in which my soul luxuriated and cast an Eastern enchantment over me. I asked for leave to go to the bazaar on Saturday night. My aunt was surprised, and hoped it was not some Freemason affair. I answered few questions in class. I watched my master's face pass from amiability to sternness; he hoped I was not beginning to idle. I could not call my wandering thoughts together. I had hardly any patience with the serious work of life which, now that it stood between me and my desire, seemed to me child's play, ugly monotonous child's play.

On Saturday morning I reminded my uncle that I wished to go to the bazaar in the evening. He was fussing at the hallstand, looking for the hat-brush, and answered me curtly:

"Yes, boy, I know."

As he was in the hall I could not go into the front parlour and lie at the window. I left the house in bad humour and walked slowly towards the school. The air was pitilessly raw and already my heart misgave me.

When I came home to dinner my uncle had not yet been home. Still it was early. I sat staring at the clock for some time and, when its ticking began to irritate me, I left the room. I mounted the staircase and gained the upper part of the house. The high, cold, empty, gloomy rooms liberated me and I went from room to room singing. From the front window I saw my companions playing below in the street. Their cries reached me weakened and indistinct and, leaning my forehead against the cool glass, I looked over at the dark house where she lived. I may have stood there for an hour, seeing nothing but the brown-clad figure cast by my imagination, touched discreetly by the lamplight at the curved neck, at the hand upon the railings and at the border below the dress.

When I came downstairs again I found Mrs. Mercer sitting at the fire. She was an old, garrulous woman, a pawnbroker's widow, who collected used stamps for some pious purpose. I had to endure the gossip of the tea-table. The meal was prolonged beyond an hour and still my uncle did not come. Mrs. Mercer stood up to go: she was sorry she couldn't wait any longer, but it was after eight o'clock and she did not like to be out late, as the night air was bad for her. When she had gone I began to walk up and down the room, clenching my fists. My aunt said:

"I'm afraid you may put off your bazaar for this night of Our Lord."

At nine o'clock I heard my uncle's latchkey in the hall door. I heard him talking to himself and heard the hallstand rocking when it had received the weight of his overcoat. I could interpret these signs. When he was midway through his dinner I asked him to give me the money to go to the bazaar. He had forgotten.

"The people are in bed and after their first sleep now," he said.

I did not smile. My aunt said to him energetically:

"Can't you give him the money and let him go? You've kept him late enough as it is."

My uncle said he was very sorry he had forgotten. He said he believed in the old saying: "All work and no play makes Jack a dull boy." He asked me where I was going and, when I told him a second time, he asked me did I know *The Arab's Farewell to His Steed*. When I left the kitchen he was about to recite the opening lines of the piece to my aunt.

I held a florin tightly in my hand as I strode down Buckingham Street towards the station. The sight of the streets thronged with buyers and glaring with gas recalled to me the purpose of my journey. I took my seat in a third-class carriage of a deserted train. After an intolerable delay the train moved out of the station slowly. It crept onward among ruinous houses and over the twinkling river. At Westland Row Station a crowd of people pressed to the carriage doors; but the porters moved them back, saying that it was a special train for the bazaar. I remained alone in the bare carriage. In a few minutes the train drew up beside an improvised wooden platform. I passed out on to the road and saw by the lighted dial of a clock that it was ten minutes to ten. In front of me was a large building which displayed the magical name.

I could not find any sixpenny entrance and, fearing that the bazaar would be closed, I passed in quickly through a turnstile, handing a shilling to a weary-looking man. I found myself in a big hall girded at half its height by a gallery. Nearly all the stalls were closed and the greater part of the hall was in darkness. I recognized a silence like that which pervades a church after a service. I walked into the center of the bazaar timidly. A few people were gathered about the stalls which were still open. Before a curtain, over which the words *Café Chantant* were written in coloured lamps, two men were counting money on a salver. I listened to the fall of the coins.

Remembering with difficulty why I had come, I went over to one of the stalls and examined porcelain vases and flowered tea-sets. At the door of the stall a young lady was talking and laughing with two young gentlemen. I remarked their English accents and listened vaguely to their conversation.

"O, I never said such a thing!"

"O, but you did!"

"O, but I didn't!"

"Didn't she say that?"

"Yes. I heard her."

"O, there's a ... fib!"

Observing me, the young lady came over and asked me did I wish to buy anything. The tone of her voice was not encouraging; she seemed to have spoken to me out of a sense of duty. I looked humbly at the great jars that stood like eastern guards at either side of the dark entrance to the stall and murmured:

"No, thank you."

The young lady changed the position of one of the vases and went back to the two young men. They began to talk of the same subject. Once or twice the young lady glanced at me over her shoulder.

I lingered before her stall, though I knew my stay was useless, to make my interest in her wares seem the more real. Then I turned away slowly and walked down the middle of the bazaar. I allowed the two pennies to fall against the sixpence in my pocket. I heard a voice call from one end of the gallery that the light was out. The upper part of the hall was now completely dark.

Gazing up into the darkness I saw myself as a creature driven and derided by vanity; and my eyes burned with anguish and anger.

（选自 Joyce, James. *Dubliners*. Beijing: Beijing World Publishing Corporation, 1995: 30 - 35.）

Questions

1. Why does the opening of the story mention a dead priest, his room and books?
2. The story describes in detail the Saturday on which the boy is to visit Araby, from morning to evening. What do you think is the function of such a detailed description?
3. Examine two conversations, the conversation between the boy and Mangan's sister, and the conversation at the end. What messages do the conversations carry?
4. What symbols have been used to represent the boy's love?
5. In addition to examples discussed in "Cutting-edge topic," what other evidences could you find in the story that carry the idea of isolation?

Unit 2

Stendhal: *The Red and the Black*

  Stendhal (pseudonym of Marie-Henri Beyle) was born in 1783 into a respectable, middle-class family. Stendhal's father was an industrious, narrow-minded bourgeois. He detested his father. He loved his mother tenderly, but this delightful woman, died when he was only seven. Of a fiery and rebellious nature, Stendhal declared himself early to be an atheist or liberal—an expression of revolt.

  Stendhal studied at the Ecole Centrale in Grenoble when he was young until 1799. He excelled in mathematics and art. Then, he went to Paris, and securing a commission in the army, stayed briefly in Italy, a country he came to love above France. Back in Paris, Stendhal resigned from the army, and from 1802 until 1806, he studied the eighteenth-century materialistic philosophy. He aspired to become a playwright but failed. A relative of his obtained for Stendhal an administrative position in the army that took him to Germany, with periodic trips back to Paris. In 1812, he participated in Napoleon's Russian retreat. Following Napoleon's fall in 1814, Stendhal retired permanently from the army and settled in Milan, where he began to write in earnest. He soon produced *Lives of Haydn, Mozart, and Metastasio* (1814), followed by the two-volume *History of Painting in Italy* (1817). His next book—a travel guide entitled *Rome, Naples, and Florence* in 1817—was the first to bear the pen name Stendhal, the most famous of the more than two hundred pseudonyms he employed in his lifetime.

  At the age of forty-four, Stendhal wrote his first novel, *Armance*, which was not well received. Turning away from the novel, Stendhal composed *Promenades dans Rome* (1829), which has been called a glorified guidebook. In this work, Stendhal exposed the concept of

relativism in esthetics, proclaiming that the concept of beauty varies from age to age and among different cultures. The realistic note that runs through Stendhal's literary endeavors stems from his need to anchor himself solidly in reality as a point of departure. Everything he wrote begins in the realm of facts.

Following the July Revolution of 1830, which brought Louis-Philippe to the throne, Stendhal returned to government service. In 1831 he was appointed consul to the port of Civitavecchia, some forty miles from Rome, where he spent many of his final years. During the 1830s Stendhal began two novels, *Lucien Leuwen* and *Lamiel*, both of which remained unfinished and were not published until long after his death. He also undertook two autobiographical works, *Memoirs of an Egotist* and *The Life of Henri Brulard*, which likewise appeared posthumously. In 1835 Stendhal was awarded the Legion of Honor for services to literature; the following year he returned to Paris on an extended leave of absence. There he started to write biography of Napoleon and completed *Memoirs of a Tourist* (1838), which is a popular travel guide to France.

Stendhal returned to his consular post in 1839 in Italy, where he began his last novel, *Lamiel*, which never to be completed. When Stendhal died in Paris in 1842, his burial in the Montmartre cemetery was attended by three faithful friends, one of whom was Mérimée. "I will be famous around 1880," Stendhal once said. This is true. He began to attract and is attracting widespread attention, and many of his previously unpublished books appeared—including *A Life of Napoleon* (1876), *Journal of Stendhal* (1888), *Lamiel* (1889), *The Life of Henri Brulard* (1890), *Memoirs of an Egotist* (1892), and *Lucien Leuwen* (1894). In the twentieth century such writers as Paul Léautaud, André Gide, and Paul Valéry have acclaimed Stendhal's work. "We should never be finished with Stendhal," said Valéry. "I can think of no greater praise than that." Stendhal had written for himself and for the "happy few," and his most appreciative audience has been that of the twentieth century.

Written in 1829 and published in 1831, *The Red and the Black*, fictionalizes an actual happening of which Stendhal had read in records of court proceedings. The historical person who served as a model for Julien Sorel was a certain Antoine Berthet, convicted of murder in December 1827. Julien is a bookish boy, son of a brutal peasant who beats him and whose family doesn't understand him, sees a way out of his situation by studying for the priesthood and taking a job as a tutor in a prosperous bourgeois family, the Rênals. During this period of time, he has an affair with Madame de Rênal, and urthers his career, learning manners and the ways of the world. He is intelligent and good-looking, the epitome of a romantic hero with his large, dark eyes and tousled curls. He has "an unshakable determination to undergo a thousand deaths rather than fail to achieve success." However, after many adventures and twists of events, things are to end tragically. Julien committed murder. During his last days in prison, Julien finds peace and happiness in his reflections and through the reunion with Madame de Rênal, who visits him daily. Julien faces death courageously.

Julien Sorel is Stendhal's greatest creation, perhaps because Stendhal himself embodied

some of the contradictions of Julien's nature. To demonstrate Julien's muddle of inexperience, romantic delusion, ambition and naïveté, pride and timidity, Stendhal betrays his own exasperation with these qualities. It is the harshness and tragedy of Julien's fate which has sealed posterity's view of Stendhal as a severe, even bitter realist rather than the romantic, which he takes pains to hide, and he emerges despite himself.

Theme

The story of Julien is narrated against a background of contemporary events, which is the novel's political and social dimensions. The novel draws attention to the circumstances of the composition of the novel and to its political implications. Stendhal conceived the novel at the end of the autocratic reign of Charles X.

Stendhal's protagonists, as projections of himself, are portrayed as being in conflict with their milieu. For instance, Julien Sorel is an outsider, a peasant, nurtured by the example of Napoleon, the army officer become emperor, who would become an aristocrat in a caste society where the equality promised by the revolution was no longer a possibility. The insuperable difficulties and obstacles are the necessary conditions of the Stendhalian heroes. Without the obstacles, his heroes would no longer be heroes. Otherwise, these people would not be worthy of analysis and portrayal. Society presents itself quite naturally in the role of the obstacle. Julien has not only the exterior world as an obstacle, but also he is likewise endowed with a contradictory nature that compounds his dilemma. His extreme sensibility, virtue, and generosity will prevent him from succeeding. He is far from being unscrupulous or calculating.

Stendhal reacted violently against the personal effusions and unbridled subjectivity of the Romanticists. He was of the opinion that even passion has its modesty. Thus, Stendhal carefully controls the expression of Julien's emotions. Julien's inner struggle is waged between ambition and a predisposition to an idyllic happiness. His conflict against society engages both aspects of his nature. Psychological study of a superior being is fused with the social and political aspects, which constitutes the artistic unity of the work. *The Red and the Black* demonstrates Stendhal's belief that art is the expression of intense emotion, presented with simplicity and directness.

Cutting-edge Topic

It's very hard and unreasonable to put labels on writers like Stendhal. They are far more complicated to be categorized as realism or romanticism. *The Red and the Black* was written and published during the heyday of French Romanticism and the novel itself and the author are in many ways "romantic." Thus, it is very natural if the work carries the features of romanticism. However, Stendhal seems to detach himself from his time, like all great writers and thinkers do. Stendhal's personal "system of happiness" shows a curious combination of romantic and realistic influences. The ideal of the system is romantic, assuming the existence

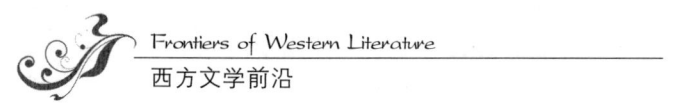

of a superior elite dedicated to the enjoyment of happiness, consisting of the combined satisfaction of the intellect, imagination, and the will.

The writer's confidence in man's ability to "systematize" happiness through experimentation seems to be optimistic. He believes that human beings are capable of doing this. Stendhal's romantic tendencies are shown in the following aspects: the cult of the superior individual in revolt against society and its ideology; the indirect presentation of himself idealized in his protagonists, indicating a basic subjectivity; the portrayal of sensitive, passionate souls in the pursuit of happiness, which is conceived by the author himself.

Stendhal seems to be a combination of romanticism and realism. His romantic traits are constantly oppressed by his traits as a realist. For instance, he is attached to contemporary reality, not only reality, and he wrote with scrupulous honesty and exactness. The antagonist of *The Red and the Black*, Julien, is what Stendhal would want to be. Many of Stendhal's characters are formed by their environment, as registered by their sensorial impressions. Stendhal portrayed and analyzed the psychological process. In this aspect, he is a writer and psychologist rolled into one. His psychological analysis of his characters is very profound. In the classical tradition, Stendhal studies man's conflicting inner life. His own hypercritical attitude toward himself leads to his treatment of his characters and he puts them to test constantly, throwing them into troubles and sufferings where their worth may be manifested. This is what makes his characters worth portraying and analyzing. His detachment from his characters results in an ironic objectivity. His style is a direct reaction to the lyrical, hyperbolic, flowery style of Romanticism.

Stendhal's language style is direct and this directness is shown in his dry and terse sentences. His language has an irregular cadence in its rapidity. His style can be said to be realistic. It is fair to say that his works communicates a direct impression of life being lived at the present moment, which is also a manifestation of his realism.

Excerpt

Chapter Twenty-Four: A Capital City

He finally saw it, set on a distant mountain; its walls were black. This was the fortress of Besançon. "What a difference for me," he said with a sigh, "if I were coming to this great military center as a second lieutenant, serving in one of the regiments sent to defend it!"

Besançon isn't simply one of the prettiest towns in France: it holds an abundance of passionate, spirited people. But Julien was only a little peasant, who had no way of approaching these distinguished men.

When he'd been at Fouqué's, he'd taken to dressing as a bourgeois, and it was thus costumed that he crossed over the drawbridges. Knowing quite well the history of the siege of 1674, he wanted to see, before he closed himself up in the seminary, the ramparts and the citadel. Two or three times, he came close to being stopped by the sentries; he got into places forbidden to the general public, on grounds of military security, but in fact so the armies could sell hay, for twelve or fifteen francs a year. The walls' great height, the depth of the surrounding ditches, the frightening appearance of the cannons, had held his attention for some hours, by the time he went past the huge café on the rampart walkway. He stood looking at it, motionless in wonder. He could quite readily read the word café, written in large letters above the two great doors; he could not believe his eyes. Shyness held him back, and then he risked going in, and found himself in a room thirty or forty feet long, with a ceiling at least twenty feet high. That day, it was all magical to him.

Two games of billiards were being played. Waiters called out the scores; the players hurried around the tables, about which spectators crowded. Billows of tobacco smoke, pouring from every mouth, wrapped them in a blue cloud. The men's height, their rounded shoulders, their heavy step, their enormous beards, the long frock coats they wore—everything attracted Julien's notice. These noble sons of ancient Besançon spoke only at the top of their lungs; they thought of themselves as terrifying warriors. Julien stood there, wondering; his mind was full of the immensity, the magnificence, of a great capital like Besançon. He did not feel entirely capable of ordering a cup of coffee, not from one of these gentlemen with their haughty looks, shouting out the billiard scores.

But the barmaid had spotted his charming face, this young bourgeois from the countryside, standing three steps from the stove, with his little bundle under his arm, contemplating a bust of the king in handsome white plaster. This tall Franche-Comté girl, with a good figure and dressed very fashionably (to enhance the café's reputation), had already twice said to him, in a soft voice meant for his ears alone, "Monsieur! Monsieur!" Julien's glance met her blue eyes, big and compassionate, and saw she'd been talking to him.

He went over to the bar, and to the pretty girl, quick-stepping exactly as he would have marched toward a hostile army. But in performing this notable maneuver, he dropped his bundle.

What pity for our country bumpkin would have sprung in the hearts of Paris high school students, who at fifteen already know how to make a polished, terribly distinguished entrance to a café. Yet these children, so eminently accomplished at fifteen, at eighteen turn common. The passionate shyness one finds in the provinces sometimes rises above itself, and then it shapes the will. Approaching this very pretty girl, who'd taken the trouble to speak to him, Julien—becoming courageous, precisely because he'd overcome shyness—thought: "I have to tell her the truth."

"Madame, I'm here in Besançon for the first time in my life. I should like to have, and to pay for, some bread and a cup of coffee."

She smiled, and then reddened: she worried that this handsome young fellow would bring down on himself, from the billiard players, sarcastic remarks and jokes. He'd be frightened and would not come again.

"Sit here, near me," she said, pointing to a marble table, almost completely hidden by the huge mahogany bar that projected out into the room.

The girl leaned down over the bar, allowing herself to show off her splendid figure. Julien noted it; all his ideas changed. The pretty girl had just set a cup in front of him, along with sugar and a roll. She was hesitating to call over a waiter, so he could have coffee, quite aware that when the waiter arrived, her tête-à-tête with Julien was going to end.

Julien was thoughtful, comparing this bright, blonde beauty with memories that frequently stirred him. Thinking of the passion he'd evoked was almost enough to drive away his shyness. The pretty girl had very little time; she understood what she saw in Julien's eyes.

"All this pipe smoke makes you cough. Come for breakfast, tomorrow morning, before eight: I'm almost always alone."

"What's your name?" said Julien, with a tender smile of happy shyness.

"Amanda Binet."

"May I send you, in an hour, a little package the size of this one?"

Lovely Amanda considered it.

"I'm watched. That could get me into trouble. All the same, I'll write my name on a card, so you put it on your package. Send it, don't worry."

"My name's Julien Sorel," said the young man. "I have neither family nor friends, here in Besançon."

"Ah! I understand," she said cheerfully. "You've come for the law school?"

"Alas, no," said Julien. "I've been sent to the seminary."

Utter dejection crossed her face. She summoned a waiter: now she had the courage. The waiter poured Julien's coffee without looking at him.

Amanda was busy at the bar, taking in money. Julien was proud of having dared to speak to her. A quarrel started, over at the billiard tables. The shouting and arguing echoed through the whole huge room, creating an uproar that astonished Julien. Amanda was sitting dreamily, her eyes lowered.

"If you like, miss," he said to her, suddenly confident, "I'll say I'm your cousin."

This touch of authority pleased her. "He's not a young nobody," she thought. Quickly, without looking at him, her eyes busily watching for people coming toward the bar, she said:

"Me, I come from Genlis, near Dijon. Say you're from Genlis, too, and you're my mother's cousin."

"Without fail," he said.

"Every Wednesday at five, during the summer, the seminarians go by, right here in front of the café."

"If you're thinking of me, as I go by, have a bouquet of violets in your hand."

She looked at him, very surprised. Her look turned his timidity to bravery, though he blushed quite deeply as he said:

"I think I already love you most passionately."

"Don't talk so loud," she told him, very frightened.

Julien tried to recall the words he'd read in a broken set of *La Nouvelle Héloïse*, which he'd found at Vergy. His memory served him well: for ten minutes he recited Rousseau to Miss Amanda, who was in raptures. He was delighted at his gallantry, when suddenly her face took on a glacial coldness. One of her lovers had just walked in.

He came over to the bar, whistling and swinging his shoulders. He glanced at Julien. Immediately, our hero's mind, always disposed to extremes, could not help brimming with thoughts of a duel. He turned very pale, shoved his cup away, set himself in a stalwart posture, and stared fixedly toward his rival. As this gentleman bent his head, leaning down on the bar and casually ordering a glass of brandy, Amanda looked at Julien, silently commanding him to turn away his eyes. He obeyed and, for two minutes, stayed as he was, pale, determined, and thinking of nothing except what was coming. At that moment, he looked resplendent. The rival had been startled by Julien's stare: tossing down his brandy, he said something to Amanda, stuck both hands in the side pockets of his long frock coat, and went toward the billiard tables, whistling and watching Julien. Our hero leaped up, wild with anger. But he did not know how to act the part of someone who's been insulted. He put down his little bundle and, strutting as well as he knew how, went toward the billiard tables.

Prudence spoke, but in vain: "Fighting a duel as soon as you get to Besançon, you throw away your career in the Church."

"Who cares? No one's going to say I put up with an insult."

Amanda saw his courage. It made a pretty contrast to the naïveté of his behaviour. In a flash, she chose him over the tall young man in his frock coat. She got up and, acting as if she were looking at someone going by, out on the street, she quickly got herself between him and the billiard tables.

"Be careful with this gentleman. He's my brother-in-law."

"Who cares? He was looking at me."

"Do you want to make me miserable? Sure, he was looking at you, he may even have been thinking of coming over and talking to you. I told him you were my mother's cousin, just arrived from Genlis. He's a Franche-Comté hick who's never been anywhere past Dôle, on the road to Burgundy, so you can tell him anything you like and never worry about a thing."

Julien still hesitated. She quickly added, drawing on her barmaid's wit to supply all the lies she needed:

"Sure, he looked at you, but that was when he was asking who you were. This is a man who's rude to everyone: he didn't mean to insult you."

Julien was watching the fake brother-in-law. He saw him buying a number at the table where the most energetic billiard game was going on. He heard his coarse voice crying, in menacing tones, "It's my turn!" He stepped swiftly around Miss Amanda and took a step toward the billiard table. Amanda gripped him by the arm.

"First pay me," she said.

"That's fair," thought Julien. "She's afraid I'll leave without paying." Amanda was quite as excited as he was, and very red in the face. She gave him his change as slowly as she could, and kept repeating, in a soft voice:

"Get out of the café right away, or I'm finished with you, no matter how much you love me."

Julien did leave, but very slowly. "Isn't it my duty," he kept asking himself, "to take my turn and walk over, whistling, and stare at this rude fellow?" His doubts kept him on the street, in front of the café, for an entire hour, watching everyone who came out. The rude fellow did not appear, and Julien left.

He'd been in Besançon for no more than a few hours, and he'd already mastered one of his qualms. In spite of his gout, the old surgeon-major, once upon a time, had given him a few fencing lessons; that was the only knowledge Julien possessed, of which his anger could make any use. But that difficulty would not have mattered, had he known how to show his anger except by striking out with his hands—and, if it had come to a fistfight, his rival, an enormous man, would have thrashed him and left him lying flat on the floor.

"For a poor devil like me," Julien said to himself, "without protectors and without money, there won't be much difference between a seminary and a prison. I've got to store my clothing in an inn, where I can change into my black clothing. If I ever get to leave the seminary for an hour or two, I might very well—wearing my bourgeois clothes—get to see Miss Amanda again." It was all very logical, but Julien walked by every inn he saw, not daring to enter any of them.

At last, when he went by the Ambassador Hotel for the second time, his worried glance met that of a fat woman, still fairly young, very red-faced, who seemed cheerful and pleasant. He went over to her and told his story.

"Of course, my handsome little priest," she told him, "I'll hold on to your bourgeois clothes, and I'll even keep them well dusted. At this time of year, it's not a good idea to leave clothes untouched." She took down a key and personally conducted him to a room, suggesting he make a list of what he was leaving.

"Good Lord! How fine you look like that, Father Sorel," said the fat woman when he came down to the kitchen. "I'm going to give you a good dinner. And," she added in a soft voice, "it's only going to cost you twenty pence, instead of the fifty everyone else has to pay, because we really have to be nice to that little purse of yours."

"I've got two hundred francs," said Julien rather proudly.

"Ah, my God!" said the good lady, startled. "Don't talk so loud: there are lots of bad eggs in Besançon. They'd rob you of that in no time at all. Stay out of the cafés, especially: they're full of crooks."

"Really!" said Julien, her words giving him something to think about.

"Don't ever go anywhere but right here; I'll make you coffee. Remember, this is where you'll always find yourself a friend and a good dinner, and for twenty pence; that's saying something, it seems to me. Right? Now go sit down at the table, and I'll serve you myself."

"I couldn't eat a thing," Julien told her. "I'm too nervous. When I leave here, I'll go right to the seminary."

The good woman wouldn't let him go until she'd stuffed his pockets with food. Finally, Julien set out on his terrifying path. Standing in her doorway, she gave him directions.

(选自 Stendhal. *The Red and the Black*. Translated by Burton Raffel. New York: The Modern Library, 2003:105-108.)

Questions

1. Try to analyze different levels of conflicts depicted in the novel.
2. What aspects of the novel make it a psychological novel?
3. What do "red" and "black" represent?
4. Is it fair to say the Stendhalian heroes are in need of obstacles and sufferings to become mentally strong and mature?
5. Is it the realism or romanticism of the novel that appeals to the contemporary readers of Stendhal?

Unit 3
Gustave Flaubert: *Madame Bovary*

Gustave Flaubert was one of the most important European writers of the 19th century, and he embodied a high level of development of French novel. Gustave Flaubert was born on December 12, 1821, in Rouen, France and died on May 8, 1880. His father was a distinguished doctor who was the head of the hospital in Rouen. When he was young, Gustave was sensitive and quiet. He enjoyed reading very much and gained a knowledge of scientific techniques and ideas as a young boy. In the year 1841, he was sent to study law in Paris against his will. In Paris he started to move in literary circles. In 1844, Flaubert suffered from a serious nervous illness, probably related to epilepsy. Therefore, he gave up law and spent most of his time at Le Croisset where he enjoyed his tranquil life and writing and his studies. During the years 1849 to 1850, Flaubert travelled to Egypt, Syria, Turkey, and Greece. Gradually, he became acquainted with many of the important literary figures at that time, such as Victor Hugo, Turgenev, Georges Sand, Sainte-Beuve, Gautier, de Goncourts, and de Maupassant. These writers admired Flaubert's talent greatly.

Flaubert had two unusual relationships with women in his life. The first was a married older woman whom he met at Trouville when he was fifteen. This lady remained the object of his platonic and idealized affection. The other was a poetess, who was his mistress between 1846 and 1854. They communicated with each other mainly in letters. Generally, he usually preferred a solitary life at Le Croisset like a recluse. He was characterized by pessimism, which may have been partly due to his illness, and by a violent contempt for middle-class society. He was often bitter and unhappy because of the great disparity between his unattainable dreams and fantasies and the realities of his life. His famous remark, "Madame Bovary, this is me."

manifested his unhappiness and loneliness clearly. Although Flaubert gained reputation as a writer within his own lifetime, he was not financially successful. What's more, the enmity and misunderstanding of his critics and readers hurt his feelings. In 1857, he and his publisher of *Madame Bovary* were tried for an "outrage to public morals and religion." But the case was acquitted.

Flaubert's works include *Madame Bovary* (1857); *Salammbo* (1862), a historical novel about the war between Rome and Carthage; *Sentimental Education* (1869), a novel dealing with the theme of the frustrations of middle-class life and human aspirations; and *The Temptation of Saint Anthony* (1874). In 1877 he published *Three Tales*, which contains the beautiful short stories, *A Simple Heart*, *The Legend of Saint Julian Hospitator*, and *Herodias*. These famous stories are masterpieces of short fiction and are among his finest and most moving works. Flaubert also wrote a play, *The Candidate*, which failed after a few performances in 1874. His last novel, *Bouvard and Pechuhet*, which was unfinished on his death, was published posthumously in 1881. Among all his works, *Madame Bovary* was the most accomplished one. In this work Flaubert combined a feeling for the ideals of the Romantic era with the objective outlook and scientific principles of Realism.

Here is a brief summary of the novel *Madame Bovary*. Charles Bovary was the only son of a middle-class family. He was a doctor and set up his practice in a rural village. He married a woman older than himself not out of love. After his wife died, he married an attractive young woman named Emma Roualt, who was the daughter of one of his patients. At the beginning, Emma was excited and pleased by her marriage, but because of her superficial romantic ideals, she was soon bored and disillusioned by her new matrimonial life. Then she became ill because of this unbearable boredom and dissatisfaction. Then the couple moved to a new town, where their daughter was born. Emma was still unhappy, and she began to have romantic yearnings toward a young law clerk, Leon. Emma's frustration became more and more intense after Leon left the town in order to attend law school. Mr. Bovary did everything to please her but unsuccessfully. Ultimately, Emma had an adulterous affair with a local landowner, Rodolphe, who abandoned her later. Emma became seriously ill. After her recovery Emma met Leon in Rouen and began an affair with him. Emma spent her husband's money freely and went into debts. At last, her unpaid bills went long overdue and a judgment was obtained against her by her creditors. The sheriff's officers arrived to confiscate the family property. Emma tried frantically to raise the money and finally turned to both Rodolphe and Leon, but neither was willing or able to help. She poisoned herself because of shame and despair. Her husband died a ruined and broken man, leaving their daughter in a state of abject poverty.

In terms of character analysis, Emma Bovary was a middle-class woman who could not stand the middle-class life. She tried very hard to attempt to escape from this middle-class existence by dreams, love affairs, and false pretensions. Emma has a dream of life that allows her to look for ideals and feelings greater than she is. She is aware that there are feelings greater than those found in her middle-class surroundings. She could not give herself in prostitution in order to solve her financial problem. She tried to live by her dreams, and when that failed, she died without compromising her vision of something greater than herself.

Theme

Madame Bovary has been recognized as being the forerunner and model of literary genre: the realistic novel. It is now considered a book of great intrinsic worth. It provides a standard against which to compare the works and writers that have followed the novel. It is a study of human stupidity and the "romantic malady," the despair and unhappiness faced by those who are unwilling or unable to resolve the conflicts between their dreams and reality. It examines middle-class conventions and the myth of progress, exposing weaknesses and hypocrisies, dealing with the inability of the different characters to communicate with each other.

One of the important points is that though time and the setting change, human nature and human problems remain constant. Therefore, this novel is still as relevant today as when it was written. Provincial life remains the same everywhere. Madame Bovary was afflicted by many problems and frustrations that are typical of the provincial life. The characters in the novel are common people and are very much like ourselves and our neighbors. This makes the readers easier to sympathize with the characters and to view the problems and frustrations of themselves in a new perspective, which help people understand themselves better and deeper. Nothing about the characters is romanticized or exalted, which is also a clear manifestation of the author's realism. The characters in *Madame Bovary* have their cultural, social and intellectual limitations. They are so true to life that they can serve as a mirror for the people who read the novel and reflect deeply about it and their own situation and personality.

Cutting-edge Topic

Madame Bovary is considered one of the finest "realistic" novels, not only because the characters in the novel are true to life, but also because its unadorned, unromantic portrayals of everyday life. At the same time, we as readers have to bear in mind that in literary realism, we get a view of the real world as seen through the eyes of the author, that is, from his particular perspective. Another important point to know is that realism does not equal to journalism. Realism is not a true description of all the things with all the details. Every incident and episode in the novel are carefully and intentionally selected. They are not randomly selected. They are chosen for definite purposes and are perfectly embedded in the whole work, to form an overall picture. Selection means omission. The author has to omit those unimportant incidents and details. One of Flaubert's talents is that he has the profound technique and style to depict the dullness of middle-class people without making his novel boring. Every aspect of the novel rings true to life. For instance, Flaubert's handling of Homais is a talented stroke of realistic description, which shows that Homais' conversations are extremely boring. The remarkable point is that when you read those boring conversations, you

sense acutely of the dullness of Homais without feeling bored by the description. This miraculous effect is due to Flaubert's genius in selecting details.

Apart from realism, Flaubert also made extensive use of symbolism in this novel. Here is a rough definition of symbolism. Symbolic things have an objective and limited function but they can be interpreted also to embody a wider and more profound meaning in a particular context. In *Madame Bovary*, readers could search for additional layers of meaning where the omission of a particular detail would not have affected the narration of the story. The meanings are not stated directly but symbolized. In this way, the meanings are for deeply felt and more striking than expressed explicitly. It is a bit of challenging for the readers to interpret the symbols but definitely a rewarding and enlightening experience. Here are some examples of symbolism in the novel. For instance, in the first chapter of part one, the elaborate description of Charles' hat is not necessary to realistic account of his school days, but this is an important hat in the sense that it symbolizes many aspects of his personality and his future development. Another example of symbolism is the blind beggar. In addition, the wedding bouquet of Charles' first wife and Emma's pet greyhound are also cases of symbolism. Critics have pointed out that even the names of the characters in *Madame Bovary* have symbolic meanings; for instance, Bovary is indeed "bovine," with the meaning of being stupid. In the last chapter of the novel, that Charles would want to bury Emma in her wedding dress is also an embodiment of symbolism. The wedding dress is a symbol of purity and Homais' receipt of the cross of the Legion of Honor shows the pettiness of the society against which Emma rebelled.

Excerpt

Part III CHAPTER XI

The next day Charles sent for his little daughter. She asked for her mama, and was told that she'd gone away, and would be bringing her some toys when she came home. Berthe mentioned her again several times; then, eventually, forgot about her. The child's cheerfulness broke Bovary's heart; he had also to endure the insufferable commiserations of the pharmacist.

Money problems soon resurfaced, with Lheureux again urging on his friend Vincrt. Charles signed his name to notes for exorbitant sums, for never would he even consider selling the smallest object that had belonged to *her*. His mother lost her patience with him, but he was far angrier than she. He was a changed man. She left the house for good.

Then everyone began scrambling for "his share of the spoils." Mademoiselle Lempereur presented her bill for six months' lessons; Emma had never actually taken a single one (despite that signed invoice she had shown Bovary), but the two women had had an arrangement; the owner of the lending-library claimed Emma had owed him three years' subscriptions; Mère Rollet demanded the cost of delivering a score or so of letters, and when Charles asked for details, was tactful enough to reply:

"Oh, I've no idea! It was business."

Each time he settled a debt, Charles thought it was the last. But, always, there was another, and then another, on and on.

He wrote asking his patients to settle their overdue accounts. They showed him the letters his wife had sent, and he had to apologize.

Félicité went round wearing Madame's dresses, now; not all of them, because he had kept back a few, which he would go and look at, in her dressing room, first locking the door; the maid was more or less her size, and often Charles, catching sight of her from behind, would imagine she was Emma, and cry out:

"Don't go! Don't go!"

But, at Pentecost, she decamped from Yonville, running off with Théodore and carrying away with her everything that remained of Emma's wardrobe.

It was about this time that the widow Dupuis "had the honour to inform him of the marriage of her son, Monsieur Léon Dupuis, notary at Yvetot, to Mademoiselle Léocadie Leboeuf, of Bondeville." Charles, in his congratulatory letter to Léon, wrote these words:

"How delighted my poor wife would have been!"

One day when, wandering aimlessly round the house, he had climbed up to the attic, he felt something under his slipper: it was a crumpled-up sheet of thin paper. Opening it out, he read "Be brave, Emma, be brave! I can't let myself wreck your life." It was Rodolphe's letter, which had fallen on the floor between some boxes and, after lying there for a time, had now been blown near the door by the breeze from the skylight. Charles stood there, open-mouthed, transfixed, on that same spot where Emma, in despair, her face whiter even than his, had once longed for death. Eventually, he noticed a tiny "R" at the foot of the second page. Who was it? He remembered Rodolphe's attentiveness, his sudden disappearance and his constrained manner on the two or three occasions when they had subsequently met. But he was deceived by the letter's respectful tone.

"Perhaps their feelings were purely platonic," he thought.

In any case, Charles was not a man given to examining anything too closely; he shrank back from concrete proof, and his wavering jealousy melted away into the immensity of his pain.

Everyone, he thought, must have adored her. Every single man, without a doubt, must have lusted after her. Because of this she became, in his eyes, only the more beautiful, and he conceived for her an unremitting, raging desire that fed his despair, and was unbounded, because it could never be satisfied now.

To please her, as if she were still alive, he adopted her preferences and her ideas; he bought himself patent-leather boots and began wearing white cravats. He waxed his moustaches, and, like her, signed his name to promissory notes. She was corrupting him from beyond the grave.

He was forced to sell the silver piece by piece, and then he sold the parlour furniture. All the rooms were stripped; but the bedroom, her bedroom, remained just as it had always been. After dinner, Charles went up there. He would push the round table in front of the fire, and draw up *her* armchair. He took his seat opposite. A candle was burning in one of the gilded candlesticks. Berthe sat beside him, colouring pictures.

The poor man hated seeing Berthe so badly dressed, her boots with laces missing and the armholes of her smock gaping open to below her waist, for the daily woman never bothered about her. But she was so sweet, so good, with her little head bending so gracefully over her work and her thick blond hair falling over her rosy cheeks, that he was filled with immeasurable delight, with a pleasure tainted by bitterness, like those wines of poor quality that taste of resin. He would repair her toys, make puppets for her from cardboard, and sew up the torn stomachs of her dolls. Then, if his glance chanced upon the workbox, or a ribbon left about, or even a pin lying in a crack of the table, he would lapse into a daydream, and look so sad, that she would, like him, become sad as well. No one, now, came to see them. Justin had fled to Rouen, where he had found employment as a grocer's boy, and the apothecary's children spent less and less time with the child, for Monsieur Homais had no wish to encourage the relationship, given the difference in the social status of the two families.

The blind beggar, whom he had not succeeded in curing with his ointment, had returned to his former haunts on the Bois-Guillaume hill, where he entertained travellers with accounts of Homais's futile efforts, with so much persistence that the pharmacist, on his trips to the city, would cower behind the curtains of the Hirondelle to avoid encountering him. The pharmacist loathed the wretch; and wanting, in the interests of his own reputation, to be rid of him at all costs, he mounted a covert campaign against him, thereby revealing the depth of his intelligence and the unscrupulousness of his egotism. For six consecutive months, readers of the *Fanal de Rouen* were treated to paragraphs like the following:

"Every traveller heading for the fertile fields of Picardy cannot fail to have observed the presence, on the hillside of Bois-Guillaume, of a wretched creature afflicted with a hideous lesion of the face. He pesters and persecutes wayfarers, and quite literally exacts a toll from each one of them. Have we then not progressed beyond those horrendous Middle Ages, when vagabonds were permitted to display, in public places, the leprous sores and strumae they had carried back with them from the Crusades?"

Or again:

"In spite of the laws forbidding vagrancy, the outskirts of our large cities continue to be infested by bands of paupers. Some of them—and these may well not be the least dangerous—operate singlehanded. Whatever can our Aediles be thinking?"

Then Homais began concocting anecdotes:

"Yesterday, on the hill at Bois-Guillaume, a skittish horse ... "

And he launched into the description of an accident caused by the presence of the blind man. His campaign was so effective that the offender was incarcerated. But, later, he was released again. He resumed his former occupation, as did Homais. The battle was joined. The pharmacist emerged victorious, for his enemy was condemned to spend the remainder of his days in an asylum.

This victory emboldened him: from that moment on there was not a dog run over, nor a barn burnt down, nor a woman beaten up in his district but Homais, inspired always by his love of progress and his hatred of priests, promptly reported the event to the public. He drew parallels between primary schools and those run by the Ignorantine Friars (to the detriment of the latter), wrote about the St Bartholomew Massacre in connection with a 100-franc grant to the church, denounced abuses, and shot off some damaging broadsides. At least, that was the way he put it. Homais persisted with his undermining operations, and grew dangerous.

Stifled by the restrictions of journalism, however, he soon felt the need to produce a book, a major work! So he wrote his *General Statistical Study of the Canton of Yonville, followed by Various Climatological Observations*; then, from statistics, he quickly progressed to philosophy. He became preoccupied by the great questions of the day: social reforms, raising the moral standards of the poor, pisciculture, rubber, the railways, etc. He even grew ashamed of being a bourgeois, and began to affect the appearance and lifestyle of the artist; he began smoking! He bought himself two chic Pompadour-style statuettes to decorate his parlour.

He did not abandon the pharmacy: quite the contrary! He kept abreast of the latest discoveries, and followed every phase of the spreading fashion for chocolate. It was due to his efforts that *cho-ca* and *revalentia* were introduced into the department of the Seine-Inférieure. He became a great devotee of Pulvermacher electric belts; he wore one himself; and at night, when he removed his flannel undershirt, Madame Homais would lie there quite dazzled by the golden spirals that almost obscured him from her view, feeling her passion redouble for this man who was more heavily girdled than a Scythian and as magnificent as any of the Magi.

He had some splendid ideas for Emma's tomb. First he suggested a broken column with drapery, then a pyramid, then a Temple to Vesta, perhaps in the shape of a rotunda ... even "a heap of ruins." Every single plan specified a weeping willow, which Homais considered the mandatory symbol of grief.

Charles and he went to Rouen together to look at tombstones made by a mason who specialized in memorials. A painter accompanied them, one Vaufrylard, a friend of Bridoux's, who spent the entire time regaling them with puns. Finally, after examining about a hundred designs, obtaining an estimate, and making a second trip to Rouen, Charles decided on a mausoleum that would display, on its two principal walls, "a guardian spirit bearing an extinguished torch."

As for the inscription, in Homais's opinion nothing could match "*Sta viator*" for beauty, but no matter how hard he racked his brain, he could not come up with the rest; he kept repeating "*Sta viator* ..." At last, he remembered: "*amabilem conjugem calcas*!!" and this was adopted.

It was a curious fact that Bovary, while constantly thinking about Emma, was actually forgetting her; and he was filled with despair at how this image kept fading from his memory at the very time when he was struggling so hard to retain it. Every night, however, he dreamt of her; the dream was always the same: he came up to her, but just as he took her in his arms, she dissolved into dust in his embrace.

Unit 3 Gustave Flaubert: *Madame Bovary*

During one week he was seen entering the church every single evening. Monsieur Bournisien even paid him a visit or two, but eventually gave up on him. In any case, the priest, according to Homais, was becoming increasingly intolerant, in fact almost fanatical; he ranted on against the spirit of the age and never failed, every couple of weeks or so, in his sermon, to describe the death of Voltaire, who died devouring his own excrement, as everybody knows.

In spite of his frugal ways, Bovary was still quite unable to pay off his old debts. Lheureux refused to renew any of the promissory notes. Seizure became imminent. At that point he turned to his mother, who wrote agreeing to let him take out a mortgage on her property, but used the opportunity to revile Emma, and demanded, as compensation for her sacrifice, a shawl that had escaped Félicité's plundering. Charles refused to give it to her. They quarrelled.

She made the first attempt at reconciliation, by suggesting that the child be sent to her; it would make things easier for her at home. Charles agreed. But, when the moment came to part, his courage failed him. This time the breach was final, irrevocable.

As he became increasingly alienated from others, the love he felt for Berthe bound him ever more closely to her. But she worried him; she coughed intermittently, and patches of red would colour her cheeks.

Always on display in the house across the square, the pharmacist's boisterous family prospered. Everything was going right for Homais. Napoléon served as his laboratory assistant, Athalie made him an embroidered smoking cap, Irma cut out the paper rounds to cover his jams, and Franklin could recite the entire multiplication table at one go. He was the happiest of fathers, the most fortunate of men.

But no, not so! A secret ambition tormented him: Homais yearned for the cross of the Legion of Honour. His claim was not without foundation: (1) He had distinguished himself, at the time of the cholera epidemic, by his complete and unconditional devotion to duty. (2) He had published, at his own expense, various works of public utility, among them … (and he cited his treatise entitled: "Cider: Its manufacture and its effects … "; also some "Observations on the woolly aphis, submitted to the Academy"; also his statistical opus, and he even included his pharmaceutical thesis); "and that's leaving aside the fact that I belong to a number of learned societies"(he belonged to only one).

"And," he exclaimed, giving a hop and a skip, "even if they only looked at my outstanding record as a firefighter!" So Homais began making overtures to Power. In secret, he rendered important services to the Prefect in the elections. In fact he sold himself, prostituted himself. He even addressed a petition to the sovereign in which he begged him to "see justice done him," addressing him as "our good king," and comparing him to Henri Ⅳ.

And, each morning, the apothecary would grab the newspaper, expecting to find his nomination in it; but it was never there. Finally, unable to bear it any longer, he had a grass plot laid out in his garden in the shape of the star, with two narrow strips coming from the apex to represent the ribbon. He would stroll round it, his arms crossed, meditating upon the ineptitude of government and the ingratitude of men.

From feelings of respect, or from a kind of sensuality that made him want to spin out his investigations, Charles had not yet opened the secret drawer in a rosewood desk that Emma had always used. But finally, one day, he did sit down at it, turned the key, and pressed the spring. All Léon's letters were there. There could be no further doubt, this time! He devoured them all, to the very last one, then ransacked every corner, every piece of furniture, searching every drawer and even behind the panelling, sobbing, howling with rage, frantic, quite demented. Discovering a box, he kicked it open. There lay Rodolphe's portrait, staring straight at him, on top of a jumble of love letters.

His deep despondency caused general amazement. He no longer went out, he saw no one, he even refused to visit his patients. People began saying that he "shut himself away to drink."

Occasionally, however, an inquisitive passer-by would peer over the top of the garden hedge, and stare in astonishment at this long-bearded, wild-looking man infilthy clothes who paced up and down, weeping noisily.

On summer evenings he used to take his little girl with him to the cemetery. By the time they returned, darkness had fallen, and the only light showing in the square would be the one shining from Binet's attic window.

But something prevented him from fully luxuriating in his grief—he had no one close to him to share it with; and he started dropping in on Madame Lefrancois is simply to talk about *her*. But the innkeeper only listened with half an ear, having troubles of her own, for Monsieur Lheureux had finally started his own coach service, "Les Favorites du commerce," and Hivert, who had made quite a name for himself carrying out errands in town, was demanding better pay and threatening to go over "to the competition."

One day when he had gone to the market at Argueil to sell his horse—his last remaining asset—he bumped into Rodolphe. On seeing each other, both men turned white. Rodolphe, who had merely sent his card, at first stammered some excuses, but then, growing bolder, had the nerve (it was August, and very hot) to invite Bovary to come to the tavern for a beer.

Sitting opposite to him at a table, Rodolphe leant on his elbows and chewed his cigar while he talked; and Charles drifted off into a daydream as he gazed at this face that she had loved. He felt he was seeing some part of her again. He was filled with wonder. He would have liked to be that man.

Rodolphe chattered on about farming, livestock, manure, plugging with small talk any gaps where an allusion might slip in. Charles was not listening to him; and Rodolphe, noticing this, watched the other's mobile features record the successive passage of memories. Slowly Charles's face grew crimson; his nostrils pulsated rapidly, his lips trembled; there even came a moment when, filled with somber fury, he focused his gaze upon Rodolphe with such intensity that the latter almost felt afraid, and stopped what he was saying. But soon Charles's habitual expression of dismal lassitude returned.

"I don't hold it against you," he said.

Rodolphe sat there in silence. And Charles, his head in his hands, went on, his voice flat, his resigned tone heavy with infinite suffering:

"No, now I don't hold it against you any longer!"

And then, for the only time in his life, he even uttered a memorable phrase:

"Fate is to blame."

Rodolphe, who had orchestrated that fate, thought him remarkably tolerant for a man in his situation, a trifle comical, even despicable.

The next day, Charles went to sit on the bench in the arbour. The sky was blue, and the sunlight, filtering through the trellis, traced the shadows of the vine leaves on the sandy floor; jasmine scented the air, cantharides beetles droned busily round the flowering lilies, and Charles sat sobbing like an adolescent, overwhelmed by the nebulous wafts of love that swelled his sorrowing heart.

At seven o'clock, little Berthe, who had not seen him all afternoon, came to fetch him for dinner.

His head was leaning against the wall, his eyes were closed, his mouth open, and his hands held a lock of long black hair.

"Come on, papa!" she said.

Thinking he was playing a game with her, she pushed him gently. He fell to the ground. He was dead.

Thirty-six hours later, at the request of the apothecary, Monsieur Canivet arrived. He opened him up, but found nothing.

When everything had been sold up, there remained twelve francs seventy-five centimes, which paid Mademoiselle Bovary's fare to her grandmother's house. The good woman died that very same year; and, as Père Rouault was now paralysed, Berthe became the responsibility of an aunt. She is poor, and sends the child to earn her keep at a cotton mill.

Since Bovary's death, three doctors, in turn, have tried, and failed, to build up a practice in Yonville, so promptly and thoroughly did Monsieur Homais demolish their attempts. He is doing devilishly well; the authorities treat him with great circumspection, and public opinion is on his side.

He has just been awarded the Legion of Honour.

(选自 Flaubert, Gustave. *Madame Bovary*. Translated by Margaret Mauldon. New York: Oxford University Press, 2004: 303 – 311.)

Questions

1. How is the personality of Emma Bovary responsible for her own downfall?
2. Give some examples of contrast and irony in *Madame Bovary*.
3. Why is *Madame Bovary* considered as a realistic novel?
4. How symbolism is reflected in *Madame Bovary*?
5. What is the social significance of *Madame Bovary*?

Unit 4
Leo Tolstoy: *War and Peace*

Leo Tolstoy, Tolstoy also spelled Tolstoi (born on August 28 [September 9, New Style], 1828, Yasnaya Polyana, Tula Province, Russian Empire—died on November 7 [November 20], 1910, Astapovo, Ryazan Province), Russian author, a master of realistic fiction and one of the world's greatest novelists.

Tolstoy is best known for his two longest works, *War and Peace* (1865–69) and *Anna Karenina* (1875–77), which are commonly regarded as among the finest novels ever written. *War and Peace* in particular seems virtually to define this form for many readers and critics. Among Tolstoy's shorter works, *The Death of Ivan Ilyich* (1886) is usually classed among the best examples of the novella. Especially during his last three decades Tolstoy also achieved world renown as a moral and religious teacher. His doctrine of nonresistance to evil had an important influence on Gandhi.

Most readers will agree with the assessment of the 19th-century British poet and critic Matthew Arnold that "a novel by Tolstoy is not a work of art but a piece of life"; the Russian author Isaak Babel commented that, "if the world could write by itself, it would write like Tolstoy." Critics of diverse schools have agreed that somehow Tolstoy's works seem to elude all artifice. Most have stressed his ability to observe the smallest changes of consciousness and to record the slightest movements of the body. What another novelist would describe as a single act of consciousness, Tolstoy convincingly breaks down into a series of infinitesimally small steps. According to the English writer Virginia Woolf, who took for granted that Tolstoy was "the greatest of all novelists," these observational powers elicited a kind of fear in readers, who "wish to escape from the gaze which Tolstoy fixes on us." Those who visited Tolstoy as an old man also reported feelings of great discomfort when he appeared to understand their unspoken thoughts. It was commonplace to describe him as godlike in his powers and titanic in his struggles to escape the limitations of the human condition. Some viewed Tolstoy as the embodiment of nature and pure vitality, others saw him as the incarnation of the world's conscience, but for almost all who knew him or read his works, he was not just one of the greatest writers who ever lived but a living symbol of the search for life's meaning.

The scion of prominent aristocrats, Tolstoy was born at the family estate, about 130 miles south of Moscow, where he was to live the better part of his life and write his most-important works. His mother, Mariya Nikolayevna, née Princess Volkonskaya, died before he was two years old, and his father Nikolay Ilich, Graf (count) Tolstoy, followed her in 1837. His grandmother died 11 months later, and then his next guardian, his aunt Aleksandra, in 1841. Tolstoy and his four siblings were then transferred to the care of another aunt in Kazan, in western Russia. Tolstoy remembered a cousin who lived at Yasnaya Polyana, Tatyana Aleksandrovna Yergolskaya ("Aunt Toinette," as he called her), as the greatest influence on his childhood, and later, as a young man, Tolstoy wrote some of his most-touching letters to her. Despite the constant presence of death, Tolstoy remembered his childhood in idyllic terms. His first published work, *Childhood* (1852), was a fictionalized and nostalgic account of his early years.

In 1847 Tolstoy began keeping a diary, which became his laboratory for experiments in self-analysis and, later, for his fiction. Happily married and ensconced with his wife and family at Yasnaya Polyana, Tolstoy reached the height of his creative powers. He devoted the remaining years of the 1860s to writing *War and Peace*. Then, after an interlude during which he considered writing a novel about Peter the Great and briefly returned to pedagogy (bringing out reading primers that were widely used), Tolstoy wrote his other great novel, *Anna Karenina*. These two works share a vision of human experience rooted in an appreciation of everyday life and prosaic virtues.

War and Peace (1865–69) contains three kinds of material—a historical account of the Napoleonic wars, the biographies of fictional characters, and a set of essays about the philosophy of history. Critics from the 1860s to the present have wondered how these three parts cohere, and many have faulted Tolstoy for including the lengthy essays, but readers continue to respond to them with undiminished enthusiasm. The work's historical portions narrate the campaign of 1805 leading to Napoleon's victory at the Battle of Austerlitz, a period of peace, and Napoleon's invasion of Russia in 1812. Contrary to generally accepted views, Tolstoy portrays Napoleon as an ineffective, egomaniacal buffoon, Tsar Alexander I as a phrasemaker obsessed with how historians will describe him, and the Russian general Mikhail Kutuzov (previously disparaged) as a patient old man who understands the limitations of human will and planning. Particularly noteworthy are the novel's battle scenes, which show combat as sheer chaos. Generals may imagine they can "anticipate all contingencies," but battle is really the result of "a hundred million diverse chances" decided on the moment by unforeseeable circumstances. In war as in life, no system or model can come close to accounting for the infinite complexity of human behavior.

In *Anna Karenina* (1875 – 77) Tolstoy applied these ideas to family life. The novel's first sentence, which indicates its concern with the domestic, is perhaps Tolstoy's most famous: "All happy families resemble each other; each unhappy family is unhappy in its own way." *Anna Karenina* interweaves the stories of three families, the Oblonskys, the Karenins, and the Levins.

Probably even more than Dostoyevsky, Tolstoy has been praised as being the greatest novelist in world literature. The novel begins at the Oblonskys, where the long-suffering wife Dolly has discovered the infidelity of her genial and sybaritic husband Stiva. In her kindness, care for her family, and concern for everyday life, Dolly stands as the novel's moral compass. By contrast, Stiva, though never wishing ill, wastes resources, neglects his family, and regards pleasure as the purpose of life. The figure of Stiva is perhaps designed to suggest that evil, no less than good, ultimately derives from the small moral choices human beings make moment by moment.

Stiva's sister Anna begins the novel as the faithful wife of the stiff, unromantic but otherwise a decent government minister Aleksey Karenin, and the mother of a young boy, Seryozha. But Anna, who imagines herself the heroine of a romantic novel, allows herself to fall in love with an officer, Aleksey Vronsky. Schooling herself to see only the worst in her husband, she eventually leaves him and her son to live with Vronsky. Throughout the novel, Tolstoy indicates that the romantic idea of love, which most people identify with love itself, is entirely incompatible with the superior kind of love, the intimate love of good families. As the novel progresses, Anna, who suffers agonies of conscience for abandoning her husband and child, develops a habit of lying to herself until she reaches a state of near madness and total separation from reality. She at last commits suicide by throwing herself under a train. The realization that she may have been thinking about life incorrectly comes to her only when she is lying on the track, and it is too late to save herself.

The third story concerns Dolly's sister Kitty, who first imagines she loves Vronsky but then recognizes that real love is the intimate feeling she has for her family's old friend, Konstantin Levin. Their story focuses on courtship, marriage, and the ordinary incidents of family life, which, in spite of many difficulties, shape real happiness and a meaningful existence. Throughout the novel, Levin is tormented by philosophical questions about the meaning of life in the face of death. Although these questions are never answered, they vanish when Levin begins to live correctly by devoting himself to his family and to daily work. Like his creator Tolstoy, Levin regards the systems of intellectuals as spurious and as incapable of embracing life's complexity.

In the early 1880s he wrote some other works, including novels, essays and tracts, but these works are generally regarded as markedly inferior to *War and Peace* and *Anna Karenina*.

Theme

Both *War and Peace* and *Anna Karenina* advance the idea that ethics can never be a matter of timeless rules applied to particular situations. Rather, ethics depends on a sensitivity, developed over a lifetime, to particular people and specific situations. Tolstoy's preference for particularities over abstractions is often described as the hallmark of his thought.

The essays in *War and Peace*, which begin in the second half of the book, satirize all attempts to formulate general laws of history and reject the ill-considered assumptions supporting all historical narratives. In Tolstoy's view, history, like a battle, is essentially the product of contingency, has no direction, and fits no pattern. The causes of historical events are infinitely varied and forever unknowable, and so historical writing, which claims to explain the past, necessarily falsifies it. The shape of historical narratives reflects not the actual course of events but the essentially literary criteria established by earlier historical narratives.

In contrast to other psychological writers, such as Dostoyevsky, who specialized in unconscious processes, Tolstoy described conscious mental life with unparalleled mastery. His name has become synonymous with an appreciation of contingency and of the value of everyday activity. Oscillating between skepticism and dogmatism, Tolstoy explored the most-diverse approaches to human experience. Above all, his greatest works, *War and Peace* and *Anna Karenina*, endure as the summit of realist fiction.

Cutting-edge Topic

As world classics, Tolstoy's great novel *War and Peace* has been analyzed in diversified approaches. It is something of a surprise to realize that *War and Peace*, which has now become so much a part of the literary heritage of Western culture, was initially greeted with some bewilderment and perplexities.

Rewriting of Tolstoy's works have been attempted. Exploration into Tolstoy's philosophy of love and human connection has been made to make his opera acceptable for the Soviet stage. Moving away from Tolstoy's family ideal in Peace, with its basis on intimate sibling bonds, Prokofiev shifted the family to War.

Some contemporary new approaches have been employed to interpret Tolstoy's works such as Michel Foucault's theory on Discipline; gender study (analyzing the female characters in *War and Peace*); Cultural Studies ("Photography and the Crisis of Authorship: Tolstoy and the Popular Photographic Press"); interdisciplinary studies ("The Search for Narrative Control: Music and Female Sexuality in Tolstoy's 'Family Happiness' and 'The Kreutzer Sonata'"); comparative studies and cross-cultural studies are two most common methodologies that contemporary scholars tend to employ. For instance, "Hemingway and Tolstoy: A

Pugilistic Encounter" and "Tolstoy and Homer" (Epic and the Russian Novel from Gogol to Pasternak, Academic Studies Press).

In addition, Tolstoy's non-fiction has been dealt with in recent years. For instance, from the pedagogical essays of the 1860s to the intensely personal treatise on poverty, and first-person writings, whether they are diaries and letters or articles and treatises, written by Tolstoy have been studied in depth. Research on these non-fiction has expanded the scope of Tolstoy study.

Excerpt

Part Four

15

At the end of January Pierre went to Moscow and stayed in an annexe of his house, which had not been burnt. He called on Count Rastopchin and on some acquaintances who were back in Moscow, and he intended to leave for Petersburg two days later. Everybody was celebrating the victory, everything was bubbling with life in the ruined but reviving city. Everyone was pleased to see Pierre, everyone wished to meet him, and everyone questioned him about what he had seen. Pierre felt particularly well disposed towards them all, but was now instinctively on his guard for fear of binding himself in any way. To all questions put to him—whether important or quite trifling—such as, Where would he live? Was he going to rebuild? When was he going to Petersburg and would he mind taking a parcel for someone? —he replied: "Yes, perhaps," or, "I think so," and so on.

He had heard that the Rostovs were at Kostroma but the thought of Natasha seldom occurred to him. If it did, it was only as a pleasant memory of the distant past. He felt himself not only free from social obligations but also from that feeling which it seemed to him he had aroused in himself.

On the third day after his arrival he heard from the Drubetskoys that Princess Marya was in Moscow. The death, sufferings, and last days of Prince Andrei had often occupied Pierre's thoughts and now recurred to him with fresh vividness. Having heard at dinner that Princess Marya was in Moscow and living in her house—which had not been burnt—in Vozdvizhenka street, he drove that same evening to see her.

On his way to the house Pierre kept thinking of Prince Andrei, of their friendship, of his various meetings with him, and especially of the last one at Borodino.

"Is it possible that he died in the bitter frame of mind he was then in? Is it possible that the meaning of life was not disclosed to him before he died?" thought Pierre. He recalled Karataev and his death, and involuntarily began to compare those two men, so different and yet so similar in that they had both lived and both died and in the love he felt for both of them.

Pierre drove up to the house of the old prince in a most serious mood. The house had escaped; it showed signs of damage but its general aspect was unchanged. The old footman, who met Pierre with a stern face as if wishing to make the visitor feel that the absence of the old prince had not disturbed the order of things in the house, informed him that the princess had gone to her own apartments, and that she received on Sundays.

"Announce me. Perhaps she will see me," said Pierre.

"Yes, sir," said the man. "Please step into the portrait-gallery."

A few minutes later the footman returned with Dessalles, who brought word from the princess that she would be very glad to see Pierre if he would excuse her want of ceremony and come upstairs to her apartment.

In a rather low room lit by one candle sat the princess, and with her another person dressed in black. Pierre remembered that the princess always had lady companions, but who they were and what they were like he never knew or remembered. "This must be one of her companions," he thought, glancing at the lady in the black dress.

The princess rose quickly to meet him and held out her hand.

"Yes," she said, looking at his altered face after he had kissed her hand, "so this is how we meet again. He often spoke of you even at the very last," she went on, turning her eyes from Pierre to her companion with a shyness that surprised him for an instant.

"I was so glad to hear of your safety. It was the first piece of good news we had received for a long time."

Again the princess glanced round at her companion with even more uneasiness in her manner, and was about to add something but Pierre interrupted her.

"Just imagine—I knew nothing about him!" said he. "I thought he had been killed. All I know I heard at second-hand from others. I only know that he fell in with the Rostovs... What a strange coincidence!"

Pierre spoke rapidly and with animation. He glanced once at the companion's face, saw her attentive and kindly gaze fixed on him and, as often happened when one was talking, felt somehow that this companion in the black dress was a good, kind, excellent creature, who would not hinder his conversing freely with Princess Marya.

But when he mentioned the Rostovs, Princess Marya's face expressed still greater embarrassment. She again glanced rapidly from Pierre's face to that of the lady in the black dress, and said:

"Do you really not recognize her?"

Pierre looked again at the companion's pale delicate face, with its black eyes and peculiar mouth, and something near to him, long forgotten and more than sweet, looked at him from those attentive eyes.

"But no, it can't be!" he thought. "This stern, thin, pale face that looks so much older! It cannot be she. It merely reminds me of her." But at that moment Princess Marya said "Natasha!" And with difficulty, effort, and stress, like the opening of a door grown rusty on its hinges, a smile appeared on the face with the attentive eyes, and from that opening door came a breath of fragrance which suffused Pierre with a happiness he had long forgotten and of which he had not even been thinking—especially at that moment. It suffused him, seized him, and enveloped him completely. When she smiled, doubt was no longer possible, it was Natasha and he loved her.

At that moment Pierre involuntarily betrayed to her, to Princess Marya, and above all to himself, a secret of which he himself had been unaware. He flushed joyfully yet with painful distress. He tried to hide his agitation. But the more he tried to hide it the more clearly—clearer than any words could have done—did he betray to himself, to her, and to Princess Marya, that he loved her.

"No, it's only the unexpectedness of it," thought Pierre. But as soon as he tried to continue the conversation he had begun with Princess Marya he again glanced at Natasha, and a still deeper flush suffused his face and a still stronger agitation of mingled joy and fear seized his soul. He became confused in his speech and stopped in the middle of what he was saying.

Pierre had failed to notice Natasha because he did not at all expect to see her there, but he had also failed to recognize her because the change in her since he last saw her was immense. She had grown thin and pale, but that was not what made her unrecognizable; she was unrecognizable at the moment he entered because on that face whose eyes had always shone with a suppressed smile of the joy of life, when he first entered and glanced at her there was not the least shadow of a smile: only her eyes were kindly attentive and sadly interrogative.

Pierre's confusion was not reflected by any confusion on Natasha's part, but only by the pleasure that just perceptibly lit up her whole face.

16

"She has come to stay with me," said Princess Marya. "The count and countess will be here in a few days. The countess is in a terrible condition. But it was necessary for Natasha herself to see a doctor. They insisted on her coming with me."

"Yes, is there a family free from sorrow now?" said Pierre, addressing Natasha. "You know it was on the very day they liberated us. I saw him. What an enchanting boy he was!"

Natasha looked at him, and by way of answer to his words her eyes widened and lit up.

"What can I say or think of as a consolation?" said Pierre. "Nothing! Why did such a splendid boy, so full of life, have to die?"

"Yes, in our time it would be hard to live without faith … " remarked Princess Marya.

"Yes, yes, that is the honest truth," Pierre swiftly interjected.

"Why is that?" Natasha asked, looking attentively into Pierre's eyes.

"How can you ask why?" said Princess Marya. "Only the thought of that which awaits us there … "

Natasha, without waiting for Princess Marya to finish, again looked inquiringly at Pierre.

"And because," Pierre continued, "only someone who believes in this: that there is a God, guiding us, can sustain such a loss as hers and … yours."

Natasha had already opened her mouth to speak but suddenly stopped. Pierre turned quickly away from her and again addressed Princess Marya, asking her about his friend's last days.

Pierre's confusion had now almost vanished, but at the same time he felt that all his former freedom had also completely gone. He felt that there was now a judge of his every word and action whose judgement mattered more to him than that of all the rest of the world. As he spoke now he was considering what impression his words would make on Natasha. He did not purposely say things to please her, but whatever he was saying he judged from her standpoint.

Princess Marya—reluctantly, as usual in such cases—began telling of the condition in which she had found Prince Andrei. But Pierre's face quivering with emotion, his questions, and his eager restless expression, gradually compelled her to go into details which she feared to recall for her own sake.

"Yes, yes, so ... so ...?" Pierre kept saying as he leant towards her with his whole body and eagerly listened to her story. "Yes, yes, so he grew tranquil, and tender? He always sought one thing with his whole soul—to be perfectly good—so he could not be afraid of death. The faults he had—if he had any—were not of his making. So he did soften? ... What happiness that he saw you again," he added, suddenly turning to Natasha and looking at her with his eyes full of tears.

Natasha's face twitched. She frowned and lowered her eyes for a moment. She hesitated for an instant whether to speak or not.

"Yes, that was a happiness," she then said in her quiet voice with its deep chest notes. "For me it certainly was a happiness." she paused. "And he ... he ... he said he was wishing for it at the very moment I came to him ..."

Natasha's voice broke. She blushed, pressed her clasped hands on her knees, and then, controlling herself with an evident effort, lifted her head and began to speak rapidly.

"We knew nothing of it when we started from Moscow. I did not dare to ask about him. Then suddenly Sonya told me he was travelling with us. I had no idea and could not imagine what state he was in, all I wanted was to see him and be with him," she said, trembling and breathing quickly.

And not letting them interrupt her, she went on to tell what she had never yet mentioned to anyone—all she had lived through during those three weeks of their journey and life at Yaroslavl.

Pierre listened to her with lips parted and gazing at her with his eyes full of tears. As he listened he did not think of Prince Andrei, nor of death, nor of what she was telling. He listened to her, and felt only pity for her, for what she was suffering now while she was speaking.

Princess Marya, her face contorted in the effort to hold back her tears, sat beside Natasha, and heard for the first time the story of those last days of her brother's and Natasha's love.

Apparently it was essential for Natasha to relate that painful and joyous narrative.

She spoke, mingling most trifling details with the intimate secrets of her soul, and it seemed as if she could never finish. Several times over she repeated the same thing twice.

Dessalles's voice was heard outside the door asking whether Nikolushka might come in to say goodnight.

"Well, that's all—everything," said Natasha.

She got up quickly just as Nikolai entered, almost ran to the door which was hidden by curtains, struck her head against it, and rushed from the room with a moan either of pain or sorrow.

Pierre gazed at the door through which she had disappeared, and did not understand why he suddenly felt alone in all the world.

Princess Marya roused him from his abstraction by drawing his attention to her nephew, who had entered the room.

At that moment of emotional tenderness, Nikolushka's face, which resembled his father's, affected Pierre so much that when he had kissed the boy he got up quickly, took out his handkerchief, and went to the window. He wished to take leave of Princess Marya, but she would not let him go.

"No, Natasha and I sometimes don't go to sleep till after two, so please don't go. I will order supper. Go downstairs, we will come immediately."

Before Pierre left the room Princess Marya told him: "This is the first time she has spoken of him like that."

17

Pierre was shown into the large brightly-lit dining-room; a few minutes later he heard footsteps and Princess Marya entered with Natasha. Natasha was calm, though a severe and grave expression had again settled on her face. They all three of them now experienced that feeling of awkwardness which usually follows after a serious and heartfelt talk. It is impossible to go back to the same conversation, to talk of trifles is awkward, and yet the desire to speak is there and silence seems like affectation. They went silently to table. The footman drew back the chairs and pushed them up again. Pierre unfolded his cold table-napkin and, resolving to break the silence, looked at Natasha and at Princess Marya. They had evidently both formed the same resolution, the eyes of both shone with satisfaction and a confession that besides its sorrow life also has joy.

"Do you take vodka, Count?" asked Princess Marya, and those words suddenly banished the shadows of the past. "Now tell us about yourself," said she. "They tell such incredible wonders about you."

"Yes," replied Pierre with the smile of mild irony now habitual to him. "They even tell me of wonders I myself never dreamt of! Marya Abramovna invited me to her house and kept telling me what had happened, or ought to have happened, to me. Stepan Stepanych also instructed me how I ought to relate my experiences. In general I have noticed that it is very easy to be an interesting man (I am an interesting man now); people invite me out and tell me all about myself."

Natasha smiled and was on the point of speaking.

"We have been told," Princess Marya interrupted her, "that you lost two millions in Moscow. Is that true?"

"But I am three times as rich as before," returned Pierre.

Though the position was now altered by his decision to pay his wife's debts and to rebuild his houses, Pierre still maintained that he had become three times as rich as before.

"What I have certainly gained is freedom," he began seriously, but did not continue, noticing that this theme was too egotistic.

"And are you building?"

"Yes. Savelich says I must!"

"Tell me, you did not yet know of the Countess's death when you decided to remain in Moscow?" asked Princess Marya, and immediately blushed, noticing that her question, following his mention of freedom, ascribed to his words a meaning he had perhaps not intended.

"No," answered Pierre, evidently not considering the meaning Princess Marya had given to his words awkward. "I heard of it in Oryol and you cannot imagine how it shocked me. We were not an exemplary couple," he added quickly, glancing at Natasha and noticing on her face curiosity as to how he would speak of his wife, "but such a death shocked me terribly. When two people quarrel both are always at fault. And your own guilt suddenly becomes dreadfully oppressive before the one who already is no more. And then such a death ... without friends, without consolation! I am very, very sorry for her," he concluded, and was pleased to notice a look of glad approval on Natasha's face.

"Yes, and so you are once more an eligible bachelor," said Princess Marya.

Pierre suddenly flushed crimson and for a long time tried not to look at Natasha. When he ventured to glance her way again her face was cold, stern, and he fancied even contemptuous.

"And did you really see and speak to Napoleon, as we have been told?" said Princess Marya.

Pierre laughed.

"No, never once! Everybody seems to imagine that being taken prisoner means being Napoleon's guest. Not only did I never see him, but I heard nothing about him—I was in much lower company!"

Supper was over, and Pierre, who at first declined to speak about his captivity, was gradually led on to do so.

"But is it true that you remained in Moscow to kill Napoleon?" Natasha asked with a slight smile. "I guessed it then, when we met at the Sukharev Tower, do you remember?"

Pierre admitted that it was true, and from that was gradually led on by Princess Marya's questions and especially by Natasha's to giving a detailed account of his adventures.

At first he spoke with the amused and mild irony now customary with him towards everybody and especially towards himself, but when he came to describe the horrors and sufferings he had witnessed he was unconsciously carried away, and began speaking with the suppressed emotion of a man re-experiencing in recollection strong impressions he has lived through.

Princess Marya with a gentle smile looked now at Pierre and now at Natasha. In the whole narrative she saw only Pierre and his goodness. Natasha, leaning on her elbow, the expression of her face constantly changing with the narrative, watched Pierre with an attention that never wandered—evidently herself experiencing all that he described. Not only her look, but her exclamations and the brief questions she put, showed Pierre that she understood just what he wished to convey. It was clear that she understood not only what he said, but also what he wished to, but could not, express in words. The account Pierre gave of the incident with the child and the woman for protecting whom he was arrested, was this: "It was a horrible spectacle—children abandoned, some in the flames ... they snatched a child right under my eyes ... women with their things ripped off and their ear-rings torn out ... " he flushed and grew confused. "Then a patrol arrived and all the men—all those who were not looting that is—were arrested, and I among them."

"I am sure you're not telling us everything; I am sure you did something ... " said Natasha, and pausing added "something fine?"

Pierre continued. When he spoke of the execution he wanted to pass over the horrible details, but Natasha insisted that he should not omit anything.

Pierre began to tell about Karataev, but paused. By this time he had risen from table and was pacing the room, Natasha following him with her eyes. Then he added:

"No, you can't understand what I learned from that uneducated man—that simple fool."

"No, no: tell us!" said Natasha. "Where is he now?"

"They killed him almost before my eyes."

And Pierre, his voice trembling continually, went on to tell of the last days of their retreat, of Karataev's illness, and of his death.

He told of his adventures as he had never yet recalled them. He now, as it were, saw a new meaning in all he had gone through. Now that he was telling it all to Natasha, he experienced that pleasure which a man has when women listen to him—not clever women who when listening either try to remember what they hear to enrich their minds, and when opportunity offers to re-tell it, or who wish to adapt it to some thought of their own and promptly contribute their own clever comments prepared in their own little mental workshop—but the pleasure real women give who are gifted with a capacity to select and absorb the very best a man shows of himself. Natasha, without knowing it, was all attention: she did not lose a word, no single quiver in Pierre's voice, no look, no twitch of a muscle in his face, or a single gesture. She caught the unfinished word in its flight and took it straight into her open heart, divining the secret meaning of all Pierre's mental travail.

Princess Marya understood his story and sympathized with him, but she now saw something else that absorbed all her attention. She saw the possibility of love and happiness between Natasha and Pierre, and from the first moment this thought came to her, it filled her heart with joy.

It was three o'clock in the morning. The footmen came in with sad and stern faces to change the candles, but no one noticed them.

Pierre finished his story. Natasha continued to look at him intently and attentively with bright animated eyes, as if trying to understand something more, which he had perhaps left untold. Pierre in shame-faced and happy confusion glanced occasionally at her and tried to think what to say next to introduce a fresh subject. Princess Marya was silent. It occurred to none of them that it was three o'clock and time to go to bed.

"They say: misfortunes and sufferings," remarked Pierre, "yes, but if right now, right this minute they asked me: 'Would you rather be what you were before you were taken prisoner, or go through this all again?' For God's sake let me again have captivity and horse flesh! We imagine that when we are thrown out of our familiar rut all is lost, but that is only when something new and good can begin. While there is life there is happiness. There is much, much before us. I say this to you," he added, turning to Natasha.

"Yes, yes," she said, answering something quite different. "I too would wish nothing but to re-live it all from the beginning."

Pierre looked intently at her.

"Yes, and nothing more," said Natasha.

"It's not true, not true!" cried Pierre. "I am not to blame for being alive and wishing to live—nor you either."

Suddenly Natasha bent her head, covered her face with her hands, and began to cry.

"What is it, Natasha?" said Princess Marya.

"Nothing, nothing." She smiled at Pierre through her tears. "Goodnight. It's time for bed."

Pierre rose and took his leave.

Princess Marya and Natasha met as usual in the bedroom. They talked of what Pierre had told them. Princess Marya did not express her opinion of Pierre nor did Natasha speak of him.

"Well, goodnight, Marie!" said Natasha. "You know, I am often afraid that we don't speak of him" (she meant Prince Andrei) "for fear of not doing justice to our feelings, and so we forget him."

Princess Marya sighed deeply, and thereby acknowledged the justice of Natasha's remark, but she did not express agreement in words.

"Is it possible to forget?" said she.

"It was very good for me to talk about everything today; and it was hard and it was painful, but good. Very good!" said Natasha. "I am sure that he truly loved him. That is why I told him ... Was it all right that I told him?" she added, suddenly blushing.

"To tell Pierre? Oh, yes! What a splendid man he is!" said Princess Marya.

"You know, Marie ... " Natasha suddenly said with a mischievous smile such as Princess Marya had not seen on her face for a long time, "he has somehow grown so clean, smooth, and fresh—as if he had just come out of a Russian bath: do you understand? Out of a moral bath. Isn't it true?"

"Yes," replied Princess Marya. "He has greatly improved."

"With a short little coat and his hair close cropped; just as if, well, just as if he had come straight from the bath ... Papa used to ... "

"I understand why he" (Prince Andrei) "liked no one as much as him," said Princess Marya.

"Yes, and he is quite different. They say men are friends when they are quite different. That must be true. Really he is quite unlike him—in everything."

"Yes, but he's wonderful."

"Well, good night," said Natasha.

And the same mischievous smile lingered for a long time on her face as if it had been forgotten there.

18

It was a long time before Pierre could fall asleep that night. He paced up and down his room, now turning his thoughts on a difficult problem and frowning, now suddenly shrugging his shoulders and wincing, and now smiling happily.

He was thinking of Prince Andrei, of Natasha, and of their love, one moment jealous of her past, then reproaching himself for that feeling. It was already six in the morning and he still paced up and down the room.

"Well, what's to be done if it cannot be avoided? What's to be done? Evidently it has to be so," said he to himself, and hastily undressing he got into bed, happy and agitated but free from hesitation or indecision.

"Strange and impossible as such happiness seems, I must do everything that she and I may be man and wife," he told himself.

A few days previously Pierre had decided to go to Petersburg on the Friday. When he awoke on the Thursday, Savelich came to ask him about packing for the journey.

"What, to Petersburg? What is Petersburg? Who is there in Petersburg?" he asked involuntarily, though only to himself. "Oh, yes, long ago, before this happened, I did for some reason mean to go to Petersburg," he reflected. "Why? But perhaps I shall go. What a good fellow he is and how attentive, and how he remembers everything," he thought, looking at Savelich's old face, "and what a pleasant smile he has!"

"Well, Savelich, do you still not wish to accept your freedom?" Pierre asked him.

"What's the good of freedom to me, your Excellency? We lived under the late count—the Kingdom of Heaven be his! —and we have lived under you too, without ever being wronged."

"And your children?"

"The children will live just the same. With such masters one can live."

"But what about my heirs?" said Pierre. "Supposing I suddenly marry ... it might happen," he added with an involuntary smile.

"If I may take the liberty, your Excellency, it would be a good thing."

"How easy he thinks it," thought Pierre. "He doesn't know how terrible it is and how dangerous. Too soon or too late ... it is terrible!"

"So what are your orders? Are you starting tomorrow?" asked Savelich.

"No, I'll put it off for a bit. I'll tell you later. You must forgive the trouble I have put you to," said Pierre, and seeing Savelich smile, he thought: "But how strange it is that he should not know that now there is no Petersburg for me, and that *that* must be settled first of all! But probably he knows it well enough and is only pretending. Shall I have a talk with him and see what he thinks?" Pierre reflected. "No, another time."

At breakfast Pierre told the princess, his cousin, that he had been to see Princess Marya the day before and had there met—"Whom do you think? Natasha Rostova!"

The princess seemed to see nothing more extraordinary in that than if he had seen Anna Semyonovna.

"Do you know her?" asked Pierre.

"I have seen the princess," she replied. "I heard that they were arranging a match for her with young Rostov. It would be a very good thing for the Rostovs, they are said to be utterly ruined."

"No; I mean do you know Natasha Rostova?"

"I heard about that affair of hers at the time. It was a great pity."

"No, she either doesn't understand or is pretending," thought Pierre. "Better not say anything to her either."

The princess too had prepared provisions for Pierre's journey.

"How kind they all are," thought Pierre. "What is surprising is that they should trouble about these things now, when it can no longer be of interest to them. And all for me!"

On the same day the Chief of Police came to Pierre inviting him to send a representative to the Faceted Palace to recover things that were to be returned to their owners that day.

"And this man too," thought Pierre, looking into the face of the Chief of Police. "What a fine, good-looking officer, and how kind! Imagine bothering about such trifles now! And they actually say he is not honest and takes bribes. What nonsense! Besides, why shouldn't he take bribes? That's the way he was brought up, and everybody does it. But what a kind, pleasant face and how he smiles as he looks at me."

Pierre went to Princess Marya's to dinner.

As he drove through the streets past the houses that had been burnt down he was surprised by the beauty of those ruins. The picturesqueness of the chimney-stacks and tumble-down walls of the burnt-out quarters of the town, stretching out and concealing one another, reminded him of the Rhine and the Colosseum. The cabmen he met and their passengers, the carpenters cutting the timber for new houses with their axes, the women hawkers, and the shopkeepers, all looked at him with cheerful beaming eyes that seemed to say: "Ah, there he is! Let's see what will come of it!"

At the entrance to Princess Marya's house Pierre felt doubtful whether he had really been there the night before and had really seen Natasha and talked to her. "Perhaps I imagined it; perhaps I shall go in and find no one there." But he had hardly entered the room before he felt her presence with his whole being, by the loss of his sense of freedom. She was in the same black dress with soft folds and her hair was done the same way as the day before, yet she was quite different. Had she been like this when he entered the day before he could not for a moment have failed to recognize her.

She was as he had known her almost as a child, and later on as Prince Andrei's fiancée. A bright questioning light shone in her eyes, and on her face was a friendly and strangely roguish expression.

Pierre dined with them and would have spent the whole evening there, but Princess Marya was going to Vespers and Pierre left the house with her.

Next day he came early, dined, and spent the whole evening there. Though Princess Marya and Natasha were evidently glad to see their visitor and though all Pierre's interest was now centred in that house, by the evening they had talked over everything and the conversation passed from one trivial topic to another and repeatedly broke off. He stayed so long that Princess Marya and Natasha exchanged glances, evidently wondering when he would go. Pierre noticed this, but could not go. He felt uneasy and embarrassed, but sat on because he simply could not get up and take his leave.

Princess Marya, foreseeing no end to this, rose first, and complaining of a headache began to say goodnight.

"So you are going to Petersburg tomorrow?" she asked.

"No, I am not going," Pierre replied hastily, in a surprised tone and as though offended. "Yes ... no ... to Petersburg? Tomorrow—but I won't say goodbye yet. I will call round in case you have any commissions for me," said he, standing before Princess Marya and turning red, but not taking his departure.

Natasha gave him her hand and went out. Princess Marya on the other hand instead of going away sank into an armchair and looked sternly and intently at him with her deep, radiant eyes. The weariness she had plainly shown before had now quite passed off. With a deep and long-drawn sigh she seemed to be prepared for a lengthy talk.

When Natasha left the room Pierre's confusion and awkwardness immediately vanished and were replaced by eager excitement. He quickly moved an armchair up to Princess Marya.

"Yes, I wanted to tell you", said he, answering her look as if she had spoken. "Princess, help me! What am I to do? Can I hope? Princess, my dear friend, listen! I know it all. I know I am not worthy of her, I know it's impossible to speak of it now. But I want to be a brother to her. No, not that, I don't, I can't ... "

He paused and rubbed his face and eyes with his hands.

"Well," he went on, with an evident effort at self-control and coherence. "I don't know when I began to love her, but I have loved her, and her alone, all my life, and I love her so that I cannot imagine life without her. I cannot propose to her at present but the thought that perhaps she might some day be my wife and that I may be missing that possibility ... that possibility ... is terrible. Tell me, can I hope? Tell me what I am to do, dear Princess!" he added after a pause, and touched her hand as she did not reply.

"I am thinking of what you have told me," answered Princess Marya. "This is what I will say. You are right that to speak to her of love at present ... "

Princess Marya stopped. She was going to say that to speak of love was impossible, but she stopped because she had seen by Natasha's sudden change two days before, that she would not only not be hurt if Pierre spoke of his love, but that it was the very thing she wished for.

"To speak to her now wouldn't do," said the princess all the same.

"But what am I to do?"

"Leave it to me," said Princess Marya. "I know ... "

Pierre was looking into Princess Marya's eyes.

"Well? ... Well? ..." he said.

"I know that she loves ... will love you," Princess Marya corrected herself.

Before her words were out, Pierre had sprung up and with a frightened expression seized Princess Marya's hand.

"What makes you think so? You think I may hope? You think ... ?"

"Yes, I think so," said Princess Marya with a smile. "Write to her parents, and leave it to me. I will tell her when I can. I wish it to happen, and my heart tells me it will."

"No, it cannot be! How happy I am! But it can't be ... How happy I am! No, it can't be!" Pierre kept saying as he kissed Princess Marya's hands.

"Go to Petersburg, that will be best. And I will write to you," she said.

"To Petersburg? Go there? Very well, I'll go. But I may come again tomorrow?"

Next day Pierre came to say goodbye. Natasha was less animated than she had been the day before; but that day as he looked at her Pierre sometimes felt as if he was vanishing and that neither he nor she existed any longer, that nothing existed but happiness. "Is it possible? No, it can't be," he told himself at every look, gesture, and word that filled his soul with joy.

When on saying goodbye he took her thin slender hand he could not help holding it a little longer in his own.

"Is it possible that this hand, that face, those eyes, all this treasure of feminine charm so strange to me now, is it possible that it will one day be mine forever, as familiar to me as I am myself? ... No, that's impossible ... !"

"Goodbye, Count," she said aloud. "I shall look forward very much to your return," she added in a whisper.

And these simple words, her look, and the expression on her face which accompanied them, formed for two months the subject of inexhaustible memories, interpretations, and happy meditations for Pierre. "I shall look forward very much to your return ... " "Yes, yes, how did she say it? Yes, 'I shall look forward very much to your return.' Oh, how happy I am! What is happening to me? How happy I am!" said Pierre to himself.

19

There was nothing in Pierre's soul now at all like what had troubled it during his courtship of Hélène.

He did not repeat to himself, with a sickening feeling of shame, the words he had spoken, or say: "Oh, why did I not say that?" and, "whatever made me say 'Je vous aime'?" On the contrary, he now repeated in imagination every word that he or Natasha had spoken and pictured every detail of her face and smile, and did not wish to diminish or add anything, but only to repeat it again and again. There was now not a shadow of doubt in his mind as to whether what he had undertaken was right or wrong. Only one terrible doubt sometimes crossed his mind: "Wasn't it all a dream? Isn't Princess Marya mistaken? Am I not too conceited and self-confident? I believe all this; and suddenly Princess Marya will tell her, and she will be sure to smile and say: 'How strange! He must be deluding himself. Doesn't he know that he is a man, just a man, while I ... ? I am something altogether different and higher.'"

That was the only doubt often troubling Pierre. He did not now make any plans. The happiness before him appeared so inconceivable that if only he could attain it, it would be the end of all things. Everything ended with it.

A joyful, unexpected frenzy, of which he had thought himself incapable, possessed him. The whole meaning of life—not for him alone but for the whole world—seemed to him centred in his love and the possibility of being loved by her. At times everybody seemed to him to be occupied with one thing only—his future happiness. Sometimes it seemed to him that other people were all as pleased as he was himself, and merely tried to hide that pleasure by pretending to be busy with other interests. In every word and gesture he saw allusions to his happiness. He often surprised those he met by his significantly happy looks and smiles, which seemed to express a secret understanding between him and them. And when he realized that people might not be aware of his happiness, he pitied them with all his heart and felt a desire somehow to explain to them that all that occupied them was a mere frivolous trifle unworthy of attention.

When it was suggested to him that he should enter the Civil Service, or when the war or any general political affairs were discussed on the assumption that everybody's welfare depended on this or that issue of events, he would listen with a mild and pitying smile, and surprise people by his strange comments. But at this time he saw everybody—both those who as he imagined understood the real meaning of life (that is, what he was feeling) and those unfortunates who evidently did not understand it—in the bright light of the emotion that shone within himself, and at once without any effort saw in everyone he met everything that was good and worthy of being loved.

When dealing with the affairs and papers of his dead wife her memory aroused in him no feeling but pity that she had not known the bliss he now knew. Prince Vasili, who having obtained a new post and some fresh decorations was particularly proud at this time, seemed to him a pathetic, kindly old man, much to be pitied.

Later on Pierre often recalled this period of blissful insanity. All the views he formed of people and circumstances at this time remained true for him always. He not only did not renounce them subsequently, but when he was in doubt or inwardly at variance, he appealed to the views he had held at this time of his madness, and they always proved correct.

"I may have appeared strange and queer then," he thought, "but I was not so mad as I seemed. On the contrary, I was then wiser and had more insight than at any other time, and understood all that is worth understanding in life, because ... because I was happy."

Pierre's insanity consisted in not waiting, as he used to do, to discover personal attributes, which he termed "good qualities," in people before loving them; his heart was now overflowing with love, and by loving people without cause he discovered indubitable causes for loving them.

20

After Pierre's departure that first evening, when Natasha had said to Princess Marya with a gaily mocking smile: "He looks just, yes, just as if he had come out of a Russian bath—in a short little coat and with his hair close cropped," something hidden and unknown to herself, but irrepressible, awoke in Natasha's soul.

Everything: her face, walk, look, and voice, was suddenly altered. To her own surprise a power of life and hope of happiness rose to the surface and demanded satisfaction. From that evening she seemed to have forgotten all that had happened to her. She no longer complained of her position, did not say a word about the past, and no longer feared to make happy plans for the future. She spoke little of Pierre, but when Princess Marya mentioned him a long-extinguished light once more kindled in her eyes and her lips curved with a strange smile.

The change that took place in Natasha at first surprised Princess

Marya; but when she understood its meaning it grieved her. "Can she have loved my brother so little as to be able to forget him so soon?" she thought when she reflected on the change. But when she was with Natasha she was not vexed with her and did not reproach her. The reawakened power of life that had seized Natasha was so evidently irrepressible and unexpected by her, that in her presence Princess Marya felt that she had no right to reproach her even in her heart.

Natasha gave herself up so fully and frankly to this new feeling that she did not try to hide the fact that she was no longer sad, but bright and cheerful.

When Princess Marya returned to her room after her nocturnal talk with Pierre, Natasha met her on the threshold.

"He has spoken? Yes? He has spoken?" she repeated.

And a joyful yet pathetic expression, which seemed to beg forgiveness for her joy, settled on Natasha's face.

"I wanted to listen at the door, but I knew you would tell me."

Understandable and touching as the look with which Natasha gazed at her seemed to Princess Marya, and sorry as she was to see her agitation, these words pained her for a moment. She remembered her brother and his love.

"But what's to be done? She can't help it," thought the princess.

And with a sad and rather stern look she told Natasha all that Pierre had said. On hearing that he was going to Petersburg Natasha was astounded.

"To Petersburg!" she repeated as if unable to understand.

But noticing the grieved expression on Princess Marya's face, she guessed the reason of that sadness and suddenly began to cry.

"Marie," said she, "tell me what I should do! I am afraid of being bad. Whatever you tell me, I will do. Tell me ..."

"You love him?"

"Yes," whispered Natasha.

"Then why are you crying? I am happy for your sake," said Princess Marya, who because of those tears quite forgave Natasha's joy.

"It won't be just yet—some day. Think what fun it will be when I am his wife and you marry Nicolas!"

"Natasha, I have asked you not to speak of that. Let us talk about you."

They were silent awhile.

"But why go to Petersburg?" Natasha suddenly asked, and hastily replied to her own question. "But no, no, he must ... Yes, Marie. He must ..."

（选自 Tolstoy, Leo. *War and Peace*. Translated by Louise and Aylmer Maude. Oxford: Oxford University Press, 2010: 1196 - 1212.）

Questions

1. Why is Leo Tolstoy significant?
2. What was Leo Tolstoy's childhood like?
3. What are Leo Tolstoy's achievements?
4. What is the legacy of Leo Tolstoy?
5. Why do critics comment that a novel by Tolstoy is not a work of art but a piece of life?

Unit 5

Hermann Hesse: *Demian*

  Hermann Hesse (born on July 2, 1877, Germany—died on August 9, 1962, Switzerland), German novelist and poet. His father, a Baltic German, came from Estonia; his mother was the daughter of a Swabian and a French Swiss. His father's father was a doctor and his mother's father a missionary and Indologist. Hermann Hesse's father, too, had been a missionary in India for a short while, and his mother had spent several years of her youth in India and had done missionary work there.

  Hermann Hesse's childhood in Calw was interrupted by several years of living in Basle (1880–86). His family was composed of different nationalities; indeed, he was growing up among two different peoples, in two countries with their different dialects.

  Hermann Hesse spent most of his school years in boarding schools in Wuerttemberg and some time in the theological seminary of the monastery at Maulbronn. He was a good learner, good at Latin, but he was not a very manageable boy, and it was only with difficulty that he fitted into the framework of a pietist education that aimed at subduing and breaking the individual personality. From the age of twelve he wanted to be a poet, and since there was no normal or official road, he had a hard time deciding what to do after leaving school. He left the seminary and grammar school, became an apprentice to a mechanic, and at the age of nineteen he worked in book and antique shops in Tübingen and Basle. Late in 1899 a tiny volume of his poems appeared in print, followed by other small publications that remained equally unnoticed, until in 1904 the novel *Peter Camenzind*, written in Basle and set in

Switzerland, had a quick success. He gave up selling books, married a woman from Basle and moved to the country. At that time a rural life, far from the cities and civilization, was his aim.

Soon after he settled in Switzerland in 1912, the First World War broke out, and each year brought him more and more into conflict with German nationalism; ever since his first shy protests against mass suggestion and violence he had been exposed to continuous attacks and floods of abusive letters from Germany. The hatred of the official Germany, culminating under Hitler, was compensated for by the following he won among the young generation that thought in international and pacifist terms, by the friendship of Romain Rolland, which lasted until his death, as well as by the sympathy of men who thought like him even in countries as remote as India and Japan. In Germany he had been acknowledged again since the fall of Hitler, but his works, partly suppressed by the Nazis and partly destroyed by the war; have not yet been republished there. Of the western philosophers, he was influenced most by Plato, Spinoza, Schopenhauer, and Nietzsche as well as the historian Jacob Burckhardt. But they did not influence him as much as Indian and, later, Chinese philosophy. In 1923, he resigned German and acquired Swiss citizenship. After the dissolution of his first marriage, he lived alone for many years, and then he married again.

Hesse is known as the last knight of the German romantic school, which shows that he was deeply influenced by romantic poetry in art. He loves nature and is tired of urban civilization. His novels, poems and literature mostly use symbolic techniques and write beautifully and delicately. Influenced by psychoanalysis, his literary works focus on the exploration of the spiritual field and the fearless and honest nature of the heart.

The first phase of his writing, which began with the neoromantic treatment of the artist as a social outcast, ended with the realistic *Rosshalde* (1914; Eng. trans., 1970). At the beginning of World War Ⅰ, the strain of his pacifist beliefs and domestic crises led him to undertake psychoanalysis with a follower of Carl Gustav Jung. Jungian psychology gave his work a new dimension; *Demian* (1919; Eng. trans., 1923), *Siddhartha* (1922; Eng. trans., 1951), and *Steppenwolf* (1927; Eng. trans., 1929) also reveal the influence of Nietzsche, Dostoyevsky, Spengler, and Buddhist mysticism. These novels are based on the conviction that western civilization is doomed and that man must express himself in order to find his own nature. A third phase began in 1930. *Narziss und Goldmund* (1930; trans. as *Death and the Lover*, 1932) balances the artist's rebellion against the hierarchic continuity of social behavior. In *Journey to the East* (1932; Eng. trans., 1956) and *The Glass Bead Game* (1943; Eng. trans., 1957) the quest for freedom conflicts with tradition and leads to personal sacrifice suffused with optimism.

Hesse did not write any novels after 1943 but continued to publish essays, letters, poems, reviews, and stories. From 1912 he lived in Switzerland, of which he became a naturalized citizen in 1923. Hesse's novels became immensely popular during the 1950s in the English-speaking world, where their criticism of bourgeois values and interest in eastern religious philosophy and Jungian psychology echoed the preoccupations of the younger generation.

Hesse was awarded the Nobel Prize for Literature in 1946 for "the majestic grandeur and insight of his inspired literary works of fiction and poetry, which also serve as an example of noble humanitarian ideals and noble style."

Theme

Demian was written in the first-person perspective, describing Emil Sinclair's struggle to find his way into himself. Emil Sinclair is a young boy who was raised in a middle-class home, amidst what is described as a Scheinwelt, a play on words meaning "world of light" as well as "world of illusion." Sinclair's entire existence can be summarized as a struggle between two worlds: the show world of illusion (related to the Hindu concept of maya) and the real world, the world of spiritual truth. In the course of the novel, Sinclair is caught between good and evil, represented as the light and dark realms. Accompanied and prompted by his mysterious classmate and friend "Max Demian," he detaches from and revolts against the superficial ideals of the world of appearances and eventually awakens into a realization of self.

There are mainly two themes in *Demian*. The first one is the path to self-realization. Self-realization means becoming aware of and integrating all parts of the self, the conscious and the unconscious, into a whole. This integration is achieved by recognizing and then accepting those parts of the self a person hates or suppresses. Sinclair recognizes the devil part of himself through Frank Kromer, and he gradually accepts it under the help of Demian. The road to self-realization is full of struggles, and sometimes Sinclair flinches back, but he finally listens to his inner voice and makes it through. The second theme is the integration of the divine and the demonic. An important part of Emil Sinclair's personal and spiritual journey is to come to terms with the "two worlds" view established in his earliest childhood. In the book he describes the two worlds: one light and one dark. As a young boy, Sinclair struggles in the tension between these two worlds. Eventually he experiences both external and internal conflicts because he enters the dark world and has difficulty finding his way back to the light. He learns how to accept both the two worlds as part of the same world.

Cutting-edge Topic

The main theme of Hermann Hesse's novels is the individual's efforts to break out of the established modes of civilization so as to find an essential spirit and identity. The lack of continuity in the narrative of external events allows the reader to focus more on the inner world of the protagonist.

Sinclair's dissatisfaction towards his university and his observations of how people gathering, herd-like, in taverns and cafés brings attention not only to the "herd" behavior but also to the changes he has undergone. He no longer tries to fit in by going to taverns and drinking with his peers. Instead, he finally finds his true home in Demian's house. As Demian

says: "Human beings fly into each other's arms because they're afraid of each other—the masters afraid for themselves. They're afraid because they have never made themselves known to themselves. They are a community composed entirely of men who are afraid of the unknown element within themselves." "These men who come together in this nervous fashion are riddled with fear and evil; none of them trust each other. They cling to ideals which no longer exist, and stone everyone who sets up a new one." We can know that only a very few men have the courage to express their will. Most people come together because they are afraid of being different, so they come together without trusting each other. When Sinclair meets Frau Eva, she comments that she recognizes him immediately, implying that he bears a certain sign, the sign borne by all people of their type.

The idea of the herd mentality, and the suggestion of its origins in fear, likely appealed to Hesse's concerns about war. The connection between the formation of herds based on fear and war is suggested in the description: "From everything we collected in this way we gained a critical understanding of our time and contemporary Europe, which with prodigious efforts had created new weapons for mankind but had ended by falling into a deep and final desolation of the spirit. For it had conquered the whole world, only to lose its own soul in the process." They lost their dream, being unknown to their fate and just following the flow without doing anything. *Demian* also connects the fear that inspires the herd mentality to the Jung Carl's idea of self-realization or individuation. People are afraid when they are not at one with themselves, "afraid of the unknown in themselves."

Excerpt

Chapter 7 Eve

One time, over vacation, I went by the house where Max Demian had lived with his mother, years before. An old woman was strolling in the garden; I talked to her and learned the house was hers. I asked after the Demian family. She remembered them well. But she didn't know where they were living now. She could tell I was interested, so she took me into the house, dug up a leather photo album, and showed me a picture of Demian's mother. I could barely remember her, but when I saw the little portrait, my heart stood still. —It was the picture from my dream! It was her: the large, almost masculine figure, resembling her son; the signs of maternal love, strictness, and deep passion in her features; beautiful and enticing, beautiful and unapproachable, daemon and mother, fate and lover. It was her!

What a wild miracle that was for me, to learn that my dream-image was alive in the world! There was a woman who actually looked like that—who bore the features of my destiny! Where was she? Where? — And she was Demian's mother.

Not long afterward I went away on my trip. What a strange trip it was! I traveled restlessly from place to place, following every impulse that came to me, in search of this woman. There were days when I saw nothing but figures who reminded me of her, echoed her, resembled her—who lured me down the streets of foreign cities, through train stations, into train cars, as in a long, confused dream. There were other days when I realized how useless my search was; then I sat in some park or other, in a hotel garden, in a waiting room, doing nothing, peering into myself and trying to bring the image in me to life. But it had turned shy and fugitive. I was never able to fall asleep—at most I nodded off for fifteen minutes during train rides through unfamiliar landscapes. One time, in Zurich, a woman followed me. She was pretty, and quite brazen, but I barely noticed her and kept walking as though she were thin air. I would rather have died than take an interest in any other woman for even an hour.

I felt my destiny drawing me on—I felt that fulfillment was near, and I was insanely impatient and frustrated not to be able to bring it about. Once, at a train station in Innsbruck I think it was, I saw a shape through the window of a departing train that reminded me of her, and I was miserable for days. Suddenly the shape appeared to me again at night, in a dream, and I woke up feeling ashamed and empty, convinced of the senselessness of my hunt. I took the next train straight home.

A few weeks later I enrolled at the University of H—. Everything was a disappointment to me. The lectures I heard on the history of philosophy were as trivial and mass-produced as the hustle and bustle of the young students. Everything followed the same clichéd pattern, everyone did the same things as everyone else, and the good cheer on the flushed, boyish faces looked so depressingly empty and prefabricated! I was free, though; I had all my time to myself, and I lived in a nice, quiet, run-down place by the city walls with a couple volumes of Nietzsche on my table. I lived with him, felt the loneliness of his soul, trembled at the fate that had inexorably hounded him, suffered with him, and was overjoyed that there had been someone who had followed his path so relentlessly.

Late one night I wandered through the city, in gusts of autumn wind, and heard groups of students singing in the bars. Clouds of tobacco smoke poured out through the open windows, and torrents of song, loud and strictly rhythmical but utterly lifeless, joyless, and mechanical.

　　I stood on a street corner and listened. Right on schedule, the students' well-rehearsed high spirits echoed out into the night. Everywhere a communal huddling together, young men unburdening themselves of fate, fleeing to the warmth of the herd!

　　Two men slowly walked by, behind me, and I heard a snatch of their conversation.

　　"Isn't it exactly like the young men's house in an African village?" one of them said. "Everything is the way it's supposed to be, down to the prescribed tattoos of their dueling scars! Here you have it: the future of Europe."

　　The voice somehow reminded me of something—I knew that voice. I followed the men down the dark street. One of them was Japanese, a small, elegant man; I could see his yellow face light up in a smile under a streetlamp.

　　Then the other man spoke again.

　　"Well I'm sure it's no better with you in Japan. It is always rare to find people who don't follow the herd. Even here there are some."

　　I felt a stab of joyous shock with every word. I knew the person who was speaking—it was Demian.

　　I followed him and the Japanese man through the windy night, down dark streets; I listened to their conversation and was happy to hear the sound of Demian's voice. It had the same old tone from before, the same beautiful confidence and serenity, the same power over me. Now everything was going to be all right. I had found him.

　　At the end of a street on the edge of the city, the Japanese man said goodbye and opened his front door. Demian started to walk back; I had stopped and was waiting for him in the middle of the street. With my heart pounding I saw him walk toward me, standing up straight, a spring in his step, wearing a brown plastic raincoat and with a thin cane hanging on his arm. Without altering his stride he walked right up to me, took off his hat, and revealed the same old bright face with its decisive mouth and strangely bright forehead.

　　"Demian!" I cried.

　　He held out his hand to me.

　　"There you are, Sinclair! I've been expecting you."

　　"You knew I was here?"

　　"I wasn't sure, but I was definitely hoping. I hadn't seen you until tonight. You've been following us."

"So you recognized me right away?"

"Of course. It's true, you've changed. But you have the sign."

"The sign? What sign?"

"We used to call it the mark of Cain, if you recall. It is our special sign. You always had it—that's why I wanted to be your friend. But now it's clearer."

"I didn't know. Or, actually, I did. I painted a picture of you once, Demian, and I was amazed to see that it also looked like me. Was that the sign?"

"It was. It's good that you're here! My mother will be glad too."

I was suddenly frightened. "Your mother? Is she here? She doesn't even know me."

"Oh, she knows about you. She will know who you are even if I don't tell her ... You haven't been in touch for a long time."

"Oh, I wanted to write to you, so many times, but I couldn't. I've felt for a while that I'd find you soon. I waited for it every day."

He tucked his arm into mine and walked on with me, exuding a calm that entered me too. Soon we were chatting the same way we used to. We recalled our school days, the confirmation class, and the meeting that hadn't gone well during the school break too—the only thing we didn't discuss was the earliest, closest bond between us, the Franz Kromer story.

We unexpectedly found ourselves in the middle of a strange conversation, full of premonitions and forebodings. We had just been discussing student life, along the lines of Demian's conversation with the Japanese man, and had moved on from that to other things that seemed to be totally unrelated, but Demian's words revealed an underlying connection.

He spoke of the spirit of Europe, and the nature of our age. Everywhere, he said, conformity and the herd instinct prevail; nowhere do freedom and love have the upper hand. All this gathering together, from student fraternities and singing clubs to entire nations, is taking place under a kind of compulsion—they are communities of anxiety, fear, and shame, and on the inside they are old and rotten and about to collapse.

"Community is a beautiful thing," Demian said. "But what we see flourishing everywhere around us is no such thing. True community will arise again when actual individuals come to know each other; then will come a time when it reshapes the world. The communities we have now are just herds. People run as fast as they can to each other because they're afraid of each other—the rich come together over here, the workers over there, the educated elites somewhere else! And why are they afraid? Fear always comes from a split in yourself. They are afraid because they have never gotten to know who they really are. A whole society of people afraid of the unknown in their own hearts! They all can feel that the principles they live by are not valid anymore, that they're following the old laws; none of it, neither their religion nor their morality, is right for us today. For a hundred years and more, Europe has done nothing but go to school and build factories! They know exactly how many ounces of powder it takes to kill someone, but don't know how to pray to God. They don't even know how to be happy for an hour at a time. Just look at these student bars! Or anywhere rich people go to amuse themselves! It's hopeless!

"My dear Sinclair, nothing good can come of all this. These people huddling together so timidly are full of fear and full of wickedness; no one trusts the next. They cling to ideals that no longer exist, and throw stones at anyone who is trying to create a new one. I can feel the conflicts. They will come, believe me, and soon! And naturally they won't make the world 'better.' Whether the workers kill their capitalists or Russia and Germany blow each other to bits, the only thing that'll change is who owns whom. But still it won't have been in vain. These conflicts will clarify how worthless the current ideals have become; they will wipe out all our old stone age gods. The world as it is wants to die, it cries out to be destroyed—and it will be."

"And what about us?" I asked.

"Us? Oh, maybe we will be destroyed too. Our kind can be shot and killed too. But they can't get rid of us that easily. The will of the future will collect around whatever remains of us, or whichever ones of us survive. The will of humanity, which our European marketplace of science and technology has strangled for so long, will reveal itself. And then it will be as clear as day that the will of humanity has nothing, nothing to do with the so-called communities we have today—the nations and tribes, the clubs and churches. What Nature wants with us human beings always stands written in individuals: in you and in me. It was there in Jesus, it was there in Nietzsche. Those are the only tendencies that matter—of course their appearance may change day to day—and there will be room for them once today's collectivities collapse."

It was late when we arrived at a garden by a river, and stopped.

"This is where we live," Demian said. "Come see us soon. We're waiting for you."

I happily walked the long road home. The night had grown cool; here and there a student staggered noisily through the city to wherever he was going. I had often thought how opposed their ridiculous high spirits were to my lonely life—sometimes feeling I was missing out on something, sometimes simply looking down on them. But I had never felt so calm, so filled with secret strength, as I did that night. How little that world had to do with me, how distant and forgotten it was! I remembered civil servants from my hometown: dignified old gentlemen who clung to the memories of their drunken student nights like souvenirs from a blissful paradise, and who worshipped at the altar of the long-vanished "freedom" of their student years the way poets or other Romantics did with childhood. It was the same everywhere! Everywhere they sought "freedom" and "happiness" somewhere behind them, purely out of fear that they might be reminded of their responsibility for their own lives, might be admonished to follow their own path. A few years of boozing and carousing, then they knuckled under and turned into respectable bureaucrats. Yes, it was rotten here, putrid, and these student idiocies were not as bad or as idiotic as a hundred others.

In any case, by the time I got back to my distant apartment and went to bed, all these thoughts had vanished, and my whole soul clung expectantly to the great promise that had been made to me. Whenever I wanted to—tomorrow, even—I would see Demian's mother. Let the students go on their drinking binges and scar one another's faces, let the rotten world await its own destruction—what did I care? The only thing I awaited was the encounter with my destiny in a new form, a new image.

...

I slept deeply until late the next morning. The new day dawned for me as a glorious holiday, of a kind I had not had since the Christmas celebrations of my childhood. I was full of inner restlessness but without a hint of fear. I felt that an important day in my life had arrived; the world around me seemed transformed, solemnly and meaningfully waiting; even the soft, flowing autumn rain was beautiful: silently, ceremoniously full of serious yet joyful music. It was the first time the outside world was in pure harmony with my inner world, and that is a high holiday of the soul—a day that makes it worthwhile to be alive. Not a single building or shop window or face on the street bothered me; everything was as it should be, and yet it did not wear the empty face of the habitual and every day. Instead nature was waiting, standing worshipfully ready to meet its destiny. That was how I had seen the world as a boy, on the mornings of the important holidays, Christmas and Easter. I hadn't realized this world could still be so beautiful. I had gotten used to my inward-facing life, and had come to terms with the fact that the life out there had lost all meaning for me; I had decided that losing the glittering colors of the world inevitably went along with the loss of childhood, and that to a certain extent you had to pay for the freedom and manhood of the soul by renouncing that beloved shimmer. Now, enchanted, I saw that it had all merely been overshadowed and covered up, and that it was possible, even as a free man who had renounced childhood happiness, to see the world aglow and feel the heartfelt quiver of childlike vision.

The moment came when I found the garden on the edge of town once more, where I had parted from Demian the night before. Hidden behind tall, rain-gray trees was a small house, bright and homey, with large flowering plants behind a big glass pane, and clear, shining windows revealing dark walls with pictures and bookshelves. The front door led straight into a small heated hallway, and a silent old maid, in black with a white apron, showed me in and took my coat.

She left me alone in the hall. I looked around, and right away I was in the middle of my dream. High up on the dark wooden wall, above a door, hung a black frame, and under the glass was a picture I knew well: my bird with the golden yellow sparrow hawk head, vaulting out of the world-egg. I stood there, deeply moved—I had so much joy and sorrow in my heart, as though everything I had ever done and ever felt was coming back to me in that moment, as answer, as fulfillment. I saw image after image streak like lightning across my soul: my father's house back home, with the old stone coat of arms above the arch of the gate; Demian as a young man drawing the coat of arms; myself as a scared boy trapped in the evil clutches of my enemy, Kromer; myself as a teenager, sitting at the quiet table in my little student room and painting the bird of my yearnings, my soul tangled up in the net of its own threads—and everything, everything down to that moment echoed inside me, having been answered at last with affirmation and approval.

With tears in my eyes I stared at my picture and read myself. Then I looked farther down, and there, behind the open door, under the picture of the bird, stood a tall woman in a black dress. It was her.

I couldn't speak a word. With a face timeless and ageless and imbued with will, like her son's, the beautiful, sacred woman gave me a friendly smile. Her gaze was fulfillment, her greeting meant I had come home. I silently held out my hand to her, and she took it in both of her firm, warm hands.

"You must be Sinclair. I recognized you right away. Welcome!"

Her voice was deep and warm, and I drank it in like sweet wine. Then I looked up, into her quiet face, into her black, unfathomable eyes, at her lively, ripe mouth, and at her free and imperious brow, which bore the sign.

"How happy I am!" I said to her, and I kissed her hands. "I feel like I have been on a journey my whole life—and now I've come home."

She smiled a maternal smile.

"No one can ever go home," came her friendly reply. "But when friends' paths meet, the whole world can look like home for a time."

Her words expressed what I had been feeling on my way to her. Her voice as well as her words were very like her son's, and yet completely different. Everything was more mature and warmer, more direct. But the same way Max, long ago, had never seemed like a boy, his mother did not come across in the least like the mother of a grown son: her face and hair smelled so young and sweet, her golden skin was so taut and smooth, her mouth so radiant. She stood before me even more regal than she had been in my dream, and to be this close to her was to feel the joy of love. Her gaze was fulfillment.

So this was the new form in which my fate revealed itself to me: no longer stern and isolating but ripe and joyful! I came to no decisions at that moment, I took no vows—I had arrived, at a goal, a high point of the path, from which I could see the way ahead, long and majestic, reaching into promised lands, shaded by treetops of nearby happiness, cooled by nearby gardens of every pleasure. Whatever might happen to me now, I had been blessed with the knowledge that this woman was in the world, and was ecstatic to be able to drink in her voice and breathe in her closeness. Whether she be a mother to me, or a lover, or a goddess— as long as she was there, as long as my path ran next to hers!

She pointed up at my hawk picture.

"You never made our Max happier than with that picture," she said pensively. "And me as well. We were waiting for you, and when the picture came we knew you were on the way to us. When you were a little boy, Sinclair, my son came home from school one day and said: There's a boy there with the mark on his forehead, I have to make him my friend. It was you. You did not have it easy, but we had faith in you. One time, when you were home for the holidays, you met up with Max. You must have been around sixteen years old. Max told me about it ..."

I interrupted her. "Oh, he told you? That was the most miserable time of my life!"

"Yes. Max told me that Sinclair has the hardest part ahead of him: he is trying to flee back into a community, he's hanging around bars. But he won't be able to do it. His mark is obscured, but secretly it is burning him.—Isn't that how it was?"

"Yes, exactly. Then I found Beatrice, and then, at last, another guide came to me. His name was Pistorius. Only then did I realize why my childhood was so closely tied to Max, why I couldn't get free of him. Dear Lady—dear Mother—back then I often thought I would have to take my own life. Is the path that hard for everyone?"

She ran her hand over my hair, as soft as a gentle breeze.

"It is always hard to be born. You know it—the bird has to struggle to get out of the egg. Think back and ask yourself: Was the path really so hard? Was it only hard? Wasn't it lovely too? Do you wish you had had a prettier, easier way?"

I shook my head.

"It was hard," I said, as though asleep, "it was hard until the dream came."

She nodded and gave me a piercing look.

"Yes, we all have to find our dream, then the path becomes easy. But no dream lasts forever. Every dream is supplanted by a new one, and you can't try to hold tight to any of them."

I was suddenly frightened. Was that a warning? Was it a rejection, already? But whatever it was, I was ready to let her be my guide and not ask where she was leading me.

"I don't know how long my dream will last," I said. "I hope it's forever. Under the picture of the bird my destiny has welcomed me, like a mother and like a lover. I belong to that destiny and to no one else."

"For as long as that dream is your destiny, you should stay true to it," she affirmed in a serious voice.

I was gripped with sadness and the desperate desire to die in this enchanted hour. I felt tears well up inside me and overpower me, irresistibly—it had been so infinitely long since the last time I'd cried! I turned violently away from her, stepped over to the window, and looked out past the flowerpots with blind eyes.

Behind me I heard her voice. It sounded calm, and nonetheless as full of affection as a goblet filled to the rim with wine.

"Sinclair, you're acting like a child! Your destiny loves you. It will be completely yours someday, just how you dream it, as long as you stay true to it."

I had regained control of myself and I turned back to face her again. She gave me her hand.

"I have a few friends," she said with a smile, "a few—very few, very close—friends who call me Eve. You can use my first name too, if you want."

She led me to the door, opened it, and pointed out into the garden. "You'll find Max out there."

I stood under the tall trees, numb and shaken, either wider awake or more deeply dreaming than ever, I wasn't sure. The rain dripped gently from the branches. I walked slowly into the garden, which extended a long way up and down the riverbank. Finally I found Demian. He was in an open summer house, shirtless, practicing boxing with a hanging sandbag.

I stood rooted to the spot. Demian looked magnificent, with his broad chest, firm, manly head, and raised arms with huge, taut, strong muscles. Movements burst from his hips, shoulders, and wrists like playing fountains.

"Demian!" I called out. "What are you doing there?" He gave a cheerful laugh.

"Training. I've promised my little Japanese friend a match, and he's quick as a cat and just as spiteful. But he won't beat me. There's a tiny little humiliation I need to pay him back for."

He pulled on a shirt and jacket.

"You've already been to see my mother?" he asked.

"Yes, Demian, what a glorious mother you have! And: Eve! The name fits her perfectly, she really is like the mother of us all."

He looked thoughtfully into my face for a moment.

"She's already told you her first name? You can be proud, my boy, you are the first person she's ever told it to the first time she met him."

From that day on I came and went in their house like a son and a brother, although also like a lover. As soon as I had shut the gates behind me—actually as soon as I'd seen, from a distance, the tops of the garden's tall trees—I was rich, I was happy. Outside was "reality"; outside were streets and buildings, people and institutions, libraries and lecture halls—but here inside was light, and the soul; here dreams and fairy tales had come to life. And yet we did not live cut off from the world at all—in our thoughts and our conversations we were usually right in the middle of it, only on a different plane. It was not borders and frontiers that separated us from the mass of men, but rather a different way of seeing. Our task was to play the role of an island in the world—maybe we would be a model for others, maybe not, but either way we would proclaim that there were other possible ways to live. I, who had been lonely for so long, learned what true community means, the kind that is possible between people who have felt complete and total solitude. Never again did I yearn for the tables of the happy or the feasts of the blessed; never again did envy or longing for the past come over me at the sight of groups of people. I was slowly being initiated into the mystery of those who bore "the mark."

We, with the mark, might justly be considered strange, even crazy and dangerous, by the rest of the world. We were awakened, or at least awakening; our efforts were directed toward ever more complete awareness, while others always longed to merge their opinions, ideals, and duties, their lives and their happiness, more and more closely with those of the herd. That was a striving too—there was strength in that effort, and even a kind of greatness. But we, with the sign, felt that we embodied nature's will for the new, the individual, and the future, while the others' lives showed only a will to persist in the old. They loved humanity as much as we did, but for them it was something already finished, to be preserved and protected, while for us it lay in a distant future we were all moving toward, whose image was still unknown, and whose laws had never been written.

Aside from Eve, Max, and me, other seekers of very different kinds belonged to our circle, more or less intimately. Some of them followed strange paths, devoted themselves to bizarre goals, and clung to opinions and practices far outside the mainstream. The group included astrologers and kabbalists, a follower of Count Tolstoy, and all sorts of fragile, shy, and vulnerable types—followers of new sects, devotees of yoga, vegetarians, and others. In fact we had nothing in common with them spiritually, except for the mutual respect everyone showed for one another's esoteric ideals. We felt closer to other members of the group, the ones who pursued mankind's search for gods and new ideals in the past. Their studies often reminded me of those of my old friend Pistorius. They brought books with them, translated texts from ancient languages for us, showed us reproductions of old symbols and depictions of ancient rites, and taught us to see how every ideal the human race had ever possessed was a dream from the unconscious soul, dreams in which mankind had gropingly followed the dim premonitions of its future possibilities. And so we ran through the wondrous, thousand-headed chaos of gods from the ancient world, all the way up to the conversion to Christianity; we learned about the beliefs of the solitary saints and the changes and transformations that religions underwent from one people to the next. Everything we collected led us to the same critique of our time and the Europe of our day: its titanic endeavors had created powerful new human weapons but had finally ended in a profound and scandalous desolation of spirit. It had conquered the whole world only to lose its own soul.

Our group also included believers and adherents of various doctrines of salvation. There were Buddhists who wanted to convert Europe, Tolstoyans, and other faiths too. We in the inner circle listened to them but took none of their teachings as anything but a symbol. We who bore the sign felt no concern whatsoever for how the future would look. Every faith, every doctrine of salvation, seemed equally dead and useless to us from the start. We recognized only one thing as our duty and destiny: every one of us had to become himself, had to be true to and live for the sake of the seed of nature at work in himself, so completely that the uncertain future would find us ready for anything and everything it might bring.

For it was equally clear to us all, whether the sense was spoken or unspoken, that a new birth and the collapse of the present world were near, and already discernible. Demian sometimes told me: "No one can imagine what will come. Europe's soul is an animal that has lain in chains for an eternity. When it is free at last, its first stirrings will not be the sweetest and gentlest. But how we get there doesn't matter, as long as the true needs of the soul—so anesthetized and buried with lies for so long—see the light of day at last. Then our day will have come. They will need us, not as a guide or a giver of new laws (we will not live to see the new laws) but as the ones who are ready and willing to go and stand wherever destiny summons us. Look, anyone is prepared to do incredible things when his ideals are threatened, but when a new ideal, a new and perhaps dangerous or sinister stirring of growth comes knocking, there is no one. The few who will stand up and join in the transformation—will be us. That is what we are marked for, the same way Cain was marked to arouse fear and hate and to drive the humanity that existed then out of its cramped idyll into the wide, dangerous world. Everyone who has changed the course of human history, every last one was able to do so only because he was ready for his destiny. That's true of Moses and the Buddha, Napoleon and Bismarck. The wave that carries us, the star that guides us—we cannot choose it. If Bismarck had sympathized with the Social Democrats and joined them, he would have been an intelligent man but not a man of destiny. The same with Napoleon, with Caesar, with Ignatius of Loyola, with everyone! You have to think of these things in biological, evolutionary terms, always! When radical changes on the earth's surface hurled sea creatures onto dry land, or land animals back into the water, the specimens ready for their destiny were the ones that carried out the new, unimaginable transformation and adapted to save their species. Maybe up until then these specimens had stood out among their kind as conservative preservers of the past, or maybe they were the outsiders and revolutionaries, we don't know. But they were ready, and so they could save their species by evolving into something new. That we know. That is what we are ready for too."

Eve was often present during conversations like this, but she didn't talk the same way. All of us who expressed our thoughts found a listener in her, an echo, full of trust and understanding. It seemed as though all the thoughts originated with her and were only returning back to her. Sitting near her, hearing her voice now, and breathing in the atmosphere of soulful maturity that surrounded her—that was what made me happy.

She sensed at once when any change took place in me: any dullness of spirit or any renewal. The dreams I had in my sleep seemed to me to have been sent by her. I often told her about them, and she always found them comprehensible and natural; there were no details her sensitive feelings could not follow. For a time I had dreams that were like replicas of our daytime conversations: I dreamed that the whole world was in turmoil and that I, either alone or with Demian, was waiting anxiously for the great destiny to come. It stayed hidden, but somehow it bore Eve's features. To be chosen by her or rejected by her was what destiny meant.

Sometimes she said with a smile: "That's not your whole dream, Sinclair, you've forgotten the best part"—and then it sometimes happened that another part of the dream came back to me, and I couldn't understand how I could possibly have forgotten it.

At times, all this wasn't enough; I was tortured with desire. I thought I could not bear seeing her next to me without taking her in my arms. That too she noticed right away. One time, when I stayed away for several days and then returned distraught, she took me aside and said: "You mustn't have wishes you don't believe in. I know what you wish for. Either you can give up these wishes or you need to fully and properly wish for them. If you can ever ask in such a way that you are entirely sure your wish will be fulfilled, then fulfillment will come. But now you're just wishing and then feeling bad about it, scared the whole time. That is what you need to overcome. Let me tell you a story."

And she told me that once upon a time there was a young man in love with a star in the sky. He stood on the ocean's shore, reached out his hands, and worshipped the star; he dreamed about it and directed all his thoughts at it. But he knew, or thought he knew, that a star cannot be clasped in human arms. He thought it was his destiny to love a heavenly body without any hope of fulfillment, and from this idea he constructed an entire poetry of life based on renunciation and silent faithful suffering that would make him purer and better. Still all his dreams were of the star. One night he was standing by the ocean again, on a high cliff, and he looked at the star and burned with love for it. And at the pinnacle of his greatest longing, he leaped into thin air toward the star. But the instant he made the leap, he thought, fast as lightning: It's not possible! Then he was lying down on the beach, broken to pieces. He did not know how to love. If, at the moment he jumped, he had had the strength of soul to be firm and sure that his longing would be fulfilled, he would have flown up to the sky and become one with the star.

"Love cannot ask," she said, "or plead. Love must have the strength to reach certainty from within. Then one's love is no longer attracted, it attracts. Sinclair, your love is drawn to me. If it ever draws *me* to *it*, I will come. I don't want to do anyone a favor, I want to be won."

Another time, she told me a different fairy tale. There once was a lover who loved without hope. He withdrew completely into his heart and thought his love would consume him. He was lost to the world; he no longer saw the blue sky and the green forest, the stream did not murmur past for him, the harp did not sound, everything was gone, and he had grown poor and miserable. Still his love grew and grew, and he would have much rather died and withered away than give up on possessing the beautiful woman he loved. Then he felt how his love had turned everything else in his heart to ashes; his passion grew powerful; its force of attraction pulled and pulled, and the beautiful woman had no choice but to obey: she came to him, and he stood with outspread arms to draw her to him. But she, standing there before him, had been utterly transformed—he saw and felt with a shudder that he had drawn the whole lost world to him. It stood before him and gave itself to him, sky and forest and mountain stream, everything came to him fresh and magnificent, in new colors, and it belonged to him, spoke his language. Instead of winning just one woman, he had the whole world pressed to his heart; every star in the sky shone within him, sparkling with pleasure through his soul.—He had loved and had found himself in the process. Most people love only in order to lose themselves.

My love for Eve seemed like the only thing in my life. But every day it looked different. Sometimes I felt certain that my essential nature was not in fact struggling to reach her actual person, rather that she was only a symbol of what was inside me, trying only to lead me deeper into myself. The things she said often sounded like my own unconscious mind's answers to the burning questions I had. At other times there were moments when I was aflame with sensual desire next to her, and kissed things she had touched. Gradually my sexual and asexual love, reality and symbol, began to merge. Then, thinking about her in calm tranquility alone in my room, I sometimes seemed to feel her hand in mine, her lips on mine. Or else I would be with her, looking into her face, talking to her and hearing her voice, and I couldn't tell if she was even real or just a dream. I started to realize how a person can possess a love forever, immortally. I learned something new from reading a book and it was the exact same feeling as a kiss from Eve; she stroked my hair and smiled her fresh, sweet-smelling warmth at me and I had the same feeling as when I had made progress within myself. Everything that mattered to me, every part of my destiny, could take on her shape. She could turn into every one of my thoughts and vice versa.

I had to spend Christmas vacation with my parents, and I had been afraid of it because I thought it would be torture to be away from Eve for two weeks. But it was no such thing—it was wonderful to be at home and to think about her. When I returned to H., I stayed away from her house for another two days, savoring my security and my independence from her physical presence. I had dreams, too, in which my union with her took place in new, metaphorical ways. She was an ocean and I was a river pouring into her; she was a star and I was another star hurtling toward her, and we met, felt drawn to each other, stayed close to each other, and orbited blissfully around each other in tight, singing circles for all eternity.

I told her this dream the next time I visited her.

"That's a beautiful dream," she said quietly. "Make it come true!"

Early that spring there came a day I will never forget. I walked into the hall, where a window was open; a warm breeze wafted the thick smell of hyacinths through the house. Since no one was there, I went upstairs to Max Demian's study. I knocked lightly on the door and, as I habitually did, walked in without waiting for an answer.

The room was dark, all the curtains pulled shut. The door to a small side room where Max had set up a chemical laboratory was open, and from there came the bright white light of the spring sun shining through the rain clouds. I thought no one was in the room, and I pulled back a curtain.

Then I saw Max Demian sitting on a stool near the curtained window, hunched over and strangely altered. A feeling flashed through me like lightning: you've seen that before! His arms hung limp with his hands in his lap, his head hung slightly bent forward, and his face, with his eyes open, was dead and unseeing—a tiny glare of reflected light shone in the pupil of one eye, as though in a dead piece of glass. His wan face was as if turned in on itself, expressionless except for a horrible rigidity; it looked like an ancient, primitive animal mask at the gate of a temple. He did not seem to be breathing.

I felt a shudder of memory: I had seen him like that, exactly like that, once before, many years ago, when I was still a boy. His eyes had stared inward the same way; his hands had lain lifelessly next to each other the same way; a fly had walked across his face. And back then, maybe six years before, he had looked exactly as old and as timeless as he looked now. Not a wrinkle in his face was any different.

Gripped with fear, I quietly left the room and went downstairs. In the hall I saw Eve. She looked pale and seemed tired, in a way I had never seen her. A shadow flew in through the window; the glaring white sunlight was suddenly gone.

"I just saw Max," I whispered hurriedly. "Has something happened? He is asleep, or turned in on himself, I don't know how to put it. I've seen him like that once before."

"You didn't wake him up, did you?" she asked hurriedly.

"No. He didn't hear me. I left right away. Tell me, Eve, what's the matter with him?"

She wiped her brow with the back of her hand.

"Don't worry, Sinclair, nothing's the matter with him. He has withdrawn. It won't last long."

She stood up and went out into the garden, even though it had just started to rain. I could tell I wasn't supposed to go with her. So I paced back and forth in the hall, smelled the stupefying scent of the hyacinths, stared at my bird picture over the door, and anxiously breathed in the strange shadow that had filled the house that morning. What was it? What had happened?

Eve soon came back. There were raindrops in her dark hair. She sat down in her armchair, exhausted. I walked over to her, bent down, and kissed the drops from her hair. Her eyes were quiet and bright, but the drops tasted like tears.

"Should I check on him?" I asked in a whisper.

She smiled weakly.

"Don't be a little boy, Sinclair!" she warned, in a loud voice as though trying to break a spell she was under. "Go away now, and come back later, I can't talk to you right now."

I left the house and hurried out of the city toward the mountains, into the fine, slanting rain. The clouds moved past, low in the sky, under heavy pressure, as though in fear; beneath them there was hardly any breeze. A storm seemed to be raging on the peaks. More than once the sun burst through the steel-gray clouds for a moment, pale in hue but dazzlingly bright.

Then a fluffy yellow cloud came drifting across the sky and crashed into the gray wall, collecting there. In a matter of seconds the wind had shaped a picture out of the yellow and the blue: a gigantic bird, tearing free from the chaos of blue and disappearing into the sky with great beats of its wings. All at once you could hear the storm, and rain beat down mixed with hail. A short clap of thunder, improbably and terrifyingly loud, burst across the landscape whipped with rain, and immediately the sun broke through the clouds again, and the pale snow glowed wan and unreal on the nearby mountains above the brown trees.

When I came back wet and pale, hours later, Demian himself opened the front door for me.

He took me up to his room. A gas flame was burning in his laboratory, and papers lay strewn about—he seemed to have been working.

"Sit down," he invited me. "You must be tired. The weather's terrible. You look like you really got caught outside. There'll be tea in a minute."

"Something strange is happening today," I hesitantly began. "It can't be just the weather."

He looked searchingly at me.

"Did you see something?"

"Yes. I saw a picture in the clouds for a moment. It was perfectly clear."

"What was it?"

"A bird."

"The sparrow hawk? Was it him? From your dream?"

"Yes, it was my hawk. It was yellow and gigantic and flew into the blue-black sky."

Demian heaved a great sigh.

There was a knock at the door. The old servant brought in the tea.

"Help yourself, Sinclair, please ... I think it was probably no accident that you saw the bird?"

"Accident? Does anyone see something like that by chance?"

"No, you're right. The bird means something. Do you know what it means?"

"No. I can only feel some kind of disruption, destiny taking another step. I think it has to do with us all."

He paced furiously back and forth.

"Destiny taking another step!" he cried. "Last night I dreamed the same thing, and my mother had a premonition yesterday with the same message ... I dreamed I was climbing up a ladder that was leaning against a tree trunk or tower. When I got to the top I saw the whole countryside on fire—a vast plain with cities and villages. I can't tell you everything, it's not all clear in my mind yet."

"Do you interpret the dream as being about you?" I asked.

"About me? Of course. No one dreams anything that has nothing to do with them. But it's not only about me, you're right. There's a pretty sharp distinction in my mind between the dreams that show movements in my own soul and the other, very rare dreams that point to a shift in the fate of all mankind. I have not had many of that second kind of dream, and not a single one I could call a prophecy that later came true. The interpretations are not that specific. But I know for certain that I've dreamed something not only about me, partly because it connects up with earlier dreams of mine, it continues them. These are the dreams that have given me the hunches I've talked to you about, Sinclair. We know that our world is rotten to the core, but that's not a sufficient reason to prophesy its decline or destruction or what have you. For the past several

years, though, I have had dreams that make me conclude, or feel, or however you want to put it—that make me feel, then, that the collapse of the old world is approaching. At first they were very faint, distant intimations, but they have grown clearer and clearer, and stronger. I still don't know anything except that something major and terrible is coming, and that it will affect me. We are going to live through what we've talked about, Sinclair! The world wants to be reborn. The smell of death is in the air. Nothing new comes without death … It's worse than I ever imagined." I stared at him in horror.

"You can't tell me the rest of your dream?" I asked shyly.

He shook his head.

"No."

The door opened. Eve walked in.

"There you two are! You're not sad, are you, children?"

She looked refreshed, no longer tired at all. Demian smiled at her, and she came up to us the way a mother comes to frightened children.

"We're not sad, Mother, we've just been trying to puzzle out something from these new signs. But it doesn't matter. Whatever it is that's about to happen will suddenly be here, and then we'll find out whatever we need to know."

But I was in a bad mood, and when I said goodbye and walked out through the hallway alone, the scent of the hyacinths seemed stale and cadaverous. A shadow had fallen over us.

(选自 Hesse, Hermann. *Demian*. Translated by Damion Searls. New York: Penguin Group, 2013: 97 – 116.)

Questions

1. Why did Sinclair read Nietzsche's books in university?
2. What did Frau Eva tell Sinclair he must do in order to win her over?
3. Why did Sinclair think the people with Cain mark should get ready for the coming fate?
4. When Demian and Sinclair reunited for the final time, what did they identify as responsible for humanity's degradation?
5. How do you understand the sentence "We recognize only one thing as our duty and destiny: every one of us had to become himself, had to be true to and live for the sake of the seed of nature at work in himself, so completely that the uncertain future would find us ready for anything and everything it might bring"?

Unit 6

Nevil Shute Norway: *A Town Like Alice*

Nevil Shute Norway (17 January 1899—12 January 1960) was an English novelist and aeronautical engineer who spent his later years in Australia. He used his full name in his engineering career and Nevil Shute as his pen name to protect his engineering career from any potential negative publicity in connection with his novels, which included *On the Beach* and *A Town Like Alice*.

Born in Somerset Road, Ealing, Middlesex, Nevil Shute was educated at the Dragon School, Shrewsbury School and Balliol College; he graduated from Oxford University in 1922 with a third-class degree in engineering science. Shute's father, Arthur Hamilton Norway, became head of the post office in Ireland before the First World War and was based at the main post office in Dublin in 1916 at the time of the Easter Rising. Shute himself was later commended for his role as a stretcher-bearer during the rising. On 13 June 1915, his elder brother, Fredrick Hamilton Norway, aged 19, was wounded at Epinette, near Armentières, and was evacuated to Wimereux where he died, on 4 July, with his parents by his side. Shute attended the Royal Military Academy, Woolwich, but because of his stammer he was unable to take up a commission in the Royal Flying Corps and then he served in the Great War as a soldier in the Suffolk Regiment.

An aeronautical engineer as well as a pilot, he began his engineering career with the De Havilland Aircraft Company. Dissatisfied with the lack of opportunities for advancement, he took a position in 1924 with Vickers Ltd., where he was involved with the development of airships, working as Chief Calculator (stress engineer) on the R100 airship project for the Vickers subsidiary Airship Guarantee Company. In 1929, he was promoted to Deputy Chief

Engineer of the R100 project under Barnes Wallis and when Wallis left the project, he became the Chief Engineer.

The R100 was a prototype for passenger-carrying airships that would serve the needs of Britain's empire. The government-funded but privately-developed R100 made a successful 1930 round trip to Canada. While in Canada, it made trips from Montreal to Ottawa, Toronto and Niagara Falls. The fatal crash in France of its government-developed counterpart R101 ended British interest in dirigibles. The Secretary of State for Air, Lord Thomson, was killed in the crash along with several senior figures in the airship development program. The R100 was immediately grounded and subsequently scrapped. Shute gave a detailed account of the development of the two airships in his 1954 autobiographical work, *Slide Rule*. His account was very critical of the R101 design and management team, and strongly hinted that senior team members were complicit in concealing flaws in the airship's design and construction. In 1931, with the cancellation of the R100 project, Shute teamed up with the talented de Havilland trained designer A. Hessell Tiltman to found the aircraft construction company Airspeed Ltd.

On 7 March 1931, Shute married Frances Mary Heaton, a 28-year-old medical practitioner. They had two daughters, Heather and Shirley. By the outbreak of the Second World War, Shute was already a rising novelist. Even as war seemed imminent, he was working on military projects with his former boss at Vickers, Sir Dennistoun Burney. He was commissioned into the Royal Naval Volunteer Reserve as a sub-lieutenant and quickly ended up in what would become the Directorate of Miscellaneous Weapons Development. There, he was a head of engineering, working on secret weapons such as Panjandrum, a job that appealed to the engineer in him. He also developed the Rocket Spear, an anti-submarine missile with a fluted cast iron head. After the first U-boat was sunk by it, Charles Goodeve sent him a message concluding "I am particularly pleased as it fully substantiates the foresight you showed in pushing this in its early stages. My congratulations."

His celebrity as a writer caused the Ministry of Information to send him to the Normandy Landings on 6 June 1944 and later to Burma as a correspondent. He finished the war with the rank of lieutenant commander in the Royal Navy Volunteer Reserves (RNVR). In 1948, Shute flew his own Percival Proctor airplane to Australia and back, accompanied by the writer James Riddell, who published a book, *Flight of Fancy*, based on the trip, in 1950.

Twenty-four of his novels and novellas have been published. Many of his books have been adapted for the screen, including *Lonely Road* in 1936; *Landfall: A Channel Story* in 1949; *Pied Piper* in 1942, 1959, and as *Crossing to Freedom*, a CBS made-for-television movie, in 1990; *On the Beach* in 1959 and in 2000 as a two-part miniseries; and *No Highway* in 1951. *A Town Like Alice* was adapted in 1956 and serialized for Australian television in 1981, and was broadcast on BBC Radio 2 in 1997 starring Jason Connery, Becky Hindley, Bernard Hepton and Virginia McKenna. Shute's 1952 novel *The Far Country* was filmed for television as six one-hour episodes in 1972, and as a two-part miniseries in 1987. In the readers' list of

"Modern Library 100 Best Novels" of the 20th century, *A Town Like Alice* came in at number 17, *Trustee from the Toolroom* at 27, and *On the Beach* at 56.

On his return, concerned about what he saw as the decline of his home country, Shute decided that he and his family would emigrate to Australia. In 1950, he settled with his wife and two daughters on farmland at Langwarrin, south-east of Melbourne. Remembering his 1930 trip to Canada and his decision to emigrate to Australia, he wrote, in 1954, "For the first time in my life I saw how people live in an English-speaking country outside England." Although he intended to remain in Australia, he did not apply for Australian citizenship. Between 1956 and 1958 in Australia, he took up car racing as a hobby, driving a white Jaguar XK140. Some of this experience found its way into his book *On the Beach*. Shute died in Melbourne in 1960 after a stroke. Norway Road and Nevil Shute Road at Portsmouth Airport, Hampshire were both named after him.

Theme

A Town Like Alice, published in 1950, appeared to be a war novel on the surface, but it was written when he was presumably doing some traveling in southeast Asia and Australia. In a note to the text, Shute wrote that a forced march of women by the Japanese did indeed take place during World War II, but the women in question were Dutch rather than British in the novel, and the march was in Sumatra, but not Malaya.

The story falls broadly into three parts. In Post-World War II London, Jean Paget, a secretary in a leather goods factory, is informed by the solicitor Noel Strachan that she has inherited a considerable sum of money from an uncle she never knew. But the solicitor is now her trustee and she only has the use of the income until she inherits absolutely, at the age of thirty-five, several years in the future. In the firm's interest, but increasingly with personal interest, Strachan acts as her guide and advisor. Jean decides that her priority is to build a well in a Malayan village. The second part of the story flashes back to Jean's experiences during the war, when she was working in Malaya at the time the Japanese invaded and was taken prisoner together with a group of women and children. The third part of the book shows how Jean's entrepreneurship gives a decisive economic impact on developing Willstown into "a town like Alice" and also Jean's help in rescuing an injured stockman, which breaks down many local barriers. The story closes a few years later, with an aged Noel Strachan visiting Willstown to see what has been done with the money he has given Jean to invest. He reveals that the money which Jean inherited was originally made in an Australian gold rush, and he is satisfied to see the money returning to the site of its making.

The novel criticized the attitudes of the time: Aborigines are referred to as "boongs" or "abos" and it is also assumed that the non-whites must use different shops and bars from the whites and that they are less reliable than the whites. It reveals that the captive British women are completely lost, because the only Malayan words they have learned are orders for their Malayan servants, while Jean survives by use of her language skills and her willingness to live the Malayan way.

Cutting-edge Topic

Shute's novels are written in a simple, highly readable style, with clearly delineated plot lines. Where there is a romantic element, sex is referred to only obliquely. Many of the stories are introduced by a narrator who is not a character in the story. The most common theme in Shute's novels is the dignity of work spanning all classes. Another recurrent theme is the bridging of social barriers such as class, race or religion.

Shute deals with women situations in a broad sense. For example, Jean Paget is not given full control of the money she inherits from her uncle, but has her capital managed by male lawyers. Also, the Malayan women are subject to their husbands. Jean Paget makes a move toward female emancipation by digging a well in a Malayan village, so that the women of this village no longer have to carry their water for two miles each day, and also have a meeting place next to the well where they can discuss village affairs without being heard by the male villagers. However, this must be done with the approval of the men. Shute intricately describes the role that entrepreneurs may play in community building. Instead of living on the income from her inheritance, Jean Paget puts it to good use to make Willstown a better place.

Shute's heroes tend to be like himself: middle class solicitors, doctors, accountants, bank managers, engineers, generally university graduates. However (as in *Trustee from the Toolroom*), Shute values the honest artisans and their social integrity and contributions to society more than the contributions of the upper classes. Aviation and engineering provide the backdrop for many of Shute's novels. He identifies how engineering, science, and design could improve human life. Shute's novels explore the boundary between accepted science and rational belief on the one hand, and mystical or paranormal possibilities including reincarnation on the other hand, including elements of fantasy and science fiction in novels that were considered mainstream.

Excerpt

Chapter One

James Macfadden died in March 1905 when he was forty-seven years old; he was riding in the Driffield Point-to-Point.

He left the bulk of his money to his son Douglas. The Macfaddens and the Dalhousies at that time lived in Perth, and Douglas was a school friend of Jock Dalhousie, who was a young man then, and had gone to London to become junior partner in a firm of solicitors in Chancery

Lane, Owen, Dalhousie and Peters. I am now the senior partner, and Owen and Dalhousie and Peters have been dead for many years, but I never changed the name of the firm.

It was natural that Douglas Macfadden should put his affairs into the hands of Jock Dalhousie, and Mr. Dalhousie handled them personally till he died in 1928. In splitting up the work I took Mr. Macfadden on to my list of clients, and forgot about him in the pressure of other matters.

It was not until 1935 that any business for him came up. I had a letter from him then, from an address in Ayr. He said that his brother-in-law, Arthur Paget, had been killed in a motor car accident in Malaya and so he wanted to redraft his will to make a trust in favour of his sister Jean and her two children. I am sorry to say that I was so ignorant of this client that I did not even know he was unmarried and had no issue of his own. He finished up by saying that he was too unwell to travel down to London, and he suggested that perhaps a junior member of the firm might be sent up to see him and arrange the matter.

This fitted in with my arrangements fairly well, because when I got this letter I was just leaving for a fortnight's fishing holiday on Loch Shiel. I wrote and told him that I would visit him on my way south, and I put the file concerning his affairs in the bottom of my suitcase to study one evening during my vacation.

When I got to Ayr I took a room at the Station Hotel, because in our correspondence there had been no suggestion that he could put me up. I changed out of my plus-fours into a dark business suit, and went to call upon my client.

He did not live at all in the manner I had expected. I did not know much about his estate except that it was probably well over twenty thousand pounds, and I had expected to find my client living in a house with a servant or two. Instead, I discovered that he had a bedroom and a sitting-room on the same floor of a small private hotel just off the sea front. He was evidently leading the life of an invalid though he was hardly more than fifty years old at that time, ten years younger than I was myself. He was as frail as an old lady of eighty, and he had a peculiar grey look about him which didn't look at all good to me. All the windows of his sitting-room were shut and after the clean air of the lochs and moors I found his room stuffy and close; he had a number of budgerigars in cages in the window, and the smell of these birds made the room very unpleasant. It was clear from the furnishings that he had lived in that hotel and in that room for a good many years.

He told me something about his life as we discussed the will; he was quite affable, and pleased that I had been able to come to visit him myself. He seemed to be an educated man, though he spoke with a marked Scots accent. "I live very quietly, Mr. Strachan," he said. "My health will not permit me to go far abroad. Whiles I get out upon the front on a fine day and sit for a time, and then again Maggie—that's the daughter of Mrs. Doyle who keeps the house—Maggie wheels me out in the chair. They are very good to me here."

Turning to the matter of the will, he told me that he had no close relatives at all except his sister, Jean Paget. "Forbye my father might have left what you might call an indiscretion or two in Australia," he said. "I would not say that there might not be some of those about, though I have never met one, or corresponded. Jean told me once that my mother had been sore distressed. Women talk about these things, of course, and my father was a lusty type of man."

His sister Jean had been an officer in the WAACs in the 1914 – 1918 War, and she had married a Captain Paget in the spring of 1917. "It was not a very usual sort of marriage," he said thoughtfully. "You must remember that my sister Jean had never been out of Scotland till she joined the army, and the greater part of her life had been spent in Perth. Arthur Paget was an Englishman from Southampton, in Hampshire. I have nothing against Arthur, but we had all naturally thought that Jean would have married a Scot. Still, I would not say but it has been a happy marriage, or as happy as most."

After the war was over Arthur Paget had got a job upon a rubber estate in Malaya somewhere near Taiping, and Jean, of course, went out there with him. From that time Douglas Macfadden had seen little of his sister; she had been home on leave in 1926 and again in 1932. She had two children, Donald born in 1918 and Jean born in 1921; these children had been left in England in 1932 to live with the Paget parents and to go to school in Southampton, while their mother returned to Malaya. My client had seen them only once, in 1932 when their mother brought them up to Scotland.

The present position was that Arthur Paget had been killed in a motor accident somewhere near Ipoh; he had been driving home at night from Kuala Lumpur and had driven off the road at a high speed and hit a tree. Probably he fell asleep. His widow, Jean Paget, was in England; she had come home a year or so before his death and she had taken a small house in Bassett just outside Southampton to make a home for the children and to be near their schools. It was a sensible arrangement, of course, but it seemed to me to be a pity that the brother and the sister could not have arranged to live nearer to each other. I fancy that my client regretted the distance that separated them, because he referred to it more than once.

He wanted to revise his will. His existing will was a very simple one, in which he left his entire estate to his sister Jean. "I would not alter that," he said. "But you must understand that Arthur Paget was alive when I made that will, and that in the nature of things I expected him to be alive when Jean inherited from me, and I expected that he would be there to guide her in matters of business. I shall not make old bones."

He seemed to have a fixed idea that all women were unworldly creatures and incapable of looking after money; they were irresponsible, and at the mercy of any adventurer. Accordingly, although he wanted his sister to have the full use of his money after his death, he wanted to create a trust to ensure that her son Donald, at that time a schoolboy, should inherit the whole estate intact after his mother's death. There was, of course, no special difficulty in that. I presented to him the various pros and cons of a trust such as he envisaged, and I reminded him that a small legacy to Mrs. Doyle, in whose house he had lived for so many years, might not be out of place provided that he was still living with them at the time of his death. He agreed to that. He told me then that he had no close relations living, and he asked me if I would undertake to be the sole trustee of his estate and the executor of his will. That is the sort of business a family solicitor frequently takes on his shoulders, of course. I told him that in view of my age he should appoint a co-trustee, and he agreed to the insertion of our junior partner, Mr. Lester Robinson, to be co-trustee with me. He also agreed to a charging clause for our professional services in connection with the trust.

There only remained to tidy up the loose ends of what was, after all, a fairly simple will. I asked him what should happen if both he and his sister were to die before the boy Donald was twenty-one, and I suggested that the trust should terminate and the boy should inherit the estate absolutely when he reached his majority. He agreed to this, and I made another note upon my pad.

"Supposing then," I said, "that Donald should die before his mother, or if Donald and his mother should die in some way before you. The estate would then pass to the girl, Jean. Again, I take it that the trust would terminate when she reached her majority?"

"Ye mean," he asked, "when she became twenty-one?" I nodded. "Yes. That is what we decided in the case of her brother."

He shook his head. "I think that would be most imprudent, Mr. Strachan, if I may say so. No lassie would be fit to administer her own estate when she was twenty-one. A lassie of that age is at the mercy of her sex, Mr. Strachan, at the mercy of her sex. I would want the trust to continue for much longer than that. Till she was forty, at the very least."

From various past experiences I could not help agreeing with him that twenty-one was a bit young for a girl to have absolute control over a large sum of money, but forty seemed to me to be excessively old. I stated my own view that twenty-five would be a reasonable age, and very reluctantly he receded to thirty-five. I could not move him from that position, and as he was obviously tiring and growing irritable I accepted that as the maximum duration of our trust. It meant that in those very unlikely circumstances the trust would continue for twenty-one years from that date, since the girl Jean had been born in 1921 and it was then 1935. That finished our business and I left him and went back to London to draft out the will, which I sent to him for signature. I never saw my client again.

It was my fault that I lost touch with him. It had been my habit for a great many years to take my holiday in the spring, when I would go with my wife to Scotland for a fortnight's fishing, usually to Loch Shiel. I thought that this was going on for ever, as one does, and that next year I would call again upon this client on my way down from the north to see if there was any other business I could do for him. But things turn out differently, sometimes. In the winter of 1935 Lucy died. I don't want to dwell on that, but we had been married for twenty-seven years and—well, it was very painful. Both our sons were abroad, Harry in his submarine on the China station and Martin in his oil company at Basra. I hadn't the heart to go back to Loch Shiel, and I had never been to Scotland since. I had a sale and got rid of most of our furniture, and I sold our house on Wimbledon Common; one has to make an effort at a time like that, and a clean break. It's no good going on living in the ashes of a dead happiness.

I took a flat in Buckingham Gate opposite the Palace stables and just across the park from my club in Pall Mall. I furnished it with a few things out of the Wimbledon house and got a woman to come in and cook my breakfast and clean for me in the mornings, and here I set out to re-create my life. I knew the pattern well enough from the experience of others in the club. Breakfast in my flat. Walk through the Park and up the Strand to my office in Chancery Lane. Work all day, with a light lunch at my desk. To the club at six o'clock to read the periodicals, and gossip, and dine, and after dinner a rubber of bridge. That is the routine that I fell into in the spring of 1936, and I am in it still.

All this, as I say, took my mind from Douglas Macfadden; with more than half my mind upon my own affairs I could only manage to attend to those clients who had urgent business with my office. And presently another interest grew upon me. It was quite obvious that war was coming, and some of us in the club who were too old for active military service began to get very interested in Air Raid Precautions. Cutting the long story short, Civil Defence as it came to be called absorbed the whole of my leisure for the next eight years. I became a Warden, and I was on duty in my district of Westminster all through the London blitz and the long, slow years of war that followed it. Practically all my staff went on service, and I had to run the office almost single-handed. In those years I never took a holiday, and I doubt if I slept more than five hours in any night. When finally peace came in 1945 my hair was white and my head shaky, and though I improved a little in the years that followed I had definitely joined the ranks of the old men.

One afternoon in January 1948 I got a telegram from Ayr. It read,

> Regret Mr. Douglas Macfadden passed away last night please instruct the funeral.
>
> Doyle, Balmoral Hotel, Ayr.

I had to search my memory, I am afraid, to recollect through the war years who Mr. Douglas Macfadden was, and then I had to turn to the file and the will to refresh my memory with the details of what had happened thirteen years before. It seemed rather odd to me that there was nobody at Ayr who could manage the funeral business. I put in a trunk call to Ayr right away and very soon I was speaking to Mrs. Doyle. It was a bad line, but I understood that she knew of no relations; apparently Mr. Macfadden had had no visitors for a very long time. Clearly, I should have to go to Ayr myself, or else send somebody. I had no urgent engagements for the next two days and the matter seemed to be a little difficult. I had a talk with Lester Robinson, my partner, who had come back from the war as a brigadier, and cleared my desk, and took the sleeper up to Glasgow after dinner that night. In the morning I went down in a slow train to Ayr.

When I got to the Balmoral Hotel I found the landlord and his wife in mourning and obviously distressed; they had been fond of their queer lodger and it was probably due in a great part to their ministrations that he had lived so long. There was no mystery about the cause of death. I had a talk with the doctor and heard all about his trouble; the doctor had been with him at the end, for he lived only two doors away, and the death certificate was already signed. I took a brief look at the body for identification and went through the various formalities of death. It was all perfectly straightforward, except that there were no relations.

"I doubt he had any," said Mr. Doyle. "His sister used to write to him at one time, and she came to see him in 1938, I think it was. She lived in Southampton. But he's had no letters except just a bill or two for the last two years."

His wife said, "Surely, the sister died, didn't she? Don't you remember him telling us, sometime towards the end of the war?"

"Well, I don't know," he said. "So much was happening about that time. Maybe she did die."

Relations or not, arrangements had to be made for the funeral, and I made them that afternoon. When that was done I settled down to look through the papers in his desk. One or two of the figures in an account book and on the back of the counterfoils of his cheque book made me open my eyes; clearly I should have to have a talk with the bank manager first thing next morning. I found a letter from his sister dated in 1941 about the lease of her house. It threw no light, of course, upon her death, if she was dead, but it did reveal significant news about the children. Both of them were in Malaya at that time. The boy Donald, who must have been twenty-three years old at that time, was working on a rubber plantation near Kuala Selangor. His sister Jean had gone out to him in the winter of 1939, and was working in an office in Kuala Lumpur.

At about five o'clock I put in a trunk call to my office in London, standing in the cramped box of the hotel, and spoke to my partner. "Look, Lester," I said. "I told you that there was some difficulty about the relations. I am completely at a loss up here, I'm sorry to say. Provisionally, I have arranged the funeral for the day after tomorrow, at two o'clock, at St. Enoch's cemetery. The only relations that I know of live, or used to live, in Southampton. The sister, Mrs. Arthur Paget, was living in 1941 at No. 17 St Ronans Road, Bassett—that's just by Southampton somewhere. There were some other Paget relations in the district, the parents of Arthur Paget. Mrs. Arthur Paget—her Christian name was Jean—yes, she was the deceased's sister. She had two children, Donald and Jean Paget, but they were both in Malaya in 1941. God knows what became of them. I wouldn't waste much time just now looking for them, but would you get Harris to do what he can to find some of these Southampton Pagets and tell them about the funeral? He'd better take the telephone book and talk to all the Pagets in Southampton one by one. I don't suppose there are so very many."

Lester came on the telephone to me next morning just after I got back from the bank. "I've nothing very definite, I'm afraid, Noel," he said. "I did discover one thing. Mrs. Paget died in 1942, so she's out of it. She died of pneumonia through going out to the air raid shelter—Harris got that from the hospital. About the other Pagets, there are seven in the telephone directory and we've rung them all up, and they're none of them anything to do with your family. But one of them, Mrs. Eustace Paget, thinks the family you're looking for are the Edward Pagets, and that they moved to North Wales after the first Southampton blitz."

"Any idea whereabouts in North Wales?" I asked.

"Not a clue," he said. "I think the only thing that you can do now is to proceed with the funeral."

"I think it is," I replied. "But tell Harris to go on all the same, because apart from the funeral we've got to find the heirs. I've just been to the bank, and there is quite a sizeable estate. We're the trustees, you know."

I spent the rest of that day packing up all personal belongings, and letters, and papers, to take down to my office. Furniture at that time was in short supply, and I arranged to store the furniture of the two rooms, since that might be wanted by the heirs. I gave the clothes to Mr. Doyle to give away to needy people in Ayr. Only two of the budgerigars were left; I gave those to the Doyles, who seemed to be attached to them. Next morning I had another interview with the bank manager and telephoned to book my sleeper on the night mail down to London. And in the afternoon we buried Douglas Macfadden.

It was very cold and bleak and grey in the cemetery, that January afternoon. The only mourners were the Doyles, father, mother, and daughter, and myself, and I remember thinking that it was queer how little any of us knew about the man that we were burying. I had a great respect for the Doyle family by that time. They had been overwhelmed when I told them of the small legacy that Mr. Macfadden had left them and at first they were genuinely unwilling to take it; they said that they had been well paid for his two rooms and board for many years, and anything else that they had done for him had been because they liked him. It was something, on that bitter January afternoon beside the grave, to feel that he had friends at the last ceremonies.

So that was the end of it, and I drove back with the Doyles and had tea with them in their sitting-room beside the kitchen. And after tea I left for Glasgow and the night train down to London, taking with me two suitcases of papers and small personal effects to be examined at my leisure if the tracing of the heir proved to be troublesome, and later to be handed over as a part of the inheritance.

In fact, he found the heir without much difficulty. Young Harris got a line on it within a week, and presently we got a letter from a Miss Agatha Paget, who was the headmistress of girls' school in Colwyn Bay. She was a sister of Arthur Paget, who had been killed in the motor accident in Malaya. She confirmed that his wife, Jean, had died in Southampton in the year 1942, and she added the fresh information that the son, Donald, was also dead. He had been a prisoner of war in Malaya, and had died in captivity. Her niece, Jean, however, was alive and in the London district. The headmistress did not know her home address because she lived in rooms and had changed them once or twice, so she usually wrote to her addressing her letters to her firm. She was employed in the office of a concern called Pack and Levy Ltd, whose address was The Hyde, Perivale, London, NW.

I got this letter in the morning mail; I ran through the others and cleared them out of the way, and then picked up this one and read it again. Then I got my secretary to bring me the Macfadden box and I read the will through again, and went through some other papers and my notes on the estate. Finally I reached out for the telephone directory and looked up Pack and Levy Ltd, to find out what they did.

Presently I got up from my desk and stood for a time looking out of the window at the bleak, grey, January London street. I like to think a bit before taking any precipitate action. Then I turned and went through into Robinson's office; he was dictating, and I stood warming myself at his fire till he had finished and the girl had left the room.

"I've got that Macfadden heir," I said. "I'll tell Harris."

"All right," he replied. "You've found the son?"

"No," I said. "I've found the daughter. The son's dead."

He laughed. "Bad luck. That means we're trustees for the estate until she's thirty-five, doesn't it?"

I nodded.

"How old is she now?"

I calculated for a minute. "Twenty-six or twenty-seven."

"Old enough to make a packet of trouble for us."

"I know."

"Where is she? What's she doing?"

"She's employed as a clerk or typist with a firm of handbag manufacturers in Perivale," I said. "I'm just about to concoct a letter to her."

He smiled. "Fairy Godfather."

"Exactly," I replied.

I went back into my room and sat for some time thinking out that letter; it seemed to me to be important to set a formal tone when writing to this young woman for the first time. Finally I wrote,

DEAR MADAM,

It is with regret that we have to inform you of the death of Mr. Douglas Macfadden at Ayr on January 21st. As Executors to his will we have experienced some difficulty in tracing the beneficiaries, but if you are the daughter of Jean (*née* Macfadden) and Arthur Paget formerly resident in Southampton and in Malaya, it would appear that you may be entitled to a share in the estate.

May we ask you to telephone for an appointment to call upon us at your convenience to discuss the matter further? It will be necessary for you to produce evidence of identity at an early stage, such as your birth certificate, National Registration Identity Card, and any other documents that may occur to you.

I am,
Yours truly,
for Owen, Dalhousie and Peters,
N. H. STRACHAN

She rang me up the next day. She had quite a pleasant voice, the voice of a well-trained secretary. She said, "Mr. Strachan, this is Miss Jean Paget speaking. I've got your letter of the 29th. I wonder—do you work on Saturday mornings? I'm in a job, so Saturday would be the best day for me."

I replied, "Oh, yes, we work on Saturday mornings. What time would be convenient for you?"

"Should we say ten-thirty?"

I made a note upon my pad. "That's all right. Have you got your birth certificate?"

"Yes, I've got that. Another thing I've got is my mother's marriage certificate, if that helps."

I said, "Oh yes, bring that along. All right, Miss Paget, I shall look forward to meeting you on Saturday. Ask for me by name, Mr. Noel Strachan. I am the senior partner."

She was shown into my office punctually at ten-thirty on Saturday. She was a girl or woman of a medium height, dark-haired. She was good-looking in a quiet way; she had a tranquillity about her that I find it difficult to describe except by saying that it was the grace that you see frequently in women of a Scottish descent. She was dressed in a dark blue coat and skirt. I got up and shook hands with her, and gave her the chair in front of my desk, and went round and sat down myself. I had the papers ready.

"Well, Miss Paget," I said. "I heard about you from your aunt—I think she is your aunt? Miss Agatha Paget, at Colwyn Bay."

She inclined her head. "Aunt Aggie wrote and told me that she had had a letter from you. Yes, she's my aunt."

"And I take it that you are the daughter of Arthur and Jean Paget, who lived in Southampton and Malaya?"

She nodded. "That's right I've got the birth certificate and mother's birth certificate, as well as her marriage certificate." She took them from her bag and put them on my desk, with her identity card.

I opened these documents and read them through carefully. There was no doubt about it; she was the person I was looking for. I leaned back in my chair presently and took off my spectacles. "Tell me, Miss Paget," I said. "Did you ever meet your uncle, who died recently? Mr. Douglas Macfadden?"

She hesitated. "I've been thinking about that a lot," she said candidly. "I couldn't honestly swear that I have ever met him, but I think it must have been him that mother took me to see once in Scotland, when I was about ten years old. We all went together, Mother and I and Donald. I remember an old man in a very stuffy room with a lot of birds in cages. I think that was Uncle Douglas, but I'm not quite sure."

That fitted in with what he had told me, the visit of his sister with her children in 1932. This girl would have been eleven years old then. "Tell me about your brother Donald, Miss Paget," I asked. "Is he still alive?"

She shook her head. "He died in 1943, while he was a prisoner. He was taken by the Japs in Singapore when we surrendered, and then he was sent to the railway."

I was puzzled. "The railway?"

She looked at me coolly, and I thought I saw tolerance for the ignorance of those who stayed in England in her glance. "The railway that the Japs built with Asiatic and prisoner-of-war labour between Siam and Burma. One man died for every sleeper that was laid, and it was about two hundred miles long. Donald was one of them."

There was a little pause. "I am so sorry," I said at last. "One thing I have to ask you, I am afraid. Was there a death certificate?"

She stared at me. "I shouldn't think so."

"Oh ..." I leaned back in my chair and took up the will. "This is the will of Mr. Douglas Macfadden," I said. "I have a copy for you, Miss Paget, but I think I'd better tell you what it contains in ordinary, non-legal language. Your uncle made two small bequests. The whole of the residue of the estate was left in trust for your brother Donald. The terms of the trust were to the effect that your mother was to enjoy the income from the trust until her death. If she died before your brother attained his majority, the trust was to continue until he was twenty-one, when he would inherit absolutely and the trust would be discharged. If your brother died before inheriting, then you were to inherit the residuary estate after your mother's time, but in that event the trust was to continue till the year 1956, when you would be thirty-five years old. You will appreciate that it is necessary for us to obtain legal evidence of your brother's death."

She hesitated, and then she said, "Mr. Strachan, I'm afraid I'm terribly stupid. I understand you want some proof that Donald is dead. But after that is done, do you mean that I inherit everything that Uncle Douglas left?"

"Broadly speaking—yes," I replied. "You would only receive the income from the estate until the year 1956. After that, the capital would be yours to do what you like with."

"How much did he leave?"

I picked up a slip of paper from the documents before me and ran my eye down the figures for a final check. "After paying death duties and legacies," I said carefully, "the residuary estate would be worth about fifty-three thousand pounds at present-day prices. I must make it clear that that is at present-day prices, Miss Paget. You must not assume that you would inherit that sum in 1956. A falling stock market affects even trustee securities."

She stared at me. "Fifty-three thousand pounds?"

I nodded. "That seems to be about the figure."

"How much a year would that amount of capital yield, Mr. Strachan?"

I glanced at the figures on the slip before me. "Invested in trustee stocks, as at present—about £1550 a year, gross income. Then income tax has to be deducted. You would have about nine hundred a year to spend, Miss Paget."

"Oh ..." There was a long silence; she sat staring at the desk in front of her. Then she looked up at me, and smiled. "It takes a bit of getting used to," she remarked. "I mean, I've always worked for my living, Mr. Strachan. I've never thought that I'd do anything else unless I married, and that's only a different sort of work. But this means that I need never work again—unless I want to."

She had hit the nail on the head with her last sentence. "That's exactly it," I replied. "Unless you want to."

"I don't know what I'd do if I didn't have to go to the office," she said. "I haven't got any other life ..."

"Then I should go on going to the office," I observed.

She laughed. "I suppose that's the only thing to do."

I leaned back in my chair. "I'm an old man now, Miss Paget. I've made plenty of mistakes in my time and I've learned one thing from them, that it's never very wise to do anything in a great hurry. I take it that this legacy will mean a considerable change in your circumstances. If I may offer my advice, I should continue in your present employment for the time, at any rate, and I should refrain from talking about your legacy in the office just yet. For one thing, it will be some months before you get possession even of the income from the estate. First we have to obtain legal proof of the death of your brother, and then we have to obtain the confirmation of the executors in Scotland and realize a portion of the securities to meet estate and succession duties. Tell me, what are you doing with this firm Pack and Levy?"

"I'm a shorthand typist," she said. "I'm working now as secretary to Mr. Pack."

"Where do you live, Miss Paget?"

She said, "I've got a bed-sitting-room at No. 43 Campion Road, just off Ealing Common. It's quite convenient, but of course I have a lot of my meals out. There's a Lyons just round the corner."

I thought for a minute. "Have you got many friends in Ealing? How long have you been there?"

"I don't know very many people," she replied. "One or two families, people who work in the firm, you know. I've been there over two years now, ever since I was repatriated. I was out in Malaya, you know, Mr. Strachan, and I was a sort of prisoner of war for three and a half years. Then when I got home I got this job with Pack and Levy."

I made a note of her address upon my pad. "Well, Miss Paget," I said, "I should go on just as usual for the time being. I will consult the War Office on Monday morning and obtain this evidence about your brother as quickly as I can. Tell me his name, and number, and unit." She did so, and I wrote them down. "As soon as I get that, I shall submit the will for probate. When that is proved, then the trust commences and continues till the year 1956, when you will inherit absolutely."

She looked up at me. "Tell me about this trust," she asked. "I'm afraid I'm not very good at legal matters."

I nodded. "Of course not. Well, you'll find it all in legal language in the copy of the will which I shall give you, but what it means is this, Miss Paget. Your uncle, when he made this will, had a very poor opinion of the ability of women to manage their own money. I'm sorry to have to say such a thing, but it is better for you to know the whole of the facts."

She laughed. "Please don't apologize for him, Mr. Strachan. Go on."

"At first, he was quite unwilling that you should inherit the capital of the estate till you were forty years old," I said. "I contested that view, but I was unable to get him to agree to any less period than the present arrangement in the will. Now, the object of a trust is this. The testator appoints trustees—in this case, myself and my partner—who undertake to do their best to preserve the capital intact and hand it over to the legatee—to you—when the trust expires."

"I see. Uncle Douglas was afraid that I might spend the fifty-three thousand all at once."

I nodded. "That was in his mind. He did not know you, of course, Miss Paget, so there was nothing personal about it. He felt that in general women were less fit than men to handle large sums of money at an early age."

She said quietly, "He may have been right." She thought for a minute, and then she said, "So you're going to look after the money for me till I'm thirty-five and give me the interest to spend in the meantime? Nine hundred a year?"

"If you wish us to conduct your income-tax affairs for you, that would be about the figure," I said. "We can arrange the payments in any way that you prefer, as a quarterly or a monthly cheque, for example. You would get a formal statement of account half-yearly."

She asked curiously, "How do you get paid for doing all this for me, Mr. Strachan?"

I smiled. "That is a very prudent question, Miss Paget. You will find a clause in the will, No. 8, I think, which entitles us to charge for our professional services against the income from the trust. Of course, if you get into any legal trouble we should be glad to act for you and help you in any way we could. In that case we should charge you on the normal scale of fees."

She said unexpectedly, "I couldn't ask for anybody better." And then she glanced at me, and said mischievously, "I made some enquiries about this firm yesterday."

"Oh ... I hope they were satisfactory?"

"Very." She did not tell me then what she told me later, that her informant had described us as, "as solid as the Bank of England, and as sticky as treacle". "I know I'm going to be in very good hands, Mr. Strachan."

I inclined my head. "I hope so. I am afraid that at times you may find this trust irksome, Miss Paget; I can assure you that I shall do my utmost to prevent it from becoming so. You will see in the will that the testator gave certain powers to the trustees to realize capital for the benefit of the legatee in cases where they were satisfied that it would be genuinely for her advantage."

"You mean, if I really needed a lot of money—for an operation or something—you could let me have it, if you approved?"

She was quick, that girl. "I think that is a very good example. In case of illness, if the income were insufficient, I should certainly realize some of your capital for your benefit."

She smiled at me, and said, "It's rather like being a ward in Chancery, or something."

I was a little touched by the comparison. I said, "I should feel very much honoured if you care to look at it that way, Miss Paget. Inevitably this legacy is going to make an upset in your condition of life, and if I can do anything to help you in the transition I should be only too pleased." I handed her copy of the will. "Well, there is the will, and I suggest you take it away and read it quietly by yourself. I'll keep the certificates for the time being. After you've thought things over for a day or two I am sure that there will be a great many questions to which you will want answers. Would you like to come and see me again?"

She said, "I would. I know there'll be all sorts of things I want to ask about, but I can't think of them now. It's all so sudden."

I turned to my engagement diary. "Well, suppose we meet again about the middle of next week." I stared at the pages. "Of course, you're working. What time do you get off from your office, Miss Paget?"

She said, "Five o'clock."

"Would six o'clock on Wednesday evening suit you, then? I shall hope to have got somewhere with the matter of your brother by that time."

She said, "Well, that's all right for me, Mr. Strachan, but isn't it a bit late for you? Don't you want to get home?"

I said absently, "I only go to the club. No, Wednesday at six would suit me very well." I made a note upon my pad, and then I hesitated. "Perhaps if you are doing nothing after that you might like to come on to the club and have dinner in the Ladies Annexe," I said. "I'm afraid it's not a very gay place, but the food is good."

She smiled, and said warmly, "I'd love to do that, Mr. Strachan. It's very kind of you to ask me."

I got to my feet. "Very well, then, Miss Paget—six o'clock on Wednesday. And in the meantime, don't do anything in a great hurry. It never pays to be impetuous ..."

She went away, and I cleared my desk and took a taxi to the club for lunch. After lunch I had a cup of coffee and slept for ten minutes in a chair before the fire, and when I woke up I thought I ought to get some exercise. So I put on my hat and coat and went out and walked rather aimlessly up St. James's Street and along Piccadilly to the Park. As I walked, I wondered how that fresh young woman was spending her weekend. Was she telling her friends all about her good luck, or was she sitting somewhere warm and quiet, nursing and cherishing her own anticipations, or was she on a spending spree already? Or was she out with a young man? She would have plenty of men now to choose from, I thought cynically, and then it struck me that she probably had those already because she was a very marriageable girl. Indeed, considering her appearance and her evident good nature, I was rather surprised that she was not married already.

I had a little talk that evening in the club with a man who is in the Home Office about the procedure for establishing the death of a prisoner of war, and on Monday I had a number of telephone conversations with the War Office and the Home Office about the case. I found, as I had suspected, that there was an extraordinary procedure for proving death which could be invoked, but where a doctor was available who had attended the deceased in the prison camp the normal certification of death was the procedure to adopt. In this instance there was a general practitioner called Ferris in practice at Beckenham who had been a doctor in Camp 206 in the Takunan district on the Burma-Siam railway, and the official at the War Office advised me that this doctor would be in a position to give the normal death certificate.

I rang him up next morning, and he was out upon his rounds. I tried to make his wife understand what I wanted but I think it was too complicated for her; she suggested that I should call and see him after the evening surgery, at half past six. I hesitated over that because Beckenham is a good long way out, but I was anxious to get these formalities over quickly for the sake of the girl. So I went out to see this doctor that evening.

He was a cheerful, fresh-faced man not more than thirty-five years old; he had a keen sense of humour, if rather a macabre one at times. He looked as healthy and fit as if he had spent the whole of his life in England in a country practice. I got to him just as he was finishing off the last of his patients, and he had leisure to talk for a little.

"Lieutenant Paget," he said thoughtfully. "Oh yes, I know. Donald Paget—was his name Donald?" I said it was. "Oh, of course, I remember him quite well. Yes, I can write a death certificate. I'd like to do that for him, though I don't suppose it'll do him much good."

"It will help his sister," I remarked. "There is a question of an inheritance, and the shorter we can make the necessary formalities the better for her."

He reached for his pad of forms. "I wonder if she's got as much guts as her brother."

"Was he a good chap?"

He nodded. "Yes," he said. "He was a delicate-looking man, dark and rather pale, you know, but he was a very good type. I think he was a planter in civil life—anyway, he was in the Malay volunteers. He spoke Malay very well, and he got along in Siamese all right. With those languages, of course, he was a very useful man to have in the camp. We used to do a lot of black market with the villagers, the Siamese outside, you know. But quite apart from that, he was the sort of officer the men like. It was a great loss when he went."

"What did he die of?" I asked.

He paused with his pen poised over the paper. "Well, you could take your pick of half a dozen things. I hadn't time to do a post mortem, of course. Between you and me, I don't really know. I think he just died. But he'd recovered from enough to kill a dozen ordinary men, so I don't know that it really matters what one puts down on the certificate. No legal point depends upon the cause of death, does it?"

"Oh, no," I said. "All I want is the death certified."

He still paused, in recollection. "He had a huge tropical ulcer on his left leg that we were treating, and that was certainly poisoning the whole system. I think if he'd gone on we'd have had to have taken that leg off. He got that because he was one of those chaps who won't report sick while they can walk. Well, while he was in hospital with the ulcer, he got cerebral malaria. We had nothing to treat that damn thing with till we got around to making our own quinine solutions for intravenous injection; we took a frightful risk with that, but there was nothing else to do. We got a lot through it with that, and Paget was one of them. He got over it quite well. That was just before we got the cholera. Cholera went right through the camp—hospital and everything. We couldn't isolate the cases, or anything like that. I never want to see a show like that again. We'd got nothing, *nothing*, not even saline. No drugs to speak of, and no equipment. We were making bed-pans out of old kerosene tins. Paget got that, and would you believe it, he got over cholera. We got some prophylactic injections from the Nips and we gave him those; that may have helped. At least, I think we gave him that—I'm not sure. He was very weak when that left him, of course, and the ulcer wasn't any too good. And about a week after that, he just died in the night. Heart, I fancy. I'll tell you what I'll do, I'll put down for

Cause of Death—Cholera. There you are, sir. I'm sorry you had to come all this way for it."

As I took the certificate I asked curiously, "Did you get any of those things yourself?"

He laughed. "I was one of the lucky ones. All I got was the usual dysentery and malaria, the ordinary type malaria, not cerebral. Overwork was *my* trouble, but other people had that, too. We were in such a jam, for so long. We had hundreds of cases just lying on the floor or bamboo charpoys in palm huts—it was raining almost all the time. No beds, no linen, no equipment, and precious few drugs. You just couldn't rest. You worked till you dropped asleep, and then you got up and went on working. You never came to an end. There was never half an hour when you could slack off and sit and have a smoke, or go for a walk, except by neglecting some poor sod who needed you very badly."

He paused. I sat silent, thinking how easy by comparison my own war had been. "It went on like that for nearly two years," he said. "You got a bit depressed at times, because you couldn't even take time off to go and hear a lecture."

"Did you have lectures?" I asked.

"Oh yes, we used to have a lot of lectures by the chaps in camp. How to grow Cox's Orange Pippins, or the TT motorcycle races, or Life in Hollywood. They made a difference to the men, the lectures did. But we doctors usually couldn't get to them. I mean, it's not much of an alibi when someone's in convulsions if you're listening to a lecture on Cox's Orange Pippins at the other end of the camp."

I said, "It must have been a terrible experience."

He paused, reflecting. "It was so beautiful," he said. "The Three Pagodas Pass must be one of the loveliest places in the world. You've got this broad valley with the river running down it, and the jungle forest, and the mountains ... We used to sit by the river and watch the sun setting behind the mountains, sometimes, and say what a marvellous place it would be to come to for a holiday. However terrible a prison camp may be, it makes a difference if it's beautiful."

When Jean Paget came to see me on Wednesday evening I was ready to report the progress I had made. First I went through one or two formal matters connected with the winding up of the estate, and then I showed her the schedule of the furniture that I had put in store at Ayr. She was not much interested in that. "I should think it had all better be sold, hadn't it?" she remarked. "Could we put it in an auction?"

"Perhaps it would be as well to wait a little before doing that," I suggested. "You may want to set up a house or a flat of your own."

She wrinkled up her nose. "I can't see myself wanting to furnish it with any of Uncle Douglas's stuff, if I did," she said.

However, she agreed not to do anything about that till her own plans were more definite, and we turned to other matters. "I've got your brother's death certificate," I said, and I was going on to tell her what I had done with it when she stopped me.

"What did Donald die of, Mr. Strachan?" she asked.

I hesitated for a moment. I did not want to tell so young a woman the unpleasant story I had heard from Dr. Ferris. "The cause of death was cholera," I said at last.

She nodded, as if she had been expecting that. "Poor old boy," she said softly. "Not a very nice way to die."

I felt that I must say something to alleviate her distress. "I had a long talk with the doctor who attended him," I told her. "He died quite peacefully, in his sleep."

She stared at me. "Well then, it wasn't cholera," she said. "That's not the way you die of cholera."

I was a little at a loss in my endeavour to spare her unnecessary pain. "He had cholera first, but he recovered. The actual cause of death was probably heart failure, induced by the cholera."

She considered this for a minute. "Did he have anything else?" she asked.

Well, then of course there was nothing for it but to tell her everything I knew. I was amazed at the matter-of-fact way in which she took the unpleasant details and at her knowledge of the treatment of such things as tropical ulcers, until I recollected that this girl had been a prisoner of the Japanese in Malaya, too. "Damn bad luck the ulcer didn't go a bit quicker," she said coolly. "If there'd been an amputation they'd have had to evacuate him from the railway, and then he wouldn't have got the cerebral malaria or the cholera."

"He must have had a wonderfully strong constitution to have survived so much," I said.

"He hadn't," she said positively. "Donald was always getting coughs and colds and things. What he *had* got was a wonderfully strong sense of humour. I always thought he'd come through, just because of that. Everything that happened to him was a joke."

When I was a young man, girls didn't know about cholera or great ulcers, and I didn't quite know how to deal with her. I turned the conversation back to legal matters, where I was on firmer ground, and showed her how her case for probate was progressing. And presently I took her downstairs and we got a taxi and went over to the club to dine.

I had a reason for entertaining her, that first evening. It was obvious that I was going to have a good deal to do with this young woman in the next few years, and I wanted to find out about her. I knew practically nothing of her education or her background at that time; her knowledge of tropical diseases, for example, had already confused me. I wanted to give her a good dinner with a little wine and get her talking; it was going to make my job as trustee a great deal easier if I knew what her interests were, and how her mind worked. And so I took her to the Ladies Annexe at my club, a decent place where we could dine in our own time without music and talk quietly for a little time after dinner. I find that I get tired if there is a lot of noise and bustling about, as in a restaurant.

I showed her where she could go to wash and tidy up, and while she was doing that I ordered her a sherry. I got up from the table in the drawing-room when she came to me, and gave her a cigarette, and lit it for her, "What did you do over the weekend?" I asked as we sat down. "Did you go out and celebrate?"

She shook her head. "I didn't do anything very much. I'd arranged to meet one of the girls in the office for lunch on Saturday and to go and see the new Bette Davis film at the Curzon, so we did that."

"Did you tell her about your good fortune?"

She shook her head. "I haven't told anybody." She paused, and sipped her sherry; she was managing that and her cigarette quite nicely. "It seems such an improbable story," she said, laughing. "I don't know that I really believe in it myself."

I smiled with her. "Nothing is real till it happens," I observed. "You'll believe that this is true when we send you the first cheque. It would be a great mistake to believe in it too hard before that happens."

"I don't," she laughed. "Except for one thing. I don't believe you'd be wasting so much time on my affairs unless there was something in it."

"It's true enough for that." I paused, and then I said, "Have you thought yet what you are going to do in a month or two when the income from the trust begins? Your monthly cheque, after the tax has been deducted, will be about seventy-five pounds. I take it that you will hardly wish to go on with your present employment when those cheques begin to come in?"

"No ... " She sat staring for a minute at the smoke rising from her cigarette. "I don't want to stop working. I wouldn't mind a bit going on with Pack and Levy just as if nothing had happened, if it was a job worth doing," she said. "But—well, it's not. We make ladies' shoes and handbags, Mr. Strachan, and small ornamental attaché cases for the high-class trade—the sort that sells for thirty guineas in a Bond Street shop to stupid women with more money than sense. Fitted vanity cases in rare leathers, and all that sort of thing. It's all right if you've got to earn your living, working in that sort of place. And it's been interesting, too, learning all about that trade."

"Most jobs are interesting when you are learning them," I said.

She turned to me. "That's true. I've quite enjoyed my time there. But I couldn't go on now, with all this money. One ought to do something more worth while, but I don't know what." She drank a little sherry. "I've got no profession, you see—only shorthand and typing, and a bit of book-keeping. I never had any real education—technical education, I mean. Taking a degree, or anything like that."

I thought for a moment. "May I ask a very personal question, Miss Paget?"

"Of course."

"Do you think it likely that you will marry in the near future?"

She smiled. "No, Mr. Strachan, I don't think it's very likely that I shall marry at all. One can't say for certain, of course, but I don't think so."

I nodded without comment. "Well then, had you thought about taking a university course?"

Her eyes opened wide. "No—I hadn't thought of that. I couldn't do it, Mr. Strachan—I'm not clever enough. I couldn't get into a university." She paused. "I was never higher than the middle of my class at school, and I never got into the Sixth."

"It was just a thought," I said. "I wondered if that might attract you."

She shook her head. "I couldn't go back to school again now. I'm much too old."

I smiled at her. "Not quite such an old woman as all that," I observed.

For some reason the little compliment fell flat. "When I compare myself with some of the girls in the office," she said quietly, and there was no laughter in her now, "I know I'm about seventy."

I was finding out something about her now, but to ease the situation I suggested that we should go into dinner. When the ordering was done, I said, "Tell me what happened to you in the war. You were out in Malaya, weren't you?"

She nodded. "I had a job in an office, with the Kuala Perak Plantation Company. That was the company my father worked for, you know. Donald was with them, too."

"What happened to you in the war?" I asked. "Were you a prisoner?"

"A sort of prisoner," she said.

"In a camp?"

"No," she replied. "They left us pretty free." And then she changed the conversation very positively, and said, "What happened to you, Mr. Strachan? Were you in London all the time?"

I could not press her to talk about her war experiences if she didn't want to, and so I told her about mine — such as they were. And from that, presently, I found myself telling her about my two sons, Harry on the China station and Martin in Basra, and their war records, and their families and children. "I'm a grandfather three times over," I said ruefully. "There's going to be a fourth soon, I believe."

She laughed. "What does it feel like?"

"Just like it did before," I told her. "You don't feel any different as you get older. Only, you can't do so much."

Presently I got the conversation back on to her own affairs. I pointed out to her what sort of life she would be able to lead upon nine hundred a year. As an instance, I told her that she could have a country cottage in Devonshire and a little car, and a daily maid, and still have money to spare for a moderate amount of foreign travel. "I wouldn't know what to do with myself unless I worked at something," she said. "I've always worked at something, all my life."

I knew of several charitable appeals who would have found a first-class shorthand typist, unpaid, a perfect god-send, and I told her so. She was inclined to be critical about those. "Surely, if a thing is really worth while, it'll pay," she said. She evidently had quite a strong business instinct latent in her. "It wouldn't need to have an unpaid secretary."

"Charitable organizations like to keep the overheads down," I remarked.

"I shouldn't have thought organizations that haven't got enough margin to pay a secretary can possibly do very much good," she said. "If I'm going to work at anything, I want it to be something really worth while."

I told her about the almoner's job at a hospital, and she was very much interested in that. "That's much more like it, Mr. Strachan," she said. "I think that's the sort of job one might get stuck into and take really seriously. But I wish it hadn't got to do with sick people. Either you've got a mission for sick people or you haven't, and I think I'm one of the ones who hasn't. But it's worth thinking about."

"Well, you can take your time," I said. "You don't have to do anything in a hurry."

She laughed at me. "I believe that's your guiding rule in life—never do anything in a hurry."

I smiled. "You might have a worse rule than that."

With the coffee after dinner I tried her out on the Arts. She knew nothing about music, except that she liked listening to the radio while she sewed. She knew nothing about literature, except that she liked novels with a happy ending. She liked paintings that were a reproduction of something that she knew, but she had never been to the Academy. She knew nothing whatsoever about sculpture. For a young woman with nine hundred a year, in London, she knew little of the arts and graces of social life, which seemed to me to be a pity.

"Would you like to come to the opera one night?" I asked.

She smiled. "Would I understand it?"

"Oh yes. I'll look and see what's on. I'll pick something light, and in English."

She said, "It's terribly nice of you to ask me, but I'm sure you'd be much happier playing bridge."

"Not a bit," I said. "I haven't been to the opera or anything like that for years."

She smiled. "Well, of course I'd love to come," she said. "I've never seen an opera in my life. I don't even know what happens."

We sat talking about these things for an hour or more, till it was half past nine and she got up to go; she had three-quarters of an hour to travel out to her suburban lodgings. I went with her, because she was going from St. James's Park station, and I didn't care about the thought of so young a woman walking across the park alone late at night. At the station, standing on the dark, wet pavement by the brightly lit canopy, she put out her hand.

"Thank you so much, Mr. Strachan, for the dinner, and for everything you're doing for me," she said.

"It has been a very great pleasure to me, Miss Paget," I replied, and I meant it.

She hesitated, and then she said, smiling, "Mr. Strachan, we're going to have a good deal to do with each other. My name is Jean. I'll go crackers if you keep on calling me Miss Paget."

"You can't teach an old dog new tricks," I said awkwardly.

She laughed. "You said just now you don't feel any different as you get older. You can try and learn."

"I'll bear it in mind," I said. "Sure you can manage all right now?"

"Of course. Goodnight, Mr. Strachan."

"Goodnight," I said, lifting my hat and dodging the issue. "I'll let you know about the opera."

In the following weeks while probate was being granted I took her to a good many things. We went together to the opera several times, to the Albert Hall on Sunday afternoons, and to art galleries and exhibitions of paintings. In return, she took me to the cinema once or twice. I cannot really say that she developed any very great artistic appreciation. She liked paintings more than concerts. If it had to be music she preferred it in the form of opera and the lighter the better; she liked to have something to look at while her ears were assailed. We went twice to Kew Garden as the spring came on. In the course of these excursions she came several times to my flat in Buckingham Gate; she got to know the kitchen, and made tea once or twice when we came in from some outing together. I had never entertained a lady in that flat before except my daughters-in-law, who sometimes come and use my spare room for a night or two in London.

Her business was concluded in March, and I was able to send her first cheque. She did not give up her job at once, but continued to go to the office as usual. She wanted, very wisely, to build up a small reserve of capital from her monthly cheques before starting to live on them; moreover, at that time she had not made up her mind what she wanted to do.

That was the position one Sunday in April. I had arranged a little jaunt for her that day; she was to come to lunch at the flat and after that we were going down to Hampton Court, which she had never seen. I thought that the old palace and the spring flowers would please her, and I had been looking forward to this trip for several days. And then, of course, it rained.

She came to the flat just before lunch, dripping in her dark blue raincoat, carrying a very wet umbrella. I took the coat from her and hung it up in the kitchen. She went into my spare room and tidied herself; then she came to me in the lounge and we stood watching the rain beat against the Palace stables opposite; wondering what we should do instead that afternoon.

We had not got that settled when we sat down to coffee before the fire after lunch. I had mentioned one or two things but she seemed to be thinking about other matters. Over the coffee it came out, and she said, "I've made up my mind what I want to do first of all, Mr. Strachan."

"Oh?" I asked. "What's that?"

She hesitated. "I know you're going to think this very odd. You may think it very foolish of me, to go spending money in this way. But—well, it's what I want to do. I think perhaps I'd better tell you about it now, before we go out."

It was warm and comfortable before the fire. Outside the sky was dark, and the rain streamed down on the wet pavements.

"Of course, Jean," I replied. "I don't suppose it's foolish at all. What is it that you want to do?"

She said, "I want to go back to Malaya, Mr. Strachan. To dig a well."

(选自 Shute, Nevil. *A Town Like Alice*. New York: Vintage International, 2009: 5-35.)

Questions

1. What does Chapter one mainly talk about?
2. How is prejudice manifested in this novel?
3. Do you agree with the statement "even though cultures differ, people are basically the same"?
4. What is the situation of women in western and Asian societies at that period?
5. Why do Malayan women live a hard life and do a little improvement?

Unit 7

John Robert Fowles: *The French Lieutenant's Woman*

John Robert Fowles (31 March 1926 – 5 November 2005) was an international famous English novelist. He was born in Leigh-on-Sea in Essex, England, the son of Gladys May Richards and Robert John Fowles. In 1939, Fowles attended Bedford School until 1944. His time at Bedford coincided with the Second World War. He became head boy and was an athletic standout. After leaving Bedford School in 1944, Fowles enrolled in a Naval Short Course at Edinburgh University and was prepared to receive a commission in the Royal Marines. After completing his military service in 1947, Fowles entered New College, Oxford, where he concentrated on French for his BA. After reading Jean-Paul Sartre and Albert Camus, Fowles first considered life as a writer.

Fowles spent his early adult life as a teacher. In 1951, Fowles became an English master in Greece where he met his future wife Elizabeth Christy. In late 1960s, Fowles began working and published *The Collector* in 1963. The success of *The Collector* meant that Fowles could stop teaching and devote himself full-time to a literary career.

In 1965 Fowles left London, moving to Underhill, a farm on the fringes of Lyme Regis, Dorset. The isolated farm house became the model for the Dairy in the book Fowles was writing: *The French Lieutenant's Woman* (1969). In 1968 he and his wife moved to Belmont, in Lyme Regis, which Fowles used as a setting for parts of *The French Lieutenant's Woman*. Fowles lived the rest of his life in Lyme Regis. Despite his occasional involvement, he was generally considered reclusive. In 1990, his first wife Elizabeth died of cancer. Her death affected him severely, and he did not write for a year. In 1998, Fowles married his second wife, Sarah Smith. With Sarah by his side, Fowles died of heart failure on 5 November 2005, aged 79.

The French Lieutenant's Woman was published in 1969 and it became an instant critical and popular success. The story is set in the mid-nineteenth century, the Victorian era. There are three main characters. Charles Smithson is an orphaned gentleman. He is engaged to Ernestina Freeman, a daughter of a wealthy tradesman. On holiday with his fiancée in Lyme Regis, Charles notices a woman named Sarah Woodruff staring out to sea at the very end of The Cobb, a stone harbour breakwater. Sarah Woodruff is also known by the local nickname as "Tragedy" and as "the French lieutenant's whore." She is a former governess and then becomes a fallen woman, allegedly abandoned by a French ship's officer named Varguennes who has returned to France. Now she works as a companion to the odious Mrs. Poulteney in the town. After hearing about Sarah's story, Charles becomes curious about her. As an amateur scientist to collect fossils, Charles searches the wooded area, the Undercliff, to the west of Lyme, where he encounters Sarah several times. During these meetings, Sarah tells Charles of her history, and asks for his emotional and social support. During the same period, he learns of the possible loss of place as heir to his elderly uncle, who has become engaged to a woman young enough to bear a child. Meanwhile, Charles's servant Sam falls in love with Mary, the maid of Ernestina's aunt. Despite the difference in their backgrounds, Charles falls in love with Sarah and advises her to leave Lyme for Exeter. Returning from a journey to warn Ernestina's father about his uncertain inheritance, Charles stops in Exeter. Charles visits Sarah in a hotel room in Exeter and they have sex in which Charles realizes that Sarah is a virgin. Charles breaks his engagement to Ernestina and is disgraced by her father. Charles, intends to marry Sarah, only to find she has vanished. The narrator appears as a character sharing a railway compartment with Charles. He tosses a coin to determine the order in which he will portray the two possible endings. Charles goes abroad but after two years, Sarah is discovered in London, living as a model to Dante Gabriel Rossetti. When Charles and Sarah meet again, the novel is divided to two endings. In the first ending, Charles and Sarah are reunited together with their daughter. In the second ending Sarah rejects Charles's offer of marriage and he returns to America alone, but with the chance of leading a free, existentially authentic life.

The structure of The French Lieutenant's Woman could be summarized as the meeting, separation and reunion of two lovers. Charles is a rather typical romantic hero, a cynical yet idealistic Victorian gentleman. Sarah is one of the most enigmatic female characters in literary history because her thoughts and motivations are blocked from the perception of readers. In the novel, the narrator intervenes in the story with a personality of its own.

After the publication the novel was translated into many languages and established Fowles's international reputation. It was adapted as a feature film in 1981 with a screenplay by the noted British playwright Harold Pinter, and starring Meryl Streep and Jeremy Irons.

Theme

The subject of *The French Lieutenant's Woman* is the relationship between life and art, the artist and his creation, and the isolation resulting from an individual's struggle for selfhood. Fowles works within the tradition of the Victorian novel and consciously uses its conventions to serve his own design. His style combines a flowing nineteenth-century prose style with a twentieth-century perspective. It touches upon the theme of metafiction, gender, love and sex, convention and freedom, science and religion.

Fowles has taken two traditional romantic characters, a young hero and a mysterious woman, and has transformed them into human beings. There is no French lieutenant to pine after, and Sarah's life is not a tragedy that echoes her nickname in Lyme. Charles's gift of marriage is not a gift at all. While the novel could have ended with the couple's reconciliation, Fowles does not end it there. In the second ending, Sarah rejects the security that Charles offers and both are forced to go on alone. Fowles's novel echoes the doubts about the Victorian view of the world. The world is changing and old standards no longer apply. The novel is therefore actually a psychological study of an individual rather than a romance. It is a novel of individual growth and the awareness of one's basic isolation which accompanies that growth.

Cutting-edge Topic

In 1981, the novel *The French Lieutenant's Woman* was adapted into a movie with the same title by Karel Reisz with Harold Pinter as the screenplay. As a pastiche of the Victorian novel as well as a metafiction, the novel was full of postmodern features, such as the intrusive narrator, multiple endings and the enigmatic main character. It was really a challenge to translate them into cinematic terms.

The adaptation was a film-within-a-film, also entitled *The French Lieutenant's Woman*. It portrays the making of a film about Sarah Woodruff and Charles Smithson's affair, and the actors playing these roles, Meryl Streep and Jeremy Irons, respectively also play the actors playing Anna and Mike married to other people, but having an affair as they make the film. Anna and Mike's relationship mirrors that of the Victorian protagonists, but each affair ends differently: Sarah and Charles are reunited at the house of her patron while Anna and Mike separate when she abandons him at the party held to celebrate the end of filming. Thus the framing device is the equivalence of the novel's two endings. Scenes such as Anna researches her role as Sarah, reading out to Mike, historical facts about the mid-19th century, are the attempts made by the director to imitate the intrusive narrator of the novel and Fowles's account of Victorian times.

In the film, Sarah and Charles are united, canoeing off into the romantic sunlight through a literal tunnel of love. But in the modern story's resolution, Anna, after staring at herself in the dressing-room mirror, with Sarah's wig propped on a stand beside her, abruptly leaves the wrap party. We hear but do not see her car roaring away as Mike calls out her name from a window above. This blurs the modern and Victorian time frames that has been going on throughout the film. The cinema audience knows that the joyful, reunited Charles and Sarah are part of a film and their love is only footage and a script. So is Mike's affair with Anna. It isn't hard for the viewer to realize that their own existence might be considered as the same.

Pinter and Reisz successfully remind the audience of how artificial their lives are, with the pressures of history, ideology, psychology and social convention forming the script of their lives. The Victorian narrative, the modern frame and the lives of the audience merge, to remind us again of the fragile and ambiguous boundaries distinguishing our own realities.

Excerpt

13

For the drift of the Maker is dark, an Isis was hidden by the veil ...

TENNYSON, Maud (1855)

I do not know. This story I am telling is all imagination. These characters I create never existed outside my own mind. If I have pretended until now to know my characters, just as I have assumed some of the vocabulary and my story: that the novelist stands next to God. He may not know all, yet he tries to pretend that he does. But I live in the age of Alain Robbe-Grillet and Roland Barthes; if this is a novel, it cannot be a novel in the modern sense of the word.

So perhaps I am writing a transposed autobiography; perhaps I now live in one of the houses I have brought into the fiction; perhaps Charles is myself disguised. Perhaps it is only a game. Modern women like Sarah exist, and I have never understood them. Or perhaps I am trying to pass off a concealed book of essays on you. Instead of chapter headings, perhaps I should have written "On the Horizontality of Existence," "The Illusions of Progress," "The History of the Novel Form," "The Aetiology of Freedom," "Some Forgotten Aspects of the Victorian Age"... what you will.

Perhaps you suppose that a novelist has only to pull the right strings and his puppets will behave in a lifelike manner; and produce on request a thorough analysis of their motives and intentions. Certainly I intended at this stage (*Chap. Thirteen—unfolding of Sarah's true state of mind*) to tell all—or all that matters. But I find myself suddenly like a man in the sharp spring night, watching from the lawn beneath that dim upper window in Malborough House; I know in the context of my book's reality that Sarah would never have brushed away her tears and leaned down and delivered a chapter of revelation. She would instantly have turned, had she seen me there just as the old moon rose, and disappeared into the interior shadows.

But I am a novelist, not a man in garden—I can follow her where I like? But possibility is not permissibility. Husbands could often murder their wives—and the reverse—and get away with it. But they don't.

You may think novelists always have fixed plans to which they work, so that the future predicted by Chapter One is always inexorably the actuality of Chapter Thirteen. But novelists write for countless different reasons: for money, for fame, for reviewers, for parents, for friends, for loved ones, for vanity, for pride, for curiosity, for amusement: as skilled furniture makers enjoy making furniture, as drunkards like drinking, as judges like judging, as Sicilians like emptying a shotgun into an enemy's back. I could fill a book with reasons, and they would all be true, though not true of all. Only one same reason is shared by all of us: *we wish to create worlds as real as*, *but other than the world that is*. Or was. This is why we cannot plan. We know a world is an organism, not a machine. We also know that a genuinely created world must be independent of its creator; a planned world (a world that fully reveals its planning) is a dead world. It is only when our characters and events begin to disobey us that they begin to live. When Charles left Sarah on her cliff edge, I order him to walk straight back to Lyme Regis. But he did not; he gratuitously turned and went down to the Dairy.

Oh, but you say, come on—what I really mean is that the idea crossed my mind as I wrote that it might be more clever to have him stop and drink milk ... and meet Sarah again. That is certainly one explanation of what happened; but I can only report—and I am the most reliable witness—that the idea seemed to me to come clearly from Charles, not myself. It is not only that he has begun to gain an autonomy; I must respect it, and disrespect all my quasi-divine plans for him, if I wish him to be real.

In other words, to be free myself, I must give him, and Tina and Sarah, even the abominable Mrs. Poulteney, their freedom as well. There is only one good definition of God: the freedom that allows other freedoms to exist. And I must conform to that definition.

The novelist is still a god, since he creates (and not even the most aleatory avant-garde modern novel has managed to extirpate its author completely); what has changed is that we are no longer the gods of Victorian image, ominiscient and decreeing; but in the new theological image, with freedom our first principle, not authority.

I have disgracefully broken the illusion? No. My characters still exist, and in an reality no less, or no more, real than the one I have just broken. Fiction is woven into all, as a Greek observed some two and a half thousand years ago. I find this new reality (or unreality) more valid; and I would have you share my own sense that I do not fully control these creatures of my mind, any more than you control—however hard you try, however much of a laterday Mrs. Poulteney you may be—your children, colleagues, friends, or even yourself.

But this is preposterous? A character is either "real" or "imaginary"? If you think that, *hypocrite lecteur*, I can only smile. You do not even think of your own past as quite real; you dress it up, you gild it or blacken it, censor it, tinker with it…fictionalize it, in a word, and put it away on a shelf—your book, your romanced autobiography. We are all in flight from the real reality. That is a basic definition of *Homo sapiens*.

So if you think all this unlucky (but it *is* Chapter Thirteen) digression has nothing to do with your Time, Progress, Society, Evolution and all those other capitalized ghosts in the night that are rattling their chains behind the scenes of this book…I will not argue. But I shall suspect you.

I report, then, only the outward facts: that Sarah cried in the darkness, but did not kill herself; that she continued, in spite of the express prohibition, to haunt Ware Commons. In a way, therefore, she had indeed jumped; and was living in a kind of long fall, since sooner or later the news must inevitably come to Mrs. Poulteney of the sinner's compounding of her sin. It is true Sarah went less often to the woods than she had become accustomed to, a deprivation at first made easy for her by the wetness of the weather those following two weeks. It is true also that she took some minimal precautions of a military kind. The cart track eventually ran out into a small lane, little better than a superior cart track itself, which curved down a broad combe called Ware Valley until it joined, on the outskirts of Lyme, the main carriage road to Sidmouth and Exeter. There was a small scatter of respectable houses in Ware Valley, and it was therefore a seemly place to walk. Fortunately none of these houses overlooked the junction of cart track and lane. Once there, Sarah had merely to look round to see if she was alone. One day she set out with the intention of walking into the woods. But as in the lane she came to the track to the Dairy she saw two people come round a higher bend. She walked straight on towards them, and once round the bend, watched to make sure that the couple did not themselves take the Dairy track; then retraced her footsteps and entered her sanctuary unobserved.

She risked meeting other promenaders on the track itself; and might always have risked the dairyman and his family's eyes. But this latter danger she avoided by discovering for herself that one of the inviting paths into the bracken above the track lead round, out of sight of the Dairy, onto the path through the woods. This path she had invariably taken, until that afternoon when she recklessly—as we can now realize—emerged in full view of the two men.

The reason was simple. She had overslept, and she knew she was late for her reading. Mrs. Poulteney was to dine at Lady Cotton's that evening; and the usual hour had been put forward to allow her to prepare for what was always in essence, if not appearance, a thunderous clash of two brontosauri; with black velvet taking the place of iron cartilage, and quotations from the Bible the angry raging teeth; but no less dour and relentless a battle.

Also, Charles's down-staring face had shocked her; she felt the speed of her fall accelerate; when the cruel ground rushes up, when the fall is from such a height, what use are precautions?

...

54

> My wind is turned to bitter north
> That was so soft a south before ...
>
> A. H. CLOUGH, Poem (1841)

In fairness to Charles it must be said that he sent to find Sam before he left the White Lion. But the servant was not in the taproom or the stables. Charles guessed indeed where he was. He could not send them; and thus he left Lyme without seeing him again. He got into his four-wheeler in the yard, and promptly drew down the blinds. Two hearse-like miles passed before he opened them again, and let the slanting evening sunlight, for it was now five o'clock, brighten the dingy paint-work and upholstery of the carriage.

It did not immediately brighten Charles's spirits. Yet gradually, as he continued to draw away from Lyme, he felt as if a burden had been lifted off his shoulders; a defeat suffered, and yet he had survived it. Grogan's solemn warning—that the rest of his life must be lived in proof of the justice of what he had done—he accepted. But among the rich green fields and May hedgerows of the Devon countryside it was difficult not to see the future as fertile—a new life lay ahead of him, great challenges, but he would rise to them. His guilt seemed almost beneficial: its expiation gave his life its hitherto lacking purpose.

An image from ancient Egypt entered his mind—a sculpture in the British Museum, showing a pharaoh standing beside his wife, who had her arm round his waist, with her other hand on his forearm. It had always seemed to Charles a perfect emblem of conjugal harmony, not least since the figures were carved from the same block of stone. He and Sarah were not yet carved into that harmony; but they were of the same stone.

He gave himself then to thoughts of the future, to practical arrangements. Sarah must be suitably installed in London. They should go abroad as soon as his affairs could be settled, the Kensington house got rid of, his things stored ... perhaps Germany first, then south in winter to Florence or Rome (if the civil conditions allowed) or perhaps Spain ... Granada! The Alhambra! Moonlight, the distant sound below of singing gypsies, such grateful, tender eyes ... and in some jasmine-scented room they would lie awake, in each other's arms, infinitely alone, exiled, yet fused in that loneliness, inseparable in that exile.

Night had fallen. Charles craned out and saw the distant lights of Exeter. He called out to the driver to take him first to Endicott's Family Hotel. Then he leaned back and reveled in the scene that was to come. Nothing carnal should disfigure it, of course; that at least he owed to Ernestina as much as to Sarah. But he once again saw an exquisite tableau of tender silence, her hands in his ...

They arrived. Telling the man to wait Charles entered the hotel and knocked on Mrs. Endicott's door.

"Oh it's you, sir."

"Miss Woodruff expects me. I will find my own way."

Already he was turning away towards the stairs.

"The young lady's left, sir?"

"Left! You mean gone out?"

"No, sir. I mean left." He stared weakly at her. "She took the

London train this morning, sir."

"But I ... are you sure?"

"Sure as I'm standing here, sir. I distinctly heard her say the railway station to the cabman, sir. And he asked what train, and she said, plain as I'm speaking to you now, the London."

The plump old lady came forward. "Well I was surprised myself, sir. Her with three days still paid on her room."

"But did she leave no address?"

"Not a line, sir. Not a word to me where she was going." That black mark very evidently cancelled the good one merited by not asking for three days' money back.

"No message was left for me?"

"I thought it might very likely be you she was a—going off with, sir. That's what I took the liberty to presume."

To stand longer there became an impossibility. "Here is my card. If you hear from her—if you would let me know. Without fail. Here. Something for the service and postage." Mrs. Endicott smiled ingratiatingly. "Oh thank you, sir. Without fail." He went out; and as soon came back.

"This morning—a manservant, did he not come with a letter and packet for Miss Woodruff?"

Mrs. Endicott looked blank. "Shortly after eight o'clock?" Still the proprietress looked blank. Then she called for Betsy Anne, who appeared and was severely cross-examined by her mistress ... that is, until Charles abruptly left.

He sank back into his carriage and closed his eyes. He felt without volition, plunged into a state of abulia. If only he had not been so scrupulous, if only he had come straight back after ... but Sam. Sam! A thief! A spy! Had he been tempted into Mr. Freeman's pay? Or was his crime explicable as resentment over those wretched three hundred pounds? How well did Charles now understand the scene in Lyme—Sam must have realized he would be discovered as soon as they returned to Exeter; must therefore have read his letter ... Charles flushed a deep red in the darkness. He would break the man's neck if he ever saw him again. For a moment he even contemplated going to a police station office and charging him with ... well, theft at any rate. But at once he saw the futility of that. And what good would it do in the essential: the discovery of Sarah?

He saw only one light in the gloom that descended on him. She had gone to London; she knew he lived in London. But if her motive was to come, as Grogan had once suggested, knocking on his door, would not that motive rather have driven her back to Lyme, where she supposed him to be? And had he not decided that all her intentions were honorable? Must it not seem to her that he was renounced, and lost, forever? The one light flickered, and went out.

He did something that night he had not done for many years. He knelt by his bed and prayed; and the substance of his prayer was that he would find her; if he searched for the rest of his life, he would find her.

55

"Why, about you!" Tweedledee exclaimed, clapping his hands triumphantly. "And if he left off dreaming about you, where do you suppose you'd be?"

"Where I am now, of course," said Alice.

"Not you!" Tweedledee retorted contemptuously. "You'd be nowhere. Why, you're only a sort of thing in his dream."

"If that there King was to wake," added Tweedledum, "you'd go out—bang! just like a candle?"

"I shouldn't?" Alice exclaimed indignantly.

LEWIS CARROLL, *Through the Looking-Glass* (1872)

Charles arrived at the station in ridiculously good time the next morning; and having gone through the ungentlemanly business of seeing his things loaded into the baggage van and then selected an empty first-class compartment, he sat impatiently waiting for the train to start. Other passengers looked in from time to time, and were rebuffed by that Gorgon stare (this compartment is reserved for non-lepers) the English have so easily at command. A whistle sounded, and Charles thought he had won the solitude he craved. But then, at the very last moment, a massively bearded face appeared at his window. The cold stare was met by the even colder stare of a man in a hurry to get aboard.

The latecomer muttered a "Pardon me, sir" and made his way to the far end of the compartment. He sat, a man of forty or so, his top hat firmly square, his hands on his knees, regaining his breath. There was something rather aggressively secure about him; he was perhaps not quite a gentleman ... an ambitious butler (but butlers did not travel first class) or a successful lay preacher—one of the bullying tabernacle kind, a would-be Spurgeon, converting souls by scorching them with the cheap rhetoric of eternal damnation. A decidedly unpleasant man, thought Charles, and so typical of the age—and therefore emphatically to be snubbed if he tried to enter into conversation.

As sometimes happens when one stares covertly at people and speculates about them, Charles was caught in the act; and reproved for it. There was a very clear suggestion in the sharp look sideways that Charles should keep his eyes to himself. He hastily directed his gaze outside his window and consoled himself that at least the person shunned intimacy as much as he did.

Very soon the even movement lulled Charles into a douce daydream. London was a large city; but she must soon look for work. He had the time, the resources, the will; a week might pass, two, but then she would stand before him; perhaps yet another address would slip through his letter box. The wheels said it: she—could—not—be—so—cruel, she—could—not—be—so—cruel, she—could—not—be—so—cruel ... the train passed through the red and green valleys towards Cullompton. Charles saw its church, without knowing where the place was, and soon afterwards closed his eyes. He had slept poorly that previous night.

For a while his traveling companion took no notice of the sleeping Charles. But as the chin sank deeper and deeper—Charles had taken the precaution of removing his hat—the prophet-bearded man began to stem at him, safe in the knowledge that his curiosity could not be surprised.

His look was peculiar: sizing, ruminative, more than a shade disapproving, as if he knew very well what sort of man this was (as Charles had believed to see very well what sort of man he was) and did not much like the knowledge or the species. It was true that, unobserved, he looked a little less frigid and authoritarian a person; but there remained about his features an unpleasant aura of self-confidence—or if not quite confidence in self, at least a confidence in his judgment of others, of how much he could get out of them, expect from them, tax them.

A stare of a minute or so's duration, of this kind, might have been explicable. Train journeys are boring; it is amusing to spy on strangers; and so on. But this stare, which became positively cannibalistic in its intensity, lasted far longer than a minute. It lasted beyond Taunton, though it was briefly interrupted there when the noise on the platform made Charles wake for a few moments. But when he sank back into his slumber, the eyes fastened on him again in the same leechlike manner.

You may one day come under a similar gaze. And you may—in the less reserved context of our own century—be aware of it. The intent watcher will not wait till you are asleep. It will no doubt suggest something unpleasant, some kind of devious sexual approach ... a desire to know you in a way you do not want to be known by a stranger. In my experience there is only one profession that gives that particular look, with its bizarre blend of the inquisitive and the magistral; of the ironic and the soliciting.

Now could I use you?

Now what could I do with you?

It is precisely, it has always seemed to me, the look an omnipotent god—if there were such an absurd thing—should be shown to have. Not at all what we think of as a divine look; but one of a distinctly mean and dubious (as the theoreticians of the nouveau roman have pointed out) moral quality. I see this with particular clarity on the face, only too familiar to me, of the bearded man who stares at Charles. And I will keep up the pretense no longer.

Now the question I am asking, as I stare at Charles, is not quite the same as the two above. But rather, what the devil am I going to do with you? I have already thought of ending Charles's career here and now; of leaving him for eternity on his way to London. But the conventions of Victorian fiction allowed no place for the open, the inconclusive ending; and I preached earlier of the freedom characters must be given. My problem is simple—what Charles wants is clear? It is indeed. But what the protagonist wants is not so clear; and I am not at all sure where she is at the moment. Of course if these two were two fragments of real life, instead of two figments of my imagination, the issue of the dilemma is obvious; the one wants combats the other wants, fails or succeeds, as the actuality may be. Fiction usually pretends to conform to the reality: the writer puts the conflicting wants in the ring and then describes the fight—but in fact fixes the fight, letting that want he himself favors win. And we judge writers of fiction both by the skill they show in fixing the fights (in other words, in persuading us that they were not fixed) and by the kind of fighter they fix in favor of: the good one, the tragic one, the evil one, the funny one, and so on.

But the chief argument for fight-fixing is to show one's readers what one thinks of the world around one—whether one is a pessimist, an optimist, what you will. I have pretended to slip back into 1867; but of course that year is in reality a century past. It is futile to show optimism or pessimism, or anything else about it, because we know what has

happened since.

So I continue to stare at Charles and see no reason this time for fixing the fight upon which he is about to engage. That leaves me with two alternatives. I let the fight proceed and take no more than a recording part in it; or I take both sides in it. I stare at that vaguely effete but not completely futile face. And as we near London, I think I see a solution; that is, I see the dilemma is false. The only way I can take no part in the fight is to show two versions of it. That leaves me with only one problem: I cannot give both versions at once, yet whichever is the second will seem, so strong is the tyranny of the last chapter, the final, the "real" version.

I take my purse from the pocket of my frock coat, I extract a florin, I rest it on my right thumbnail, I flick it, spinning, two feet into the air and catch it in my left hand. So be it. And I am suddenly aware that Charles has opened his eyes and is looking at me. There is something more than disapproval in his eyes now; he perceives I am either a gambler or mentally deranged. I return his disapproval, and my florin to my purse. He picks up his hat, brushes some invisible speck of dirt (a surrogate for myself) from its nap and places it on his head.

We draw under one of the great cast-iron beams that support the roof of Paddington station. We arrive, he steps down to the platform, beckoning to a porter. In a few moments, having given his instructions, he turns. The bearded man has disappeared in the throng.

（选自 Fowles, John. *The French Lieutenant's Woman*. Beijing: Foreign Language Teaching and Research Press, 1992.）

Questions

1. Why does Sarah allow herself to be called "the French lieutenant's whore" when in fact she never had sex with him?
2. Why did Sarah start the rumor, since she was the one who first mentioned it to her employer, Mrs. Talbot?
3. How is Charles changed by his romance with Sarah?
4. Why does Fowles give the novel two conclusions? Do you consider them to be equally viable options, or is one more of a conclusion than the other?
5. To what extent is the novel *The French Lieutenant's Woman* successful?

Unit 8

Alice Walker: *The Color Purple*

Alice Walker, in full Alice Malsenior Walker, (born on 9 February, 1944, Eatonton, Georgia, U. S.), an American writer whose novels, short stories, and poems are noted for their insightful treatment of African American culture. Her novels, most notably *The Color Purple* (1982), focus particularly on women.

Alice Walker is the best known southern African American writer of the second half of the 20th century, perhaps because of the controversy generated by her Pulitzer Prize-winning *The Color Purple* (1982), the first novel by an African American woman to win this award. She has, however, published many other works—to date, five other novels, five volumes of poetry, four essay collections, two children's books, and three short story collections. But *The Color Purple* is a point of demarcation in Walker's oeuvre in that it is both the completion of the cycle of novels she announced in the early 1970s and the beginning of new emphases for her as a writer.

Walker was the eighth child of African American sharecroppers. While growing up, she was accidentally blinded in one eye, and her mother gave her a typewriter, allowing her to write instead of doing chores. She received a scholarship to attend Spelman College, where she studied for two years before transferring to Sarah Lawrence College. With the help of a scholarship, Walker was able to attend Spelman College in Atlanta. She later switched to Sarah Lawrence College in New York. While at Sarah Lawrence, Walker visited Africa as part of a study-abroad program. She graduated in 1965—the same year when she published her first short story. After college, Walker worked as a social worker, teacher and lecturer. She became active in the civil rights movement, fighting for equality for all African Americans.

She married in 1967, but the couple divorced in 1976.

Walker's experiences informed her first collection of poetry, *Once*, which was published in 1968. Better known now as a novelist, Walker showed her talents for storytelling in her debut work, *Third Life of Grange Copeland* (1970), a narrative that spans 60 years and three generations, followed two years later.

Walker continued to explore writing in all of its forms. In 1973, she published a second volume of poetry, *Revolutionary Petunias and Other Poems*, and her first collection of short stories, *In Love and Trouble: Stories of Black Woman*, which included the highly acclaimed "Everyday Use" both appeared in 1973. The following year, she delivered her first children's book, *Langston Hughes: American Poet*. Walker also emerged as a prominent voice in the Black feminist movement. The latter bears witness to sexist violence and abuse in the African American community.

In 1974, when "In Search of Our Mothers' Gardens" appeared, Walker already understood the concept of the everyday, and she articulated the practice of the everyday as crucial to a late twentieth-century understanding of the production of art and of artistic production and the art of living life fully and, as she insisted, whole. Understanding the commonplace, the ordinary, the everyday became possible as a direct result of reading the domestic landscape of quilts and gardens. The identification that Walker makes with the everyday is revolutionary.

After moving to New York, Walker completed *Meridian* (1976), a novel describing the coming of age of several civil rights workers in the 1960s. Walker later moved to California, where she wrote her most popular novel, *The Color Purple*. As an epistolary novel, it depicts the growing-up and self-realization of an African American woman in a town in Georgia. Set in the early 1900s, the novel explores the female African American experience through the life and struggles of its narrator, Celie. Celie suffers terrible abuse at the hands of her father, and later, from her husband. The compelling work won Walker both the Pulitzer Prize for Fiction and the National Book Award for Fiction in 1983.

In 1985, Walker's story made it to the big screen: Spielberg directed *The Color Purple*, which starred Whoopi Goldberg as Celie, as well as Oprah Winfrey and Danny Glover. Like the novel, the movie was a critical success, receiving 11 Academy Award nominations. Walker explored her own feelings about the film in her 1996 work, *The Same River Twice: Honoring the Difficult*. In 2005, *The Color Purple* became a Broadway musical.

Walker incorporated characters and their relations from *The Color Purple* into two of her other novels: *The Temple of My Familiar* (1989) and *Possessing the Secret of Joy* (1992). *The Temple of My Familiar* is an ambitious examination of racial and sexual tensions (1989); *Possessing the Secret of Joy* (1992) is a narrative centred on female genital mutilation. These two novels earned great critical praise and caused some controversy for its exploration of the practice of female genital mutilation. *By the Light of My Father's Smile* (1998), is a story of a family of anthropologists posing as missionaries in order to gain access to a Mexican tribe; and

Now Is the Time to Open Your Heart (2005), the story about an older woman's quest for identity. Reviewers complained that these novels employed New Age abstractions and poorly conceived characters, though Walker continued to draw praise for championing racial and gender equality in her work. She also released the volume of short stories *The Way Forward Is with a Broken Heart* (2000) and several other volumes of poetry, including *Absolute Trust in the Goodness of the Earth* (2003), *A Poem Traveled Down My Arm* (2003), *Hard Times Require Furious Dancing* (2010), and *Taking the Arrow Out of the Heart* (2018). *Her Blue Body Everything We Know: Earthling Poems* (1991) collects poetry from 1965 to 1990.

Walker's essays were compiled in *In Search of Our Mother's Gardens: Womanist Prose* (1983), *Sent by Earth: A Message from the Grandmother Spirit After the Bombing of the World Trade Center and Pentagon* (2001), *We Are the Ones We Have Been Waiting For* (2006), and *The Cushion in the Road: Meditation and Wandering as the Whole World Awakens to Being in Harm's Way* and the poetry collection *The World Will Follow Joy: Turning Madness into Flowers* (2013). Walker also wrote juvenile fiction and critical essays on such female writers as Flannery O'Connor and Zora Neale Hurston. She cofounded a short-lived press in 1984.

Walker also wrote about her experiences with the group Women for Women International in 2010's *Overcoming Speechlessness: A Poet Encounters the Horror in Rwanda, Eastern Congo and Palestine/Israel*. She published another poetry collection, *Hard Times Require Furious Dancing*, that same year.

After more than four decades as a writer, Walker shows no signs of slowing down. In the unconventional memoir *The Chicken Chronicles* (2011), Walker discussed caring for a flock of chickens while also musing on her life. The documentary *Alice Walker: Beauty in Truth* was released in 2013.

Along with her Pulitzer and National Book Award, Walker has been honored with the O. Henry Award and the Mahmoud Darwish Literary Prize for Fiction. Additionally, she was inducted into the California Hall of Fame in 2006 and received the LennonOno Grant for Peace Award in 2010. Her books have been translated into more than two dozen languages.

Theme

Alice Walker's theme can be best illustrated by the novel *The Color Purple*, a Pulitzer Prize winner in 1983. A feminist work about an abused and uneducated African American woman's struggle for empowerment, *The Color Purple* was praised for the depth of its female characters and for its eloquent use of Black English Vernacular. *The Color Purple* movingly depicts the growing-up and self-realization of Celie, who overcomes oppression and abuse to find fulfillment and independence. The novel also addresses gender equality.

Unwavering in her commitment to exploring the lives and the work of other black women, Walker coined the term "womanism" early in her career, which lies in the center of her literary concern. The word is derived from a black folk expression and Walker prefers it to feminism because it honors a long-standing tradition of strength among black women.

Walker's other themes include such topical and controversial themes as abortion and interracial relationships. Her nonfiction and poems also demonstrate her commitment to environmentalism as well as human rights.

Walker remains what she has been for more than 40 years: a gifted and prolific writer, a bold thinker, a woman who is determined to confront and embrace the contradiction of her life and the paradox of our time.

Cutting-edge Topic

Womanism perhaps is the most important issue of Alice Walker's studies. However, in the new era, Walker's studies also have witnessed the development of new perspectives. Reconstruction of southern racial space is among one of them.

Walker has slipped out of recent discourses and that her contribution to the ways in which we today think about the South, its literary and cultural production, has been occluded in part by her own adherence to what we might call New Age, non heteronormative political spiritualism. With this notice, such questions as how Alice Walker, an artist forged on the battleground of Mississippi during the height of civil rights activism, may have been one primary catalyst in naturalizing how so many scholars and artists approach the South today, and with that naturalizing a concomitant erasing of her very positionality in the process have been put forward.

Walker begins a postmodern stance toward both race and region in her deconstruction of arenas and hierarchies of power and in her transgression of the fixed and rigid notions of art, epistemologies of art, and production of art, as well as in her anticipation of the shifts in gender theory and with its cultural transformation in the very geographical matrix that was the South of her childhood and youth. When Walker brought together place and identity in her work, she destabilized both categories and began the process of the reformation of both. She invented her own "radically subjective politics" within a matrix of change, but she did not produce an identity that is fragmentary, conflicted, or contradictory despite its fluid boundaries. She produced texts, critical and creative and autobiographical, that defied the notion of clearly defined and readable meaning explicit in and based upon established transcendental precepts. She saw pluralism and relativism, rejected nostalgia and sentimentalism, and claimed political relevance for her transformative positions and subversive ideologies, all the while insisting on her own vision, certainly idiosyncratic and subjective but not fractured or paranoid. Writing in the political and cultural upheaval of the 1960s, Walker envisioned both the importance of articulating her own new southern black woman identity and the necessity of new formations and new modalities—even while asserting the changing ground for all such formations and modalities. In particular, she was able to foreground the damaging impact of racism and patriarchal authority/power in her short fiction, poetries, and novels, as well as in her essays, and in the process, to create a space for the gendering of subjectivity and reassessing gendered racial hierarchies.

In the conjunction of her political and literary works, Walker examined gender and ideological formations under segregation and displayed an ability to map the postmodern at a time when among African American writers, there was still a strong adherence to modernist aesthetic productions. Walker's emphasis on difference then becomes one of the primary ways of linking her to a postmodern aesthetic, especially by means of her collapsing the distinctions between genres and destabilizing the hierarchy of high and low culture, high and low art, and exploiting the class dynamics to challenge the hegemony of a white racialist society.

Besides what have been mentioned above, cultural studies, black lesbian writing tradition, Walker as an activist and a critic have also become the topics that many scholars have paid special attention to in recent years.

Excerpt

Dearest Celie,

Every day for the past week I've been trying to get Corrine to remember meeting you in town. I know if she can just recall your face, she will believe Olivia (if not Adam) is your child. They think Olivia looks like me, but that is only because I look like you. Olivia has your face and eyes, exactly. It amazes me that Corrine didn't see the resemblance.

Remember the main street of town? I asked. Remember the hitching post in front of Finley's dry goods store? Remember how the store smelled like peanut shells?

She says she remembers all this, but no men speaking to her.

Then I remember her quilts. The Olinka men make beautiful quilts which are full of animals and birds and people. And as soon as Corrine saw them, she began to make a quilt that alternated one square of appliqued figures with one nine-patch block, using the clothes the children had outgrown, and some of her old dresses.

I went to her trunk and started hauling out quilts.

Don't touch my things, said Corrine. I'm not gone yet.

I held up first one and then another to the light, trying to find the first one I remembered her making. And trying to remember, at the same time, the dresses she and Olivia were wearing the first months I lived with them.

Aha, I said, when I found what I was looking for, and laid the quilt across the bed.

Do you remember buying this cloth? I asked, pointing to a flowered square. And what about this checkered bird?

She traced the patterns with her finger, and slowly her eyes filled with tears.

She was so much like Olivia! she said. I was afraid she'd want her back. So I forgot her as soon as I could. All I let myself think about was how the clerk treated me! I was acting like somebody because I was Samuel's wife, and a Spelman Seminary graduate, and he treated me like any ordinary nigger. Oh, my feelings were hurt! And I was mad! And that's what I thought about, even told Samuel about, on the way home. Not about your sister—what was her name? —Celie? Nothing about her.

She began to cry in earnest. Me and Samuel holding her hands.

Don't cry. Don't cry, I said. My sister was glad to see Olivia with you. Glad to see her alive. She thought both her children were dead.

Poor thing! said Samuel. And we sat there talking a little and holding on to each other until Corrine fell off to sleep.

But, Celie, in the middle of the night she woke up, turned to Samuel and said: I believe. And died anyway.

Your Sister in Sorrow,
Nettie

Dearest Celie,

Just when I think I've learned to live with the heat, the constant dampness, even steaminess of my clothes, the swampiness under my arms and between my legs, my friend comes. And cramps and aches and pains—but I must still keep going as if nothing is happening, or be an embarrassment to Samuel, the children and myself. Not to mention the villagers, who think women who have their friends should not even be seen.

Right after her mother's death, Olivia got *her* friend; she and Tashi tend to each other is my guess. Nothing is said to me, in any event, and I don't know how to bring the subject up. Which feels wrong to me; but if you talk to an Olinka girl about her private parts, her mother and father will be annoyed, and it is very important to Olivia not to be looked upon as an outsider. Although the one ritual they do have to celebrate womanhood is so bloody and painful, I forbid Olivia to even think about it.

Do you remember how scared I was when it first happened to me? I thought I had cut myself. But thank God you were there to tell me I was all right.

We buried Corrine in the Olinka way, wrapped in barkcloth under a large tree. All of her sweet ways went with her. All of her education and a heart intent on doing good. She taught me so much! I know I will miss her always. The children were stunned by their mother's death. They knew she was very sick, but death is not something they think about in relation to their parents or themselves. It was a strange little procession. All of us in our white robes and with our faces painted white. Samuel is like someone lost. I don't believe they've spent a night apart since their marriage.

And how are you? dear Sister. The years have come and gone without a single word from you. Only the sky above us do we hold in common. I look at it often as if, somehow, reflected from its immensities, I will one day find myself gazing into your eyes. Your dear, large, clean and beautiful eyes. Oh, Celie! My life here is nothing but work, work, work, and worry. What girlhood I might have had passed me by. And I have nothing of my own. No man, no children, no close friend, except for Samuel. But I *do* have children, Adam and Olivia. And I *do* have friends, Tashi and Catherine. I even have a family—this village, which has fallen on such hard times.

Now the engineers have come to inspect the territory. Two white men came yesterday and spent a couple of hours strolling about the village, mainly looking at the wells. Such is the innate politeness of the Olinka that they rushed about preparing food for them, though precious little is left, since many of the gardens that flourish at this time of the year have been destroyed. And the white men sat eating as if the food was beneath notice.

It is understood by the Olinka that nothing good is likely to come from the same persons who destroyed their houses, but custom dies hard. I did not speak to the men myself, but Samuel did. He said their talk was all of workers, kilometers of land, rainfall, seedlings, machinery, and whatnot. One seemed totally indifferent to the people around him—simply eating and then smoking and staring off into the distance—and the other, somewhat younger, appeared to be enthusiastic about learning the language. Before, he says, it dies out.

I did not enjoy watching Samuel speaking to either of them. The one who hung on every word, or the one who looked through Samuel's head.

Samuel gave me all of Corrine's clothes, and I need them, though none of our clothing is suitable in this climate. This is true even of the clothing the Africans wear. They used to wear very little, but the ladies of England introduced the Mother Hubbard, a long, cumbersome, ill-fitting dress, completely shapeless, that inevitably gets dragged in the fire, causing burns aplenty. I have never been able to bring myself to wear one of these dresses, which all seem to have been made with giants in mind, so I was glad to have Corrine's things. At the same time, I dreaded putting them on. I remembered her saying we should stop wearing each other's clothes. And the memory pained me.

Are you sure Sister Corrine would want this? I asked Samuel.

Yes, Sister Nettie, he said. Try not to hold her fears against her. At the end she understood, and believed. And forgave—whatever there was to forgive.

I should have said something sooner, I said.

He asked me to tell him about you, and the words poured out like water. I was dying to tell someone about us. I told him about my letters to you every Christmas and Easter, and about how much it would have meant to us if he had gone to see you after I left. He was sorry he hesitated to become involved.

If only I'd understood then what I know now! he said.

But how could he? There is so much we don't understand. And so much unhappiness comes because of that.

    love and Merry Christmas to you,
    Your sister Nettie

Dear Nettie,

I don't write to God no more, I write to you.

What happen to God? ast Shug.

Who that? I say.

She look at me serious.

Big a devil as you is, I say, you not worried bout no God, surely.

She say, Wait a minute. Hold on just a minute here. Just because I don't harass it like some peoples us know don't mean I ain't got religion.

What God do for me? I ast.

She say, Celie! Like she shock. He gave you life, good health, and a good woman that love you to death.

Yeah, I say, and he give me a lynched daddy, a crazy mama, a lowdown dog of a step pa and a sister I probably won't ever see again. Anyhow, I say, the God I been praying and writing to is a man. And act just like all the other mens I know. Trifling, forgitful and lowdown.

She say, Miss Celie, You better hush. God might hear you.

Let 'im hear me, I say. If he ever listened to poor colored women the world would be a different place, I can tell you.

She talk and she talk, trying to budge me way from blasphemy. But I blaspheme much as I want to.

All my life I never care what people thought bout nothing I did, I say. But deep in my heart I care about God. What he going to think. And come to find out, he don't think. Just sit up there glorying in being deef, I reckon. But it ain't easy, trying to do without God. Even if you know he ain't there, trying to do without him is a strain.

I is a sinner, say Shug. Cause I was born. I don't deny it. But once you find out what's out there waiting for us, what else can you be?

Sinners have more good times, I say.

You know why? she ast.

Cause you ain't all the time worrying bout God, I say.

Naw, that ain't it, she say. Us worry bout God a lot. But once us feel loved by God, us do the best us can to please him with what us like.

You telling me God love you, and you ain't never done nothing for him? I mean, not go to church, sing in the choir, feed the preacher and all like that?

But if God love me, Celie, I don't have to do all that. Unless I want to. There's a lot of other things I can do that I speck God likes.

Like what? I ast.

Oh, she say. I can lay back and just admire stuff. Be happy. Have a good time.

Well, this sound like blasphemy sure nuff.

She say, Celie, tell the truth, have you ever found God in church? I never did. I just found a bunch of folks hoping for him to show. Any God I ever felt in church I brought in with me. And I think all the other folks did too. They come to church to *share* God, not find God.

Some folks didn't have him to share, I said. They the ones didn't speak to me while I was there struggling with my big belly and Mr. _____ children.

Right, she say.

Then she say: Tell me what your God look like, Celie.

Aw naw, I say. I'm too shame. Nobody ever ast me this before, so I'm sort of took by surprise. Besides, when I think about it, it don't seem quite right. But it all I got. I decide to stick up for him, just to see what Shug say.

Okay, I say. He big and old and tall and graybearded and white. He wear white robes and go barefooted.

Blue eyes? she ast.

Sort of bluish-gray. Cool. Big though. White lashes, I say.

She laugh.

Why you laugh? I ast. I don't think it so funny. What you expect him to look like, Mr. _____?

That wouldn't be no improvement, she say. Then she tell me this old white man is the same God she used to see when she prayed. If you wait to find God in church, Celie, she say, that's who is bound to show up, cause that's where he live.

How come? I ast.

Cause that's the one that's in the white folks' white bible.

Shug! I say. God wrote the bible, white folks had nothing to do with it.

How come he look just like them, then? she say. Only bigger? And a heap more hair. How come the bible just like everything else they make, all about them doing one thing and another, and all the colored folks doing is gitting cursed?

I never thought bout that.

Nettie say somewhere in the bible it say Jesus' hair was like lamb's wool, I say.

Well, say Shug, if he came to any of these churches we talking bout he'd have to have it conked before anybody paid him any attention. The last thing niggers want to think about they God is that his hair kinky.

That's the truth, I say.

Ain't no way to read the bible and not think God white, she say. Then she sigh. When I found out I thought God was white, and a man, I lost interest. You mad cause he don't seem to listen to your prayers. Humph! Do the mayor listen to anything colored say? Ask Sofia, she say.

But I don't have to ast Sofia. I know white people never listen to colored, period. If they do, they only listen long enough to be able to tell you what to do.

Here's the thing, say Shug. The thing I believe. God is inside you and inside everybody else. You come into the world with God. But only them that search for it inside find it. And sometimes it just manifest itself even if you not looking, or don't know what you looking for. Trouble do it for most folks, I think. Sorrow, lord. Feeling like shit.

It? I ast.

Yeah, It. God ain't a he or a she, but a It.

But what do it look like? I ast.

Don't look like nothing, she say. It ain't a picture show. It ain't something you can look at apart from anything else, including yourself. I believe God is everything, say Shug. Everything that is or ever was or ever will be. And when you can feel that, and be happy to feel that, you've found It.

Shug a beautiful something, let me tell you. She frown a little, look out cross the yard, lean back in her chair, look like a big rose.

She say, My first step from the old white man was trees. Then air. Then birds. Then other people. But one day when I was sitting quiet and feeling like a motherless child, which I was, it come to me: that feeling of being part of everything, not separate at all. I knew that if I cut a tree, my arm would bleed. And I laughed and I cried and I run all around the house. I knew just what it was. In fact, when it happen, you can't miss it. It sort of like you know what, she say, grinning and rubbing high up on my thigh.

Shug! I say.

Oh, she say. God love all them feelings. That's some of the best stuff God did. And when you know God loves 'em you enjoys 'em a lot more. You can just relax, go with everything that's going, and praise God by liking what you like.

God don't think it dirty? I ast.

Naw, she say. God made it. Listen, God love everything you love—and a mess of stuff you don't. But more than anything else, God love admiration.

You saying God vain? I ast.

Naw, she say. Not vain, just wanting to share a good thing. I think it pisses God off if you walk by the color purple in a field somewhere and don't notice it.

What it do when it pissed off? I ast.

Oh, it make something else. People think pleasing God is all God care about. But any fool living in the world can see it always trying to please us back.

Yeah? I say.

Yeah, she say. It always making little surprises and springing them on us when us least expect.

You mean it want to be loved, just like the bible say.

Yes, Celie, she say. Everything want to be loved. Us sing and dance, make faces and give flower bouquets, trying to be loved. You ever notice that trees do everything to git attention we do, except walk?

Well, us talk and talk bout God, but I'm still adrift. Trying to chase that old white man out of my head. I been so busy thinking bout him I never truly notice nothing God make. Not a blade of corn (how it do that?) not the color purple (where it come from?). Not the little wildflowers. Nothing.

Now that my eyes opening, I feels like a fool. Next to any little scrub of a bush in my yard, Mr. _____ 's evil sort of shrink. But not altogether. Still, it is like Shug say, You have to git man off your eyeball, before you can see anything a'tall.

Man corrupt everything, say Shug. He on your box of grits, in your head, and all over the radio. He try to make you think he everywhere. Soon as you think he everywhere, you think he God. But he ain't. Whenever you trying to pray, and man plop himself on the other end of it, tell him to git lost, say Shug. Conjure up flowers, wind, water, a big rock.

But this hard work, let me tell you. He been there so long, he don't want to budge. He threaten lightening, floods and earthquakes. Us fight. I hardly pray at all. Every time I conjure up a rock, I throw it.

Amen

Dear Nettie,

When I told Shug I'm writing to you instead of to God, she laugh. Nettie don't know these people, she say. Considering who I been writing to, this strike me funny.

It was Sofia you saw working as the mayor's maid. The woman you saw carrying the white woman's packages that day in town. Sofia Mr. _____ 's son Harpo's wife. Polices lock her up for sassing the mayor's wife and hitting the mayor back. First she was in prison working in the laundry and dying fast. Then us got her move to the mayor's house. She had to sleep in a little room up under the house, but it was better than prison. Flies, maybe, but no rats.

Anyhow, they kept her eleven and a half years, give her six months off for good behavior so she could come home early to her family. Her bigger children married and gone, and her littlest children mad at her, don't know who she is. Think she act funny, look old and dote on that little white gal she raise.

Yesterday us all had dinner at Odessa's house. Odessa Sofia's sister. She raise the kids. Her and her husband Jack. Harpo's woman Squeak, and Harpo himself.

Sofia sit down at the big table like there's no room for her. Children reach cross her like she not there. Harpo and Squeak act like a old married couple. Children call Odessa mama. Call Squeak little mama. Call Sofia "Miss." The only one seem to pay her any tention at all is Harpo and Squeak's little girl, Suzie Q. She sit cross from Sofia and squinch up her eyes at her.

As soon as dinner over, Shug push back her chair and light a cigarette. Now is come the time to tell yall, she say.

Tell us what? Harpo ast.

Us leaving, she say.

Yeah? say Harpo, looking round for the coffee. And then looking over at Grady.

Us leaving, Shug say again. Mr. _____ look struck, like he always look when Shug say she going anywhere. He reach down and rub his stomach, look off side her head like nothing been said.

Grady say, Such good peoples, that's the truth. The salt of the earth. But—time to move on.

Squeak not saying nothing. She got her chin glued to her plate. I'm not saying nothing either. I'm waiting for the feathers to fly.

Celie is coming with us, say Shug.

Mr. _____'s head swivel back straight. Say what? he ast.

Celie is coming to Memphis with me.

Over my dead body, Mr. _____ say.

You satisfied that what you want, Shug say, cool as clabber.

Mr. _____ start up from his seat, look at Shug, plop back down again. He look over at me. I thought you was finally happy, he say. What wrong now?

You a lowdown dog is what's wrong, I say. It's time to leave you and enter into the Creation. And your dead body just the welcome mat I need.

Say what? he ast. Shock.

All round the table folkses mouths be dropping open.

You took my sister Nettie away from me, I say. And she was the only person love me in the world.

Mr. _____ start to sputter. ButButButButBut. Sound like some kind of motor.

But Nettie and my children coming home soon, I say. And when she do, all us together gon whup your ass.

Nettie and your children! say Mr. _____. You talking crazy.

I got children, I say. Being brought up in Africa. Good schools, lots of fresh air and exercise. Turning out a heap better than the fools you didn't even try to raise.

Hold on, say Harpo.

Oh, hold on hell, I say. If you hadn't tried to rule over Sofia the white folks never would have caught her.

Sofia so surprise to hear me speak up she ain't chewed for ten minutes.

That's a lie, say Harpo.

A little truth in it, say Sofia.

Everybody look at her like they surprise she there. It like a voice speaking from the grave.

You was all rotten children, I say. You made my life a hell on earth. And your daddy here ain't dead horse's shit.

Mr. _____ reach over to slap me. I jab my case knife in his hand.

You bitch, he say. What will people say, you running off to Memphis like you don't have a house to look after?

Shug say, Albert. Try to think like you got some sense. Why any woman give a shit what people think is a mystery to me.

Well, say Grady, trying to bring light. A woman can't git a man if peoples talk.

Shug look at me and us giggle. Then us laugh sure nuff. Then Squeak start to laugh. Then Sofia. All us laugh and laugh.

Shug say, Ain't they something? Us say um *hum*, and slap the table, wipe the water from our eyes.

Harpo look at Squeak. Shut up Squeak, he say. It bad luck for women to laugh at men.

She say, Okay. She sit up straight, suck in her breath, try to press her face together.

He look at Sofia. She look at him and tough in his face. I already had my bad luck, she say. I had enough to keep me laughing the rest of my life.

Harpo look at her like he did the night she knock Mary Agnes down. A little spark fly cross the table.

I got six children by this crazy woman, he mutter.

Five, she say.

He so outdone he can't even say, Say what?

He look over at the youngest child. She sullen, mean, mischeevous and too stubborn to live in this world. But he love her best of all. Her name Henrietta.

Henrietta, he say.

She say, Yesssss ... like they say it on the radio.

Everything she say confuse him. Nothing, he say. Then he say, Go git me a cool glass of water.

She don't move.

Please, he say.

She go git the water, put it by his plate, give him a peck on the cheek. Say, Poor Daddy. Sit back down.

You not gitting a penny of my money, Mr. _____ say to me. Not one thin dime.

Did I ever ast you for money? I say. I never ast you for nothing. Not even for your sorry hand in marriage.

Shug break in right there. Wait, she say. Hold it. Somebody else going with us too. No use in Celie being the only one taking the weight.

Everybody sort of cut they eyes at Sofia. She the one they can't quite find a place for. She the stranger.

It ain't me, she say, and her look say, Fuck you for entertaining the thought. She reach for a biscuit and sort of root her behind deeper into her seat. One look at this big stout graying, wildeyed woman and you know not even to ast. Nothing.

But just to clear this up neat and quick, she say, I'm home. Period.

Her sister Odessa come and put her arms round her. Jack move up close.

Course you is, Jack say.

Mama crying? ast one of Sofia children.

Miss Sofia too, another one say.

But Sofia cry quick, like she do most things.

Who going? she ast.

Nobody say nothing. It so quiet you can hear the embers dying back in the stove. Sound like they falling in on each other.

Finally, Squeak look at everybody from under her bangs. Me, she say. I'm going North.

You going What? say Harpo. He so surprise. He begin to sputter, sputter, just like his daddy. Sound like I don't know what.

I want to sing, say Squeak.

Sing! say Harpo.

Yeah, say Squeak. Sing. I ain't sung in public since Jolentha was born. Her name Jolentha. They call her Suzie Q.

You ain't had to sing in public since Jolentha was born. Everything you need I done provided for.

I need to sing, say Squeak.

Listen Squeak, say Harpo. You can't go to Memphis. That's all there is to it.

Mary Agnes, say Squeak.

Squeak, Mary Agnes, what difference do it make?

It make a lot, say Squeak. When I was Mary Agnes I could sing in public.

Just then a little knock come on the door.

Odessa and Jack look at each other. Come in, say Jack.

A skinny little white woman stick most of herself through the door.

Oh, you all are eating dinner, she say. Excuse me.

That's all right, say Odessa. Us just finishing up. But there's plenty left. Why don't you sit down and join us. Or I could fix you something to eat on the porch.

Oh lord, say Shug.

It Eleanor Jane, the white girl Sofia used to work for.

She look round till she spot Sofia, then she seem to let her breath out. No thank you, Odessa, she say. I ain't hungry. I just come to see Sofia.

Sofia, she say. Can I see you on the porch for a minute.

All right, Miss Eleanor, she say. Sofia push back from the table and they go out on the porch. A few minutes later us hear Miss Eleanor sniffling. Then she really boo-hoo.

What the matter with her? Mr. _____ ast.

Henrietta say, Prob-limbszzzz ... like somebody on the radio.

Odessa shrug. She always underfoot, she say.

A lot of drinking in that family, say Jack. Plus, they can't keep that boy of theirs in college. He get drunk, aggravate his sister, chase women, hunt niggers, and that ain't all.

That enough, say Shug. Poor Sofia.

Pretty soon Sofia come back in and sit down.

What the matter? ast Odessa.

A lot of mess back at the house, say Sofia.

You got to go back up there? Odessa ast.

Yeah, say Sofia. In a few minutes. But I'll try to be back before the children go to bed.

Henrietta ast to be excuse, say she got a stomach ache.

Squeak and Harpo's little girl come over, look up at Sofia, say, You gotta go Misofia?

Sofia say, Yeah, pull her up on her lap. Sofia on parole, she say. Got to act nice.

Suzie Q lay her head on Sofia chest. Poor Sofia, she say, just like she heard Shug. Poor Sofia.

Mary Agnes, darling, say Harpo, look how Suzie Q take to Sofia.

Yeah, say Squeak, children know good when they see it. She and Sofia smile at one nother.

Go on sing, say Sofia, I'll look after this one till you come back.

You will? say Squeak.

Yeah, say Sofia.

And look after Harpo, too, say Squeak. Please ma'am.

                 Amen

Dear Nettie,

Well, you know wherever there's a man, there's trouble. And it seem like, going to Memphis, Grady was all over the car. No matter which way us change up, he want to sit next to Squeak.

While me and Shug sleeping and he driving, he tell Squeak all about life in North Memphis, Tennessee. I can't half sleep for him raving bout clubs and clothes and forty-nine brands of beer. Talking so much bout stuff to drink make me have to pee. Then us have to find a road going off into the bushes to relieve ourselves.

Mr. _____ try to act like he don't care I'm going.

You'll be back, he say. Nothing up North for nobody like you. Shug got talent, he say. She can sing. She got spunk, he say. She can talk to anybody. Shug got looks, he say. She can stand up and be notice. But what you got? You ugly. You skinny. You shape funny. You too scared to open your mouth to people. All you fit to do in Memphis is be Shug's maid. Take out her slop-jar and maybe cook her food. You not that good a cook either. And this house ain't been clean good since my first wife died. And nobody crazy or backward enough to want to marry you, neither. What you gon do? Hire yourself out to farm? He laugh. Maybe somebody let you work on they railroad.

Any more letters come? I ast.

He say, What?

You heard me, I say. Any more letters from Nettie come?

If they did, he say, I wouldn't give 'em to you. You two of a kind, he say. A man try to be nice to you, you fly in his face.

I curse you, I say.

What that mean? he say.

I say, Until you do right by me, everything you touch will crumble.

He laugh. Who you think you is? he say. You can't curse nobody. Look at you. You black, you pore, you ugly, you a woman. Goddam, he say, you nothing at all.

Until you do right by me, I say, everything you even dream about will fail. I give it to him straight, just like it come to me. And it seem to come to me from the trees.

Whoever heard of such a thing, say Mr. _____. I probably didn't whup your ass enough.

Every lick you bit me you will suffer twice, I say. Then I say, You better stop talking because all I'm telling you ain't coming just from me. Look like when I open my mouth the air rush in and shape words.

Shit, he say. I should have lock you up. Just let you out to work.

The jail you plan for me is the one in which you will rot, I say.

Shug come over to where us talking. She take one look at my face and say Celie! Then she turn to Mr. _____. Stop Albert, she say. Don't say no more. You just going to make it harder on yourself.

I'll fix her wagon! say Mr. _____, and spring toward me.

A dust devil flew up on the porch between us, fill my mouth with dirt. The dirt say, Anything you do to me, already done to you.

Then I feel Snug shake me. Celie, she say. And I come to myself.

I'm pore, I'm black, I may be ugly and can't cook, a voice say to everything listening. But I'm here.

Amen, say Snug. Amen, amen.

Dear Nettie,

So what is it like in Memphis? Shug's house is big and pink and look sort of like a barn. Cept where you would put hay, she got bedrooms and toilets and a big ballroom where she and her band sometime work. She got plenty grounds round the house and a bunch of monuments and a fountain out front. She got statues of folks I never heard of and never hope to see. She got a whole bunch of elephants and turtles everywhere. Some big, some little, some in the fountain, some up under the trees.

Turtles and elephants. And all over her house. Curtains got elephants, bedspreads got turtles.

Shug give me a big back bedroom overlook the backyard and the bushes down by the creek.

I know you use to morning sun, she say.

Her room right cross from mine, in the shade. She work late, sleep late, git up late. No turtles or elephants on her bedroom furniture, but a few statues spread out round the room. She sleep in silks and satins, even her sheets. And her bed round!

I wanted to build me a round house, say Shug, but everybody act like that's backward. You can't put windows in a round house, they say. But I made me up some plans, anyway. One of these days ... she say, showing me the papers.

It a big round pink house, look sort of like some kind of fruit. It got windows and doors and a lot of trees round it.

What it made of? I ast.

Mud, she say. But I wouldn't mind concrete. I figure you could make the molds for each section, pour the concrete in, let it get hard, knock off the mold, glue the parts together somehow and you'd have your house.

Well, I like this one you got, I say. That one look a little small.

It ain't bad, say Shug. But I just feel funny living in a square. If I was square, then I could take it better, she say.

Us talk bout houses a lot. How they built, what kind of wood people use. Talk about how to make the outside around your house something you can use. I sit down on the bed and start to draw a kind of wood skirt around her concrete house. You can sit on this, I say, when you get tired of being in the house.

Yeah, she say, and let's put awning over it. She took the pencil and put the wood skirt in the shade.

Flower boxes go here, she say, drawing some.

And geraniums in them, I say, drawing some.

And a few stone elephants right here, she say.

And a turtle or two right here.

And how us know you live here too? she ast.

Ducks! I say.

By the time us finish our house look like it can swim or fly.

Nobody cook like Shug when she cook.

She get up early in the morning and go to market. Buy only stuff that's fresh. Then she come home and sit on the back step humming and shelling peas or cleaning collards or fish or whatever she bought. Then she git all her pots going at once and turn on the radio. By one o'clock everything ready and she call us to the table. Ham and greens and chicken and cornbread. Chitlins and blackeyed peas and souse. Pickled okra and watermelon rind. Caramel cake and blackberry pie.

Us eat and eat, and drink a little sweet wine and beer too.

Then Shug and me go fall out in her room to listen to music till all that food have a chance to settle. It cool and dark in her room. Her bed soft and nice. Us lay with our arms round each other. Sometimes Shug read the paper out loud. The news always sound crazy. People fussing and fighting and pointing fingers at other people, and never even looking for no peace.

People insane, say Shug. Crazy as betsy bugs. Nothing built this crazy can last. Listen, she say. Here they building a dam so they can flood out a Indian tribe that been there since time. And look at this, they making a picture bout that man that kilt all them women. The same man that play the killer is playing the priest. And look at these shoes they making now, she say. Try to walk a mile in a pair of them, she say. You be limping all the way home. And you see what they trying to do with that man that beat the Chinese couple to death. Nothing whatsoever.

Yeah, I say, but some things pleasant.

Right, say Shug, turning the page. Mr. and Mrs. Hamilton Hufflemeyer are pleased to announce the wedding of their daughter June Sue. The Morrises of Endover Road are spearheading a social for the Episcopal church. Mrs. Herbert Edenfail was on a visit last week to the Adirondacks to see her ailing mother, the former Mrs. Geoffrey Hood.

All these faces look happy enough, say Shug. Big and beery. Eyes dear and innocent, like they don't know them other crooks on the front page. But they the same folks, she say.

But pretty soon, after cooking a big dinner and making a to-do about cleaning the house, Shug go back to work. That mean she never give a thought to what she eat. Never give a thought to where she sleep. She on the road somewhere for weeks at a time, come home with bleary eyes, rotten breath, overweight and sort of greasy. No place hardly to stop and really wash herself, especially her hair, on the road.

Let me go with you, I say. I can press your clothes, do your hair. It would be like old times, when you was singing at Harpo's.

She say, Naw. She can act like she not bored in front of a audience of strangers, a lot of them white, but she wouldn't have the nerve to try to act in front of me.

Besides, she say. You not my maid. I didn't bring you to Memphis to be that. I brought you here to love you and help you get on your feet.

And now she off on the road for two weeks, and me and Grady and Squeak rattle round the house trying to get our stuff together. Squeak been going round to a lot of clubs and Grady been taking her. Plus he seem to be doing a little farming out back the house.

I sit in the dining room making pants after pants. I got pants now in every color and size under the sun. Since us started making pants down home, I ain't been able to stop. I change the cloth, I change the print, I change the waist, I change the pocket. I change the hem, I change the fullness of the leg. I make so many pants Shug tease me. I didn't know what I was starting, she say, laughing. Pants all over her chairs, hanging all in front of the china closet. Newspaper patterns and cloth all over the table and the floor. She come home, kiss me, step over all the mess. Say, before she leave again, How much money you think you need *this* week?

Then finally one day I made the perfect pair of pants. For my sugar, naturally. They soft dark blue jersey with teeny patches of red. But what make them so good is, they totally comfortable. Cause Shug eat a lot of junk on the road, and drink, her stomach bloat. So the pants can be let out without messing up the shape. Because she have to pack her stuff and fight wrinkles, these pants are soft, hardly wrinkle at all, and the little figures in the cloth always look perky and bright. And they full round the ankle so if she want to sing in 'em and wear 'em sort of like a long dress, she can. Plus, once Shug put them on, she knock your eyes out.

Miss Celie, she say. You is a wonder to behold.

I duck my head. She run round the house looking at herself in mirrors. No matter how she look, she look good.

You know how it is when you don't have nothing to do, I say, when she brag to Grady and Squeak bout her pants. I sit here thinking bout how to make a living and before I know it I'm off on another pair pants.

By now Squeak see a pair *she* like. Oh, Miss Celie, she say. Can I try on those?

She put on a pair the color of sunset. Orangish with a little grayish fleck. She come back out looking just fine. Grady look at her like he could eat her up.

Shug finger the pieces of cloth I got hanging on everything. It all soft, flowing, rich and catch the light. This a far cry from that stiff army shit us started with, she say. You ought to make up a special pair to thank and show Jack.

What she say that for. The next week I'm in and out of stores spending more of Shug's money. I sit looking out cross the yard trying to see in my mind what a pair of pants for Jack would look like. Jack is tall and kind and don't hardly say anything. Love children. Respect his wife, Odessa, and all Odessa amazon sisters. Anything she want to take on, he right there. Never talking much, though. That's the main thing. And then I remember one time he touch me. And it felt like his fingers had eyes. Felt like he knew me all over, but he just touch my arm up near the shoulder.

I start to make pants for Jack. They have to be camel. And soft and strong. And they have to have big pockets so he can keep a lot of children's things. Marbles and string and pennies and rocks. And they have to be washable and they have to fit closer round the leg than Shug's so he can run if he need to snatch a child out the way of something. And they have to be something he can lay back in when he hold Odessa in front of the fire. And ...

I dream and dream and dream over Jack's pants. And cut and sew. And finish them. And send them off.

Next thing I hear, Odessa want a pair.

Then Shug want two more pair just like the first. Then everybody in her band want some. Then orders start to come in from everywhere Shug sing. Pretty soon I'm swamp.

One day when Shug come home, I say, You know, I love doing this, but I got to git out and make a living pretty soon. Look like this just holding me back.

She laugh. Let's us put a few advertisements in the paper, she say. And let's us raise your prices a hefty notch. And let's us just go ahead and give you this diningroom for your factory and git you some more women in here to cut and sew, while you sit back and design. You making your living, Celie, she say. Girl, you on your way.

Nettie, I am making some pants for you to beat the heat in Africa. Soft, white, thin. Drawstring waist. You won't ever have to feel too hot and overdress again. I plan to make them by hand. Every stitch I sew will be a kiss.

Amen,
Your Sister, Celie
Folkspants, Unlimited.
Sugar Avery Drive
Memphis, Tennessee

（选自 Walker, Alice. *The Color Purple*. New York: Pocket Books, 1985: 192 - 221.）

Questions

1. What is the theme of *The Color Purple*?
2. What was Alice Walker's childhood like?
3. What is Alice Walker best known for?
4. What's your understanding of "Womanism"?
5. What's the significance of *The Color Purple*?

Unit 9

Toni Morrison: *Song of Solomon*

In 1993 Toni Morrison became the first African American author to win the Nobel Prize for Literature; today she enjoys both critical acclaim and popular success on a scale rivaled by few other American writers. She has published eleven novels—*The Bluest Eye* (1970), *Sula* (1973), *Song of Solomon* (1977), *Tar Baby* (1981), *Beloved* (1987), *Jazz* (1992), *Paradise* (1998), *Love* (2003), *A Mercy* (2008), *Home* (2012), *God Help the Child* (2015), and a work of criticism, *Playing in the Dark: Whiteness and the Literary Imagination*, which was published in 1992.

Toni Morrison, original name Chloe Anthony Wofford, (born on February 18, 1931, Lorain, Ohio, U.S.—died on 5 August, 2019, Bronx, New York), American writer noted for her examination of Black experience (particularly Black female experience) within the Black community.

Morrison grew up in the American Midwest in a family that possessed an intense love of and appreciation for Black culture. Storytelling, songs, and folktales were a deeply formative part of her childhood. She attended Howard University (B.A., 1953) and Cornell University (M.A., 1955). After teaching at Texas Southern University for two years, she taught at Howard from 1957 to 1964. In 1965 Morrison became a fiction editor at Random House, where she worked for a number of years. In 1984 she began teaching writing at the State University of New York at Albany, which she left in 1989 to join the faculty of Princeton University; she retired in 2006.

Morrison's first book, *The Bluest Eye* (1970), is a novel of initiation concerning a victimized adolescent Black girl who is obsessed by white standards of beauty and longs to have blue eyes. This novel depicts what Jan Furman terms "black girlhood" and what Agnes Suranyi calls "black female experience from childhood to womanhood." As opposed to the neatly ordered world of the white Jane in the Dick-and-Jane primer, which loudly proclaims white bourgeois family values, *The Bluest Eye* concerns itself with the little known world of black girls like Pecola, Claudia, and Frieda. Claudia MacTeer narrates the tragic life of Pecola Breedlove. It has been widely noted by critics that the very name "Breedlove" heightens the tragic irony of Pecola's loveless existence in a family that breeds hatred and violence.

In 1973 a second novel, *Sula*, was published; it examines (among other issues) the dynamics of friendship and the expectations for conformity within the community. *Song of Solomon* (1977) is told by a male narrator in search of his identity; its publication brought Morrison to national attention. *Tar Baby* (1981), set on a Caribbean island, explores conflicts of race, class, and sex.

The critically acclaimed *Beloved* (1987), which won a Pulitzer Prize for fiction, is based on the true story of a runaway slave who, at the point of recapture, kills her infant daughter in order to spare her a life of slavery. A film adaptation of the novel was released in 1998 and starred Oprah Winfrey. In addition, Morrison wrote the libretto for *Margaret Garner* (2005), an opera about the same story that inspired *Beloved*.

In 1992 Morrison released *Jazz*, a story of violence and passion set in New York City's Harlem during the 1920s. Subsequent novels were *Paradise* (1998), a richly detailed portrait of a Black utopian community in Oklahoma, and *Love* (2003), an intricate family story that reveals the myriad facets of love and its ostensible opposite. *A Mercy* (2008) deals with slavery in 17th-century America. In this novel, Morrison did not limit herself to black girlhood alone but went on to focus on all of those "peripheral girls"; any girlhood impeded by peripherality deserves the attention of a writer alarmed at the colossal waste of potential through a deliberate disregard. *A Mercy* is a rich web of intertwined tales of several girls from different backgrounds, unraveling the universal vulnerability of tender-aged girls to brutal disruptions. In *God Help the Child* (2015), Morrison chronicled the ramifications of child abuse and neglect through the tale of Bride, a Black girl with dark skin who is born to light-skinned parents.

A work of criticism, *Playing in the Dark: Whiteness and the Literary Imagination*, was published in 1992. Many of Morrison's essays and speeches were collected in What *Moves at the Margin: Selected Nonfiction* (2008; edited by Carolyn C. Denard) and *The Source of Self-Regard: Selected Essays, Speeches, and Meditations* (2019). She and her son, Slade Morrison, cowrote a number of children's books, including the *Who's Got Game?* series, *The Book About Mean People* (2002), and *Please, Louise* (2014). She also penned *Remember* (2004), which chronicles the hardships of Black students during the integration of the American public school system; aimed at children, it uses archival photographs juxtaposed with captions speculating on the thoughts of their subjects. For that work, Morrison won the Coretta Scott King Award in 2005.

Critics continue to be drawn to Morrison's oeuvre, in part because her novels participate in multiple literary traditions. Morrison draws frequently on seminal texts in the western tradition. She insists on her identity as a black writer, and her works signify a range of African American texts. Morrison has also been an influential teacher. In the 1970s she taught at the State University of New York at Purchase, and also at Yale; in the 1980s, she taught at Bard College and then the State University of New York at Albany. Since 1989, she has been the Robert F. Goheen Professor of Humanities at Princeton. Morrison's profile as a public intellectual has risen steadily as a result of numerous interviews as well as the book reviews and essays she has written on major events today.

Theme

The central theme of Morrison's novels is the Black American experience; in an unjust society, her characters struggle to find themselves and their cultural identity. Song of Solomon also echoes this theme. The novel earns her recognition, including the National Book Critics Awards. The novel borrows many of its metaphors from African American folklore. It recounts a quest to uncover the history of black Americans that was never written but was preserved in fragments in the oral tradition: songs, stories, personal testimonies, jokes, and children's thymes. The protagonist, Milkman Dead, is an indulged son of the bourgeoisie; the materialism that has meant spiritual death for her father threatens him as well. Milkman is a participant in the journey who eventually achieves the prize of greater self-knowledge.

In Song of Solomon, even if Morrison recreates the traditionally male quest narrative, she revises the Western classics to give voice to women. When Milkman's falters, only the intervention and piloting of his aunt, Pilate, allows him to continue his quest. Blues singer, bootlegger, and conjure woman, Pilate is a mythical outsider whose life-affirming ideology the novel endorses. It mourns the fate of its other female characters, Milkman's mother, Ruth; his sisters, Corinthians and Lena; and his cousin/lover, Hagar, whose fidelity to conventional gender roles constrains them.

Cutting-edge Topic

Since Morrison was awarded Nobel Prize in 1993, she has become a "Beloved" in the world and attracted the attention of many scholars. Traditional approaches to interpret her works include gender study, postcolonial study, identity study, psychoanalysis, cultural studies, her works and African American folk tradition etc. In recent years, since the publication of her latest works, together with the publication of her critical book *Playing in the Dark: Whiteness and the Literary Imagination*, there emerges some new interpretations of her works. Many scholars began to interpret and attempt to make comparative studies on Morrison's early and the latest works. Gender study is still an important issue, however, it has developed rapidly and become more insightful. Many new perspectives and views have been touched upon. Among them, violence, especially mothering violence has become a salient example. Black female characters within Toni Morrison's novels are often scarred—physically and/or emotionally—by the oppressive environments around them.

Trauma is another new approach of Morrison study for contemporary scholars. The literary work of Toni Morrison is famous for its rich intertexuality, interweaving narrative, contemporary history, and tales and motifs from oral storytelling traditions.

Signifying theory, put forward by Henry Louis Gates, Jr. is also an effective new method to interpret Morrison's works. In the novels of her trilogy, *Beloved*, *Jazz*, and *Paradise*, Toni Morrison uses repetition with a difference to create multiple versions of stories, to revise dominant history, and to represent processes of healing, transformation, and insight. In *Beloved*, the former slave woman Sethe's freedom from the past comes not when she crosses the Ohio River, nor when her desperate and murderous act takes her beyond the reach of slavery. The potential for freedom comes from a ritual repetition of the trauma itself, this time with a significant difference; she aims her weapon not at her own children, but instead at the white man who threatens her children. In *Jazz*, the entire plot, structured like jazz music, repeats with a difference when the murderous triangle of Joe, "Violent," and Dorcas is transformed into the familial love of Joe, Violet, and Felice. The repetition of the story with a significant difference also forces the narrator of *Jazz* to reconsider assumptions. Morrison's recapitulation of the murder scene in *Paradise* again employs the narrative trope of repetition with a difference; the novel also contains numerous doublings of scenes, characters, and points of view that generate a constant process of repetition with a difference for the reader. But in *Paradise*, Morrison also considers what the danger of repetition without difference might be; what happens if difference is rejected in order to maintain the utopian harmony of paradise? The irony of *Paradise* is that repetition without a difference maintains itself through rigidity and exclusion and thus destroys the ideal it seeks to preserve; an unchanging *Paradise* inevitably loses its paradisiacal nature.

Excerpt

Chapter 10

When Hansel and Gretel stood in the forest and saw the house in the clearing before them, the little hairs at the nape of their necks must have shivered. Their knees must have felt so weak that blinding hunger alone could have propelled them forward. No one was there to warn or hold them; their parents, chastened and grieving, were far away. So they ran as fast as they could to the house where a woman older than death lived, and they ignored the shivering nape hair and the softness in their knees.

A grown man can also be energized by hunger, and any weakness in his knees or irregularity in his heartbeat will disappear if he thinks his hunger is about to be assuaged. Especially if the object of his craving is not gingerbread or chewy gumdrops, but gold.

Milkman ducked under the boughs of black walnut trees and walked straight toward the big crumbling house. He knew that an old woman had lived in it once, but he saw no signs of life there now. He was oblivious to the universe of wood life that did live there in layers of ivy grown so thick he could have sunk his arm in it up to the elbow. Life that crawled, life that slunk and crept and never closed its eyes. Life that burrowed and scurried, and life so still it was indistinguishable from the ivy stems on which it lay. Birth, life, and death—each took place on the hidden side of a leaf. From where he stood, the house looked as if it had been eaten by a galloping disease, the sores of which were dark and fluid.

One mile behind him were macadam and the reassuring sounds of an automobile or two—one of which was Reverend Cooper's car, driven by his thirteen-year-old nephew.

Noon, Milkman had told him. Come back at noon. He could just as easily have said twenty minutes, and now that he was alone, assaulted by what city people regard as raucous silence, he wished he had said five minutes. But even if the boy hadn't had chores to do, it would be foolish to be driven fifteen miles outside Danville on "business" and stay a hot minute.

He should never have made up that elaborate story to disguise his search for the cave; somebody might ask him about it. Besides, lies should be very simple, like the truth. Excessive detail was simply excess. But he was so tired after the long bus ride from Pittsburgh, coming right after the luxury of the flight, he was afraid he wouldn't be convincing.

The airplane ride exhilarated him, encouraged illusion and a feeling of invulnerability. High above the clouds, heavy yet light, caught in the stillness of speed ("Cruise," the pilot said), sitting in intricate metal become glistening bird, it was not possible to believe he had ever made a mistake, or could. Only one small thought troubled him—that Guitar was not there too. He would have loved it—the view, the food, the stewardesses. But Milkman wanted to do this by himself, with no input from anybody. This one time he wanted to go solo. In the air, away from real life, he felt free, but on the ground, when he talked to Guitar just before he left, the wings of all those other people's nightmares flapped in his face and constrained him. Lena's anger, Corinthians' loose and uncombed hair, matching her slack lips, Ruth's stepped-up surveillance, his father's bottomless greed, Hagar's hollow eyes—he did not know whether he deserved any of that, but he knew he was fed up and he knew he had to leave quickly. He told Guitar of his decision before he told his father.

"Daddy thinks the stuff is still in the cave."

"Could be." Guitar sipped his tea.

"Anyway, it's worth checking out. At least we'll know once and for all."

"I couldn't agree more."

"So I'm going after it."

"By yourself?"

Milkman sighed. "Yeah. Yeah. By myself. I need to get out of here. I mean I really have to go away somewhere."

Guitar put his cup down and folded his hands in front of his mouth. "Wouldn't it be easier with the two of us? Suppose you have trouble?"

"It might be easier, but it might look more suspicious with two men instead of one roaming around the woods. If I find it, I'll haul it back and we'll split it up just like we agreed. If I don't, well, I'll be back anyway."

"When you leaving?"

"Tomorrow morning."

"What's your father say about you going alone?"

"I haven't told him yet. You're the only one knows so far." Milkman stood up and went to the window that looked out on Guitar's little porch. "Shit."

Guitar was watching him carefully. "What's the matter?" he asked. "Why you so low? You don't act like a man on his way to the end of the rainbow."

Milkman turned around and sat on the sill. "I hope it is a rainbow, and nobody has run off with the pot, cause I need it."

"Everybody needs it."

"Not as bad as me."

Guitar smiled. "Look like you really got the itch now. More than before."

"Yeah, well, everything's worse than before, or maybe it's the same as before. I don't know. I just know that I want to live my own life. I don't want to be my old man's office boy no more. And as long as I'm in this place I will be. Unless I have my own money. I have to get out of that house and I don't want to owe anybody when I go. My family's driving me crazy. Daddy wants me to be like him and hate my mother. My mother wants me to think like her and hate my father. Corinthians won't speak to me; Lena wants me out. And Hagar wants me chained to her bed or dead. Everybody wants something from me, you know what I mean? Something they think they can't get anywhere else. Something they think I got. I don't know what it is—I mean what it is they really want."

Guitar stretched his legs. "They want your life, man."

"My life?"

"What else?"

"No. Hagar wants my life. My family ... they want—"

"I don't mean that way. I don't mean they want your dead life; they want your living life."

"You're losing me," said Milkman.

"Look. It's the condition our condition is in. Everybody wants the life of a black man. Everybody. White men want us dead or quiet—which is the same thing as dead. White women, same thing. They want us, you know, 'universal,' human, no 'race consciousness.' Tame, except in bed. They like a little racial loincloth in the bed. But outside the bed they want us to be individuals. You tell them, 'But they lynched my papa,' and they say, 'Yeah, but you're better than the lynchers are, so forget it.' And black women, they want your whole self. Love, they call it, and understanding. 'Why don't you *understand* me?' What they mean is, Don't love anything on earth except me. They say, 'Be responsible,' but what they mean is, Don't go anywhere where I ain't. You try to climb Mount Qomolangma, they'll tie up your ropes. Tell them you want to go to the bottom of the sea—just for a look—they'll hide your oxygen tank. Or you don't even have to go that far. Buy a horn and say you want to play. Oh, they love the music, but only after you pull eight at the post office. Even if you make it, even if you stubborn and mean and you get to the top of Mount Qomolangma, or you do play and you good, real good—that still ain't enough. You blow your lungs out on the horn and they want what breath you got left to hear about how you love them. They want your full attention. Take a risk and they say you not for real. That you don't love them. They won't even let you risk your *own* life, man, your *own* life—unless it's over them. You can't even die unless it's about them. What good is a man's life if he can't even choose what to die for?"

"Nobody can choose what to die for."

"Yes, you can, and if you can't, you can damn well try to."

"You sound bitter. If that's what you feel, why are you playing your numbers game? Keeping the racial ratio the same and all? Every time I ask you what you doing it for, you talk about love. Loving Negroes. Now you say—"

"It is about love. What else but love? Can't I love what I criticize?"

"Yeah, but except for skin color, I can't tell the difference between what the white women want from us and what the colored women want. You say they all want our life, our living life. So if a colored woman is raped and killed, why do the Days rape and kill a white woman? Why worry about the colored woman at all?"

Guitar cocked his head and looked sideways at Milkman. His nostrils flared a little. "Because she's *mine*."

"Yeah. Sure." Milkman didn't try to keep disbelief out of his voice. "So everybody wants to kill us, except black men, right?"

"Right."

"Then why did my father—who is a very black man—try to kill me before I was even born?"

"Maybe he thought you were a little girl; I don't know. But I don't have to tell you that your father is a very strange Negro. He'll reap the benefits of what we sow, and there's nothing we can do about that. He behaves like a white man, thinks like a white man. As a matter of fact, I'm glad you brought him up. Maybe you can tell me how, after losing everything his own father worked for to some crackers, after *seeing* his father shot down by them, how can he keep his knees bent? Why does he love them so? And Pilate. She's worse. She saw it too and, first, goes back to get a cracker's bones for some kind of crazy self-punishment, and second, leaves the cracker's gold right where it was! Now, is that voluntary slavery or not? She slipped into those Jemima shoes cause they fit."

"Look, Guitar. First of all, my father doesn't care whether a white man lives or swallows lye. He just wants what they have. And Pilate is a little nut, but she wanted us out of there. If she hadn't been smart, both our asses would be cooling in the joint right now."

"My ass. Not yours. She wanted you out, not me."

"Come on. That ain't even fair."

"No. Fair is one more thing I've given up."

"But to Pilate? What for? She knew what we did and still she bailed us out. Went down for us, clowned and crawled for us. You saw her face. You ever see anything like it in your life?"

"Once. Just once," said Guitar. And he remembered anew how his mother smiled when the white man handed her the four ten-dollar bills. More than gratitude was showing in her eyes. More than that. Not love, but a willingness to love. Her husband was sliced in half and boxed backward. He'd heard the mill men tell how the two halves, not even fitted together, were placed cut side down, skin side up, in the coffin. Facing each other. Each eye looking deep into its mate. Each nostril inhaling the breath the other nostril had expelled. The right cheek facing the left. The right elbow crossed over the left elbow. And he had worried then, as a child, that when his father was wakened on Judgment Day his first sight would not be glory or the magnificent head of God—or even the rainbow. It would be his own other eye.

Even so, his mother had smiled and shown that willingness to love the man who was responsible for dividing his father up throughout eternity. It wasn't the divinity from the foreman's wife that made him sick. That came later. It was the fact that instead of life insurance, the sawmill owner gave his mother forty dollars "to tide you and the kids over," and she took it happily and bought each of them a big peppermint stick on the very day of the funeral. Guitar's two sisters and baby brother sucked away at the bone-white and blood-red stick, but Guitar couldn't. He held it in his hand until it stuck there. All day he held it. At the graveside, at the funeral supper, all the sleepless nights. The others made fun of what they believed was his miserliness, but he could not eat it or throw it away, until finally, in the outhouse, he let it fall into the earth's stinking hole.

"Once," he said. "Just once." And felt the nausea all over again. "The crunch is here," he said. "The big crunch. Don't let them Kennedys fool you. And I'll tell you the truth: I hope your daddy's right about what's in that cave. And I sure hope you don't have no second thoughts about getting it back here."

"What's that supposed to mean?"

"It means I'm nervous. Real nervous. I need the bread."

"If you're in a hurt, I can let you have—"

"Not *me*. Us. We have work to do, man. And just recently"—Guitar squinted his eyes at Milkman—"just recently one of us was put out in the streets, by somebody I don't have to name. And his wages were garnisheed cause this somebody said two months rent owing. This somebody needs two months rent on a twelve-by-twelve hole in the wall like a fish needs side pockets. Now we have to take care of this man, get him a place to stay, pay the so-called back rent, and—"

"That was my fault. Let me tell you what happened ... ."

"No. Don't tell me nothing. You ain't the landlord and you didn't put him out. You may have handed him the gun, but you didn't pull the trigger. I'm not blaming you."

"Why not? You talk about my father, my father's sister, and you'll talk about my sister too if I let you. Why you trust me?"

"Baby, I hope I never have to ask myself that question."

It ended all right, that gloomy conversation. There was no real anger and nothing irrevocable was said. When Milkman left, Guitar opened his palm as usual and Milkman slapped it. Maybe it was fatigue, but the touching of palms seemed a little weak.

At the Pittsburgh airport he discovered that Danville was 240 miles northeast, and not accessible by any public transportation other than a Greyhound bus. Reluctantly, unwilling to give up the elegance he had felt on the flight, he taxied from the airport to the bus station and settled himself for two idle hours before the Greyhound left. By the time he boarded, the inactivity, the picture magazines he'd read, the strolls in the streets near the station, had exhausted him. He fell asleep fifteen minutes outside Pittsburgh. When he woke it was late in the afternoon, with an hour more to go before he reached Danville. His father had raved about the beauty of this part of the country, but Milkman saw it as merely green, deep into its Indian summer but cooler than his own city, although it was farther south. The mountains, he thought, must make for the difference in temperature. For a few minutes he tried to enjoy the scenery running past his window, then the city man's boredom with nature's repetition overtook him. Some places had lots of trees, some did not; some fields were green, some were not, and the hills in the distance were like the hills in every distance. Then he watched signs—the names of towns that lay twenty-two miles ahead, seventeen miles to the east, five miles to the northeast. And the names of junctions, counties, crossings, bridges, stations, tunnels, mountains, rivers, creeks, landings, parks, and lookout points. Everybody had to do his act, he thought, for surely anybody who was interested in Dudberry Point already knew where it was.

He had two bottles of Cutty Sark in his suitcase, along with two shirts and some underwear. The large suitcase, he thought, would have its real load on the return trip. Now he wished he had not checked it under the bus, for he wanted a drink right then. According to his watch, the gold Longines his mother had given him, it would be another twenty minutes before a stop. He lay back on the headrest and tried to fall asleep. His eyes were creasing from the sustained viewing of uneventful countryside.

In Danville he was astonished to learn that the bus depot was a diner on route 11 where the counterman sold bus tickets, hamburgers, coffee, cheese and peanut butter crackers, cigarettes, candy and a cold-cut plate. No lockers, no baggage room, no taxi, and now he realized no men's room either.

Suddenly he felt ridiculous. What was he supposed to do? Put his suitcase down and ask the man: Where is the cave near the farm where my father lived fifty-eight years ago? He knew nobody, had no names except the first name of an old lady who was now dead. And rather than call any more attention to himself in this tiny farming town than his beige three-piece suit, his button-down light-blue shirt and black string tie, and his beautiful Florsheim shoes had already brought, he asked the counterman if he could check his bag there. The man gazed at the suitcase and seemed to be turning the request over in his mind.

"I'll pay," said Milkman.

"Leave 'er here. Back a pop crates," the man said. "When you wanna pick 'er up?"

"This evening," he said.

"Fine. She'll be right here."

Milkman left the diner/bus station with a small satchel of shaving things and walked out into the streets of Danville, Pennsylvania. He'd seen places like this in Michigan, of course, but he never had to do anything in them other than buy gas. The three stores on the street were closing up for the night. It was five-fifteen and about a dozen people, all told, were walking on the sidewalks. One of them was a Negro. A tall man, elderly, with a brown peaked cap and an old-fashioned collar. Milkman followed him for a while, then caught up to him and said, "Say, I wonder if you could help me." He smiled as he spoke.

The man turned around but did not answer. Milkman wondered if he had offended him in some way. Finally the man nodded and said, "Do what I can." He had a slight country lilt, like that of the white man at the counter.

"I'm looking for ... Circe, a lady named Circe. Well, not her, but her house. Do you know where she used to live? I'm from out of town. I just got off the bus. I have some business to take care of here, an insurance policy, and I need to check on some property out there."

The man was listening and apparently not going to interrupt him, so Milkman ended his sentence lamely with: "Can you help me?"

"Reverend Cooper would know," said the man.

"Where can I find him?" Milkman felt something missing from the conversation.

"Stone Lane. Follow this here street till you come to the post office. Go on around the post office and that'll be Windsor. The next street is Stone Lane. He lives in there."

"Will there be a church there?" Milkman assumed a preacher lived next door to his church.

"No. No. Church ain't got no parsonage. Reverend Cooper lives in Stone Lane. Yella house, I believe."

"Thanks," said Milkman. "Thanks a lot."

"Mighty welcome," said the man. "Good evenin'." And he walked away.

Milkman considered whether to go back for his suitcase, abandoned the idea, and followed the directions given him. An American flag identified the post office, a frame structure next to a drugstore that served also as the Western Union office. He turned left at the corner, but noticed there were no street signs anywhere. How could he find Windsor or Stone Lane if there were no signs? He walked through a residential street, another and another, and he was just about to go back to the drugstore and look under "A. M. E." or "A. M. E. Zion" in the telephone directory when he saw a yellow-and-white house. Maybe this is it, he thought. He climbed the steps, determined to mind his manners. A thief should be polite and win goodwill.

"Good evening. Is Reverend Cooper here?"

A woman was standing in the doorway. "Yes, he's here. Would you like to come in? I'll call him."

"Thank you." Milkman entered a tiny hall and waited.

A short chubby man appeared, fingering his glasses. "Yes, sir? You wanted to see me?" His eyes ran rapidly over Milkman's clothes, but his voice betrayed no excessive curiosity.

"Yes. Uh ... how are you?"

"Fine. Fine. And you?"

"Pretty good." Milkman felt as awkward as he sounded. He had never had to try to make a pleasant impression on a stranger before, never needed anything from a stranger before, and did not remember ever asking anybody in the world how they were. I might as well say it all, he thought. "I could use your help, sir. My name is Macon Dead. My father is from around—"

"Dead? Macon Dead, you say?"

"Yes." Milkman smiled apologetically for the name. "My father—"

"Well, I'll be." Reverend Cooper took off his glasses. "Well, I'll be! Esther!" He threw his voice over his shoulder without taking his eyes off his guest. "Esther, come here!" Then to Milkman: "I know your people!"

Milkman smiled and let his shoulders slump a little. It was a good feeling to come into a strange town and find a stranger who knew your people. All his life he'd heard the tremor in the word: "I live here, but my people ..." or: "She acts like she ain't got no people," or: "Do any of your people live there?" But he hadn't known what it meant: links. He remembered Freddie sitting in Sonny's Shop just before Christmas, saying, "None of my people would take me in." Milkman beamed at Reverend Cooper and his wife. "You do?"

"Sit on down here, boy. You the son of the Macon Dead I knew. Oh, well, now, I don't mean to say I knew him all that well. Your daddy was four or five years older than me, and they didn't get to town much, but everybody round here remembers the old man. Old Macon Dead, your granddad. My daddy and him was good friends. A blacksmith, my daddy was. I'm the only one got the call. Well well well." Reverend Cooper grinned and massaged his knees. "Oh, Lord, I'm forgetting myself. You must be hungry. Esther, get him something to fill himself up on."

"Oh, no. No, thank you, sir. Maybe a little something to drink. I mean if you do drink, that is."

"Sure. Sure. Nothing citified, I'm sorry to say, but—Esther!" She was on her way to the kitchen. "Bring some glasses and get that whiskey out the cupboard. This here's Macon Dead's boy and he's tired and needs a drink. Tell me, how'd you find me? Don't tell me your daddy remembered me?"

"He probably does, but I met a man in the street and he told me how to find you."

"You asked him for me?" Reverend Cooper wanted to get all the facts straight. Already he was framing the story for his friends: how the man came to his house first, how he asked for him ...

Esther returned with a Coca-Cola tray, two glasses, and a large mayonnaise jar of what looked like water. Reverend Cooper poured it warm and neat into the two glasses. No ice, no water—just pure rye whiskey that almost tore Milkman's throat when he swallowed it.

"No. I didn't ask for you by name. I asked him if he knew where a woman named Circe used to live."

"Circe? Yes. Lord, old Circe!"

"He told me to talk to you."

Reverend Cooper smiled and poured more whiskey. "Everybody round here knows me and I know everybody."

"Well, I know my father stayed with her awhile, after they ... when they ... after his father died."

"They had a fine place. Mighty fine. Some white folks own it now. Course that's what they wanted. That's why they shot him. Upset a lot of people here, a whole lot of people. Scared 'em too. But didn't your daddy have a sister name of Pilate?"

"Yes, sir. Pilate."

"Still living, is she?"

"Oh, yes. Very much living."

"Issat so? Pretty girl, real pretty. My daddy was the one made the earring for her. That's how we knew they was alive. After Old Macon Dead was killed, nobody knew whether the children were dead too or what. Then a few weeks passed and Circe came to my daddy's shop. Right across from where the post office is now—that's where my daddy's blacksmith shop was. She came in there with this little metal box with a piece of paper bag folded up in it. Pilate's name was written on it. Circe didn't tell Daddy anything, but that he was to make a earring out of it. She stole a brooch from the folks she worked for. My daddy took the gold pin off it and soldered it to the box. So we knew they was alive and Circe was taking care of 'em. They'd be all right with Circe. She worked for the Butlers—rich white folks, you know—but she was a good midwife in those days. Delivered everybody. Me included."

Maybe it was the whiskey, which always made other people gracious when he drank it, but Milkman felt a glow listening to a story come from this man that he'd heard many times before but only half listened to. Or maybe it was being there in the place where it happened that made it seem so real. Hearing Pilate talk about caves and woods and earrings on

Darling Street, or his father talk about cooking wild turkey over the automobile noise of Not Doctor Street, seemed exotic, something from another world and age, and maybe not even true. Here in the parsonage, sitting in a cane-bottomed chair near an upright piano and drinking homemade whiskey poured from a mayonnaise jar, it was real. Without knowing it, he had walked right by the place where Pilate's earring had been fashioned, the earring that had fascinated him when he was little, the fixing of which informed the colored people here that the children of the murdered man were alive. And this was the living room of the son of the man who made the earring.

"Did anybody ever catch the men who did it—who killed him?"

Reverend Cooper raised his eyebrows. "Catch?" he asked, his face full of wonder. Then he smiled again. "Didn't have to catch 'em. They never went nowhere."

"I mean did they have a trial; were they arrested?"

"Arrested for what? Killing a nigger? Where did you say you was from?"

"You mean nobody did anything? Didn't even try to find out who did it?"

"Everybody knew who did it. Same people Circe worked for—the Butlers."

"And nobody did anything?" Milkman wondered at his own anger. He hadn't felt angry when he first heard about it. Why now?

"Wasn't nothing to do. White folks didn't care, colored folks didn't dare. Wasn't no police like now. Now we got a county sheriff handles things. Not then. Then the circuit judge came through just once or twice a year. Besides, the people what did it owned half the county. Macon's land was in their way. Folks just was thankful the children escaped."

"You said Circe worked for the people who killed him. Did she know that?"

"Course she did."

"And she let them stay there?"

"Not out in the open. She hid them."

"Still, they were in the same house, right?"

"Yep. Best place, I'd say. If they came to town somebody'd see 'em. Nobody would think of looking there."

"Did Daddy—did my father know that?"

"I don't know what he knew, if Circe ever told him. I never saw him after the murder. None of us did."

"Where are they? The Butlers. They still live here?"

"Dead now. Every one of 'em. The last one, the girl Elizabeth, died a couple of years back. Barren as a rock and just as old. Things work out, son. The ways of God are mysterious, but if you live it out, just live it out, you see that it always works out. Nothing they stole or killed for did 'em a bit a good. Not one bit."

"I don't care whether it did them good. The fact is they did somebody else harm."

Reverend Cooper shrugged. "White folks different up your way?"

"No, I guess not ... Sometimes, though, you can do something."

"What?" The preacher looked genuinely interested.

Milkman couldn't answer except in Guitar's words, so he said nothing.

"See this here?" The Reverend turned around and showed Milkman a knot the size of a walnut that grew behind his ear. "Some of us went to Philly to try and march in an Armistice Day parade. This was after the First World War. We were invited and had a permit, but the people, the white people, didn't like us being there. They started a fracas. You know, throwing rocks and calling us names. They didn't care nothing 'bout the uniform. Anyway, some police on horseback came—to quiet them down, we thought. They ran *us* down. Right under their horses. This here's what a hoof can do. Ain't that something?"

"Jesus God."

"You wouldn't be here to even things up, would you?" The preacher leaned over his stomach.

"No. I'm passing through, that's all. Just thought I'd look around. I wanted to see the farm ..."

"Cause any evening up left to do, Circe took care of."

"What'd she do?"

"Hah! What didn't she do?"

"Sorry I didn't come out here long time ago. I would have liked to meet her. She must have been a hundred years old when she died."

"Older. Was a hundred when I was a boy."

"Is the farm nearby?" Milkman appeared mildly interested.

"Not too far."

"I sort of wanted to see where it was since I'm out this way. Daddy talked so much about it."

"It's right back of the Butler place, about fifteen miles out. I can take you there. My old piece of car's in the shop, but it was supposed to be ready yesterday. I'll check on it."

Milkman waited four days for the car to be ready. Four days at Reverend Cooper's house as his guest, and the purpose of long visits from every old man in the town who remembered his father or his grandfather, and some who'd only heard. They all repeated various aspects of the story, all talked about how beautiful Lincoln's Heaven was. Sitting in the kitchen, they looked at Milkman with such rheumy eyes, and spoke about his grandfather with such awe and affection, Milkman began to miss him too. His own father's words came back to him: "I worked right alongside my father. Right alongside him." Milkman thought then that his father was boasting of his manliness as a child. Now he knew he had been saying something else. That he loved his father; had an intimate relationship with him; that his father loved him, trusted him, and found him worthy of working "right alongside" him. "Something went wild in me," he'd said, "when I saw him on the ground."

His was the genuine feeling that Milkman had faked when Reverend Cooper described the hopelessness of "doing anything." These men remembered both Macon Deads as extraordinary men. Pilate they remembered as a pretty woods-wild girl "that couldn't nobody put shoes on". Only one of them remembered his grandmother. "Good-lookin, but looked like a white woman. Indian, maybe. Black hair and slanted-up eyes. Died in childbirth, you know." The more the old men talked—the more he heard about the only farm in the county that grew peaches, real peaches like they had in Georgia, the feasts they had when hunting was over, the pork kills in the winter and the work, the backbreaking work of a going farm—the more he missed something in his life. They talked about digging a well, fashioning traps, felling trees, warming orchards with fire when spring weather was bad, breaking young horses, training dogs. And in it all was his own father, the second Macon Dead, their contemporary, who was strong as an ox, could ride bareback and barefoot, who, they agreed, outran, outplowed, outshot, outpicked, outrode them all. He could not recognize that stern, greedy, unloving man in the boy they talked about, but he loved the boy they described and loved that boy's father, with his hip-roofed barn, his peach trees, and Sunday break-of-dawn fishing parties in a fish pond that was two acres wide.

They talked on and on, using Milkman as the ignition that gunned their memories. The good times, the hard times, things that changed, things that stayed the same—and head and shoulders above all of it was the tall, magnificent Macon Dead, whose death, it seemed to him, was the beginning of their own dying even though they were young boys at the time. Macon Dead was the farmer they wanted to be, the clever irrigator, the peachtree grower, the hog slaughterer, the wild-turkey roaster, the man who could plow forty in no time flat and sang like an angel while he did it. He had come out of nowhere, as ignorant as a hammer and broke as a convict, with nothing but free papers, a Bible, and a pretty black-haired wife, and in one year he'd leased ten acres, the next ten more. Sixteen years later he had one of the best farms in Montour County. A farm that colored their lives like a paintbrush and spoke to them like a sermon. "You see?" the farm said to them. "See? See what you can do? Never mind you can't tell one letter from another, never mind you born a slave, never mind you lose your name, never mind your daddy dead, never mind nothing. Here, this here, is what a man can do if he puts his mind to it and his back in it. Stop sniveling," it said. "Stop picking around the edges of the world. Take advantage, and if you can't take advantage, take disadvantage. We live here. On this planet, in this nation, in this county right here. Nowhere else! We got a home in this rock, don't you see! Nobody starving in my home; nobody crying in my home, and if I got a home you got one too! Grab it. Grab this land! Take it, hold it, my brothers, make it, my brothers, shake it, squeeze it, turn it, twist it, beat it, kick it, kiss it, whip it, stomp it, dig it, plow it, seed it, reap it, rent it, buy it, sell it, own it, build it, multiply it, and pass it on—can you hear me? Pass it on!"

But they shot the top of his head off and ate his fine Georgia peaches. And even as boys these men began to die and were dying still. Looking at Milkman in those nighttime talks, they yearned for something. Some words from him that would rekindle the dream and stop the death they were dying. That's why Milkman began to talk about his father, the boy they knew, the son of the fabulous Macon Dead. He bragged a little and they came alive. How many houses his father owned (they grinned); the new car every two years (they laughed); and when he told them how his father tried to buy the Erie Lackawanna (it sounded better that way), they hooted with joy. That's him! That's Old Macon Dead's boy, all right! They wanted to know everything and Milkman found himself rattling off assets like an accountant, describing deals, total rents income, bank loans, and this new thing his father was looking into—the stock market.

Suddenly, in the midst of his telling, Milkman wanted the gold. He wanted to get up right then and there and go get it. Run to where it was and snatch every grain of it from under the noses of the Butlers, who were dumb enough to believe that if they killed one man his whole line died. He glittered in the light of their adoration and grew fierce with pride.

"Who'd your daddy marry?"

"The daughter of the richest Negro doctor in town."

"That's him! That's Macon Dead!"

"Send you all to college?"

"Sent my sisters. I work right alongside him in our office."

"Hah! Keep you home to get that money! Macon Dead gonna always make him some money!"

"What kinda car he drive?"

"Buick. Two-twenty-five."

"Great God, a deuce and a quarter! What year?"

"This year!"

"That's him! That's Macon Dead! He gonna buy the Erie Lacka*wan*na. If he want it, he'll get it! Bless my soul. Bet he worry them white folks to death. Can't nobody keep him down! Not no Macon Dead! Not in this world! And not in the next! Haw! Goddam! The Erie Lacka*wan*na!"

After all the waiting, Reverend Cooper couldn't go. His preaching income was supplemented by freight yard work and he was called for an early shift. His nephew, called Nephew since he was their only one, was assigned to drive Milkman out to the farm—as close as they could get. Nephew was thirteen and barely able to see over the steering wheel.

"Does he have a license?" Milkman asked Mrs. Cooper.

"Not yet," she said, and when she saw his consternation she explained that farm kids drove early—they had to.

Milkman and Nephew started out right after breakfast. It took them the better part of an hour because the roads were curving two lanes and they spent twenty minutes behind a light truck they couldn't pull around. Nephew spoke very little. He seemed interested only in Milkman's clothes, which he took every opportunity to examine. Milkman decided to give him one of his shirts, and asked him to stop by the bus station to pick up the suitcase he'd left there.

Finally Nephew slowed down on a stretch of road that showed no houses at all. He stopped.

"What's the matter? You want me to drive?"

"No, sir. This is it."

"What's it? Where?"

"Back in there." He pointed to some bushes. "The road to the Butler place is in there and the farm's back behind it. You got to walk it. Car won't make it."

Nothing was truer; as it turned out, Milkman's feet could hardly make it over the stony road covered with second growth. He had asked Nephew to wait, thinking he would survey the area quickly and come back later on his own. But the boy had chores, he said, and would be back whenever Milkman wanted him to be there.

"An hour," said Milkman.

"Take me an hour just to get back to town," said Nephew.

"Reverend Cooper said you were to take me. Not leave me stranded."

"My mama whip me, I don't do my chores."

Milkman was annoyed, but because he didn't want the boy to think he was nervous about being left out there alone, he agreed to having him come back at—he glanced at his heavy, overdesigned watch—at noon. It was nine o'clock then.

His hat had been knocked off by the first branches of the old walnut trees, so he held it in his hand. His cuffless pants were darkened by the mile-long walk over moist leaves. The quiet fairly roared in his ears. He was uncomfortable and a little anxious, but the gold loomed large in his mind, as did the faces of the men he'd drunk with last night, and he stepped firmly onto the gravel and leaves of the driveway which circled the biggest house he'd ever seen.

This is where they stayed, he thought, where Pilate cried when given cherry jam. He stood still a moment. It must have been beautiful, must have seemed like a palace to them, but neither had ever spoken of it in any terms but how imprisoned they felt, how difficult it was to see the sky from their room, how repelled they were by the carpets, the draperies. Without knowing who killed their father, they instinctively hated the murderers' house. And it did look like a murderer's house. Dark, ruined, evil. Never, not since he knelt by his window sill wishing he could fly, had he felt so lonely. He saw the eyes of a child peering at him over the sill of the one second-story window the ivy had not covered. He smiled. "Must be myself I'm seeing—thinking about how I used to watch the sky out the window." Or maybe it's the light trying to get through the trees. Four graceful columns supported the portico, and the huge double-door featured a heavy, brass knocker. He lifted it and let it fall; the sound was soaked up like a single raindrop in cotton. Nothing stirred. He looked back down the path and saw the green maw out of which he had come, a greenish-black tunnel, the end of which was nowhere in sight.

The farm, they said, was right in back of the Butler place, but knowing how different their concept of distance was, he thought he'd better get moving. If he found what he was looking for he would have to come back at night—with equipment, of course, but also with some familiarity with the area. On impulse he reached out his hand and tried to turn the doorknob. It didn't budge. Half turning to leave—literally as an after-thought—he pushed the door and it swung open with a sigh. He leaned in. The smell prevented him from seeing anything more than the absence of light did. A hairy animal smell, ripe, rife, suffocating. He coughed and looked for somewhere to spit, for the odor was in his mouth, coating his teeth and tongue. He pulled a handkerchief from his back pocket, held it over his nose, backed away from the open door, and had just begun to spill the little breakfast he'd eaten when the odor disappeared and, quite suddenly, in its place was a sweet spicy perfume. Like ginger root—pleasant, clean, seductive. Surprised and charmed by it, he retraced his steps and went inside. After a second or two he was able to see the hand-laid and hand-finished wooden floor in a huge hall, and at its farther end a wide staircase spiraling up into the dark. His eyes traveled up the stairs.

He had had dreams as a child, dreams every child had, of the witch who chased him down dark alleys, between lawn trees, and finally into rooms from which he could not escape. Witches in black dresses and red underskirts; witches with pink eyes and green lips, tiny witches, long rangy witches, frowning witches, smiling witches, screaming witches and laughing witches, witches that flew, witches that ran, and some that merely glided on the ground. So when he saw the woman at the top of the stairs there was no way for him to resist climbing up toward her outstretched hands, her fingers spread wide for him, her mouth gaping open for him, her eyes devouring him. In a dream you climb the stairs. She grabbed him, grabbed his shoulders and pulled him right up against her and tightened her arms around him. Her head came to his chest and the feel of that hair under his chin, the dry bony hands like steel springs rubbing his back, her floppy mouth babbling into his vest, made him dizzy, but he knew that always, always at the very instant of the pounce or the gummy embrace he would wake with a scream and an erection. Now he had only the erection.

Milkman closed his eyes, helpless to pull away before the completion of the dream. What made him surface from it was a humming sound around his knees. He looked down and there, surrounding him, was a pack of golden-eyed dogs, each of which had the intelligent child's eyes he had seen from the window. Abruptly the woman let him go and he looked down at her too. Beside the calm, sane, appraising eyes of the dogs, her eyes looked crazy. Beside their combed, brushed gun-metal hair, hers was wild and filthy.

She spoke to the dogs. "Go on away. Helmut, go on. Horst, move." She waved her hands and the dogs obeyed.

"Come, come," she said to Milkman. "In here." She took his hand in both of hers, and he followed her—his arm outstretched, his hand in hers—like a small boy being dragged reluctantly to bed. Together they weaved among the bodies of the dogs that floated around his legs. She led him into a room, made him sit on a gray velvet sofa, and dismissed all the dogs but two that lay at her feet.

"Remember the Weimaraners?" she asked, settling herself, pulling her chair close to him.

She was old. So old she was colorless. So old only her mouth and eyes were distinguishable features in her face. Nose, chin, cheekbones, forehead, neck all had surrendered their identity to the pleats and crochetwork of skin committed to constant change.

Milkman struggled for a clear thought, so hard to come by in a dream: Perhaps this woman is Circe. But Circe is dead. This woman is alive. That was as far as he got, because although the woman was talking to him, she might in any case still be dead—as a matter of fact, she *had* to be dead. Not because of the wrinkles, and the face so old it could not be alive, but because out of the toothless mouth came the strong, mellifluent voice of a twenty-year-old girl.

"I knew one day you would come back. Well, that's not entirely true. Some days I doubted it and some days I didn't think about it at all. But you see, I was right. You did come."

It was awful listening to that voice come from that face. Maybe something was happening to his ears. He wanted to hear the sound of his own voice, so he decided to take a chance on logic.

"Excuse me. I'm his son. I'm Macon Dead's son. Not the one you knew."

She stopped smiling.

"My name is Macon Dead too, but I'm thirty-two years old. You knew my father and his father too." So far, so good. His voice was the same. Now he needed only to know if he had assessed the situation correctly. She did not answer him. "You're Circe, aren't you?"

"Yes; Circe," she said, but she seemed to have lost all interest in him. "My name is Circe."

"I'm just visiting," he said. "I spent a couple of days with Reverend Cooper and his wife. They're the ones brought me out here."

"I thought you were him. I thought you came back to see me. Where is he? *My* Macon?"

"Back home. He's alive. He told me about you..."

"And Pilate. Where is she?"

"There too. She's fine."

"Well, you look like him. You really do." But she didn't sound convinced.

"He's seventy-two years old now," said Milkman. He thought that would clear things up, make her know he couldn't be the Macon she knew, who was sixteen when she last saw him. But all she said was "Uhn," as though seventy-two, thirty-two, any age at all, meant nothing whatsoever to her. Milkman wondered how old she really was.

"Are you hungry?" she asked.

"No. Thank you. I ate breakfast."

"So you've been staying with that little Cooper boy?"

"Yes, ma'am."

"A runt. I told him not to smoke, but children don't listen."

"Do you mind if I do?" Milkman was relaxing a little and he hoped the cigarette would relax him more.

She shrugged. "Do what you like. Everybody does what he likes nowadays anyway."

Milkman lit the cigarette and the dogs hummed at the sound of the match, their eyes glittering toward the flame.

"Ssh!" whispered Circe.

"Beautiful," said Milkman.

"What's beautiful?"

"The dogs."

"They're not beautiful, they're strange, but they keep things away. I'm completely worn out taking care of 'em. They belonged to Miss

Butler. She bred them, crossbred them. Tried for years to get them in the AKC. They wouldn't permit it."

"What did you call them?"

"Weimaraners. German."

"What do you do with them?"

"Oh, I keep some. Sell some. Till we all die in here together." She smiled.

She had dainty habits which matched her torn and filthy clothes in precisely the way her strong young cultivated voice matched her wizened face. Her white hair—braided, perhaps; perhaps not—she touched as though replacing a wayward strand from an elegant coiffure. And her smile—an opening of flesh like celluloid dissolving under a drop of acid—was accompanied by a press of fingers on her chin. It was this combination of daintiness and cultivated speech that misled Macon and invited him to regard her as merely foolish.

"You should get out once in a while."

She looked at him.

"Is this your house now? Did they will you this? Is that why you have to stay here?"

She pressed her lips over her gums. "The only reason I'm here alone is because she died. She killed herself. All the money was gone, so she killed herself. Stood right there on the landing where you were a minute ago and threw herself off the banister. She didn't die right away, though; she lay in the bed a week or two and there was nobody here but us. The dogs were in the kennel then. I brought her in the world, just like I did her mother and her grandmother before that. Birthed just about everybody in the county, I did. Never lost one either. Never lost nobody but your mother. Well, grandmother, I guess she was. Now I birth dogs."

"Some friend of Reverend Cooper said she looked white. My grandmother. Was she?"

"No. Mixed. Indian mostly. A good-looking woman, but fierce, for the young woman I knew her as. Crazy about her husband too, overcrazy. You know what I mean? Some women love too hard. She watched over him like a pheasant hen. Nervous. Nervous love."

Milkman thought about this mixed woman's great-granddaughter, Hagar, and said, "Yes. I know what you mean."

"But a good woman. I cried like a baby when I lost her. Like a baby. Poor Sing."

"What?" He wondered if she lisped.

"I cried like a baby when I—"

"No. I mean what did you call her?"

"Sing. Her name was Sing."

"Sing? Sing Dead. Where'd she get a name like that?"

"Where'd you get a name like yours? White people name Negroes like race horses."

"I suppose so. Daddy told me how they got their name."

"What'd he tell you?"

Milkman told her the story about the drunken Yankee.

"Well, he didn't have to keep the name. She made him. She made him keep that name," Circe said when he was through.

"She?"

"Sing. His wife. They met on a wagon going North. Ate pecans all the way, she told me. It was a wagonful of ex-slaves going to the promised land."

"Was she a slave too?"

"No. No indeed. She always bragged how she was never a slave. Her people neither."

"Then what was she doing on that wagon?"

"I can't answer you because I don't know. Never crossed my mind to ask her."

"Where were they coming from? Georgia?"

"No. Virginia. Both of them lived in Virginia, her people and his. Down around Culpeper somewhere. Charlemagne or something like that."

"I think that's where Pilate was for a while. She lived all over the country before she came to us."

"Did she ever marry that boy?"

"What boy?"

"The boy she had the baby by."

"No. She didn't marry him."

"Didn't think she would. She was too ashamed."

"Ashamed of what?"

"Her stomach."

"Oh, that."

"Borned herself. I had very little to do with it. I thought they were both dead, the mother and the child. When she popped out you could have knocked me over. I hadn't heard a heartbeat anywhere. She just came on out. Your daddy loved her. Hurt me to hear they broke away from one another. So it does me good to hear they're back together again." She had warmed up talking about the past and Milkman decided not to tell her that Macon and Pilate just lived in the same city. He wondered how she knew about their split, and if she knew what they broke apart about.

"You knew about their quarrel?" he asked quietly, non-chalantly.

"Not the substance. Just the fact. Pilate came back here just after her baby was born. One winter. She told me they split up when they left here and she hadn't seen him since."

"Pilate told me they lived in a cave for a few days after they left this house."

"Is that right? Must have been Hunters Cave. Hunters used it to rest up in there sometimes. Eat. Smoke. Sleep. That's where they dumped Old Macon's body."

"They who? I thought ... My father said he buried him. Down by a creek or a river someplace where they used to fish."

"He did. But it was too shallow and too close to the water. The body floated up at the first heavy rain. Those children hadn't been gone a month when it floated up. Some men were fishing down there and saw this body, a Negro. So they knew who it was. Dumped it in the cave, and it was summer too. You'd think they would have buried a body in the summer. I told Mrs. Butler I thought it was a disgrace."

"Daddy doesn't know that."

"Well, don't tell him. Let him have his peace. It's hard enough with a murdered father; he don't need to know what happened to the body."

"Did Pilate tell you why she came back here?"

"Yes. She said her father told her to. She had visits from him, she said."

"I'd like to see that cave. Where he's ... where they put him."

"Won't be anything left to see now. That's been a long time ago."

"I know, but maybe there's something I can bury properly."

"Now, that's a thought worth having. The dead don't like it if they're not buried. They don't like it at all. You won't have trouble finding it. You go back out the road you came in on. Go north until you come to a stile. It's falling down, but you'll see it's a stile. Right in there the woods are open. Walk a little way in and you'll come to a creek. Cross it. There'll be some more woods, but ahead you'll see a short range of hills. The cave is right on the face of those hills. You can't miss it.

It's the only one there. Tell your daddy you buried him properly, in a graveyard. Maybe with a headstone. A nice headstone. I hope they find me soon enough and somebody'll take pity on me." She looked at the dogs. "Hope they find me soon and don't let me lay in here too long."

Milkman swallowed as her thought touched his mind. "People come to see you, don't they?"

"Dog buyers. They come every now and then. They'll find me, I guess."

"Reverend Cooper ... They think you're dead."

"Splendid. I don't like those Negroes in town. Dog people come and the man that delivers the dog food once a week. They come. They'll find me. I just hope it's soon."

He loosened his collar and lit another cigarette. Here in this dim room he sat with the woman who had helped deliver his father and Pilate; who had risked her job, her life, maybe, to hide them both after their father was killed, emptied their slop jars, brought them food at night and pans of water to wash. Had even sneaked off to the village to have the girl Pilate's name and snuffbox made into an earring. Then healed the ear when it got infected. And after all these years was thrilled to see what she believed was one of them. Healer, deliverer, in another world she would have been the head nurse at Mercy. Instead she tended Weimaraners and had just one selfish wish: that when she died somebody would find her before the dogs ate her.

"You should leave this place. Sell the damn dogs. I'll help you. You need money? How much?" Milkman felt a flood of pity and thought gratitude made her smile at him. But her voice was cold.

"You think I don't know how to walk when I want to walk? Put your money back in your pocket."

Rebuffed from his fine feelings, Milkman matched her cold tone: "You loved those white folks that much?"

"Love?" she asked. "Love?"

"Well, what are you taking care of their dogs for?"

"Do you know why she killed herself? She couldn't stand to see the place go to ruin. She couldn't live without servants and money and what it could buy. Every cent was gone and the taxes took whatever came in. She had to let the upstairs maids go, then the cook, then the dog trainer, then the yardman, then the chauffeur, then the car, then the woman who washed once a week. Then she started selling bits and pieces—land, jewels, furniture. The last few years we ate out of the garden. Finally she couldn't take it anymore. The thought of having no help, no money—well, she couldn't take that. She had to let everything go."

"But she didn't let you go." Milkman had no trouble letting his words snarl.

"No, she didn't let me go. She killed herself."

"And you still loyal."

"You don't listen to people. Your ear is on your head, but it's not connected to your brain. I said she killed herself rather than do the work I'd been doing all my life!" Circe stood up, and the dogs too. "Do you hear me? She saw the work I did all her days and *died*, you hear me, *died* rather than live like me. Now, what do you suppose she thought I was! If the way I lived and the work I did was so hateful to her she killed herself to keep from having to do it, and you think I stay on here because I loved her, then you have about as much sense as a fart!"

The dogs were humming and she touched their heads. One stood on either side of her. "They loved this place. Loved it. Brought pink veined marble from across the sea for it and hired men in Italy to do the chandelier that I had to climb a ladder and clean with white muslin once every two months. They loved it. Stole for it, lied for it, killed for it. But I'm the one left. Me and the dogs. And I will never clean it again. Never. Nothing. Not a speck of dust, not a grain of dirt, will I move. Everything in this world they lived for will crumble and rot. The chandelier already fell down and smashed itself to pieces. It's down there in the ballroom now. All in pieces. Something gnawed through the cords. Ha! And I want to see it all go, make sure it does go, and that nobody fixes it up. I brought the dogs in to make sure. They keep strangers out too. Folks tried to get in here to steal things after she died. I set the dogs on them. Then I just brought them all right in here with me. You ought to see what they did to her bedroom. Her walls didn't have wallpaper. No. Silk brocade that took some Belgian women six years to make. She loved it—oh, how much she loved it. Took thirty Weimaraners one day to rip it off the walls. If I thought the stink wouldn't strangle you, I'd show it to you." She looked at the walls around her. "This is the last room."

"I wish you'd let me help you," he said after a while.

"You have. You came in here and pretended it didn't stink and told me about Macon and my sweet little Pilate."

"Are you sure?"

"Never surer."

They both stood and walked down the hall. "Mind how you step. There's no light." Dogs came from everywhere, humming. "Time for their feeding," she said. Milkman started down the stairs. Halfway down, he turned and looked up at her.

"You said his wife made him keep the name. Did you ever know his real name?"

"Jake, I believe."

"Jake what?"

She shrugged, a Shirley Temple, little-girl-helpless shrug. "Jake was all she told me."

"Thanks," he called back, louder than he needed to, but he wanted his gratitude to cut through the stink that was flooding back over the humming of the dogs.

But the humming and the smell followed him all the way back down the tunnel to the macadam road. When he got there it was ten-thirty. Another hour and a half before Nephew would be back. Milkman paced the shoulder of the road, making plans. When should he return? Should he try to rent a car or borrow the preacher's? Had Nephew got his suitcase? What equipment would he need? Flashlight and what else? What story should be in his mind in case he was discovered? Of course: looking for his grandfather's remains—to collect them and take them for a proper burial. He paced further, and then began to stroll in the direction Nephew would be coming from. After a few minutes, he wondered if he was going the right way. He started back, but just then saw the ends of two or three wooden planks sticking out of the brush. Maybe this was the stile Circe had described to him. Not exactly a stile, but the remains of one. Circe had not left that house in years, he thought. Any stile she knew of would have to be in disrepair now. And if her directions were accurate, he might make it there and back before twelve. At least he would be able to check it out in the daylight.

Gingerly, he parted the brush and walked a little way into the woods. He didn't see even a trace of a track. But as he kept on a bit, he heard water and followed the sound, which seemed to be just ahead of the next line of trees. He was deceived. He walked for fifteen minutes before he came to it. "Cross it," she'd said, and he thought there would be a bridge of some sort. There was none. He looked across and saw hills. It must be there. Right there. He calculated that he could just make it in the hour or so left before he should be back on the road. He sat down, took off his shoes and socks, stuffed the socks in his pocket, and rolled up his pants. Holding his shoes in his hand, he waded in. Unprepared for the coldness of the water and the slimy stones at the bottom, he slipped to one knee and soaked his shoes trying to break his fall. He righted himself with difficulty and poured the water out of his shoes. Since he was already wet, there was no point in turning back; he waded on out. After half a minute, the creek bed dropped six inches and he fell again, only now he went completely under and got a glimpse of small silvery translucent fish as his head went down. Snorting water, he cursed the creek, which was too shallow to swim and too rocky to walk. He should have pulled a stick to check depth before he put his foot down, but his excitement had been too great. He went on, feeling with his toes for firm footing before he put his weight down. It was slow moving—the water was about two or three feet deep and some twelve yards wide. If he hadn't been so eager, maybe he could have found a narrower part to cross. Thoughts of what he should have done instead of just plunging in, fruitless as they were, irritated him so that they kept him moving until he made it to the other side. He threw his shoes on the dry ground and hoisted himself up and out on the bank. Breathless, he reached for his cigarettes and found them soaked. He lay back on the grass and let the high sunshine warm him. He opened his mouth so the clear air could bathe his tongue.

After a while he sat up and put on the wet socks and shoes. He looked at his watch to check the time. It ticked, but the face was splintered and the minute hand was bent. Better move, he thought, and struck out for the hills, which, deceptive as the sound of the creek, were much farther away than they seemed. He had no idea that simply walking through trees, bushes, on untrammeled ground could be so hard. Woods always brought to his mind City Park, the tended woods on Honoré Island where he went for outings as a child and where tiny convenient paths led you through. "He leased ten acres of virgin woods and cleared it all," said the men describing the beginning of Old Macon Dead's farm. Cleared this? Chopped down this? This stuff he could barely walk through?

He was sweating into his wet shirt and just beginning to feel the result of sharp stones on his feet. Occasionally he came to a clear space and he'd alter his direction as soon as the low hills came back into view.

Finally flat ground gave way to a gentle upward slope of bushes, saplings, and rock. He walked along its edge, looking for an opening. As he moved southward, the skirts of the hills were rockier and the saplings fewer. Then he saw, some fifteen to twenty feet above him, a black hole in the rock which he could get to by a difficult, but not dangerous, climb, made more difficult by the thin smooth soles of his shoes. He wiped sweat from his forehead on his coat sleeve, slipped off the narrow black tie that hung open around his collar and put it in his pocket.

The salt taste was back in his mouth and he was so agitated by what he believed, hoped, he would find there, he had to put his hands on warm stone to dry them. He thought of the pitiful hungry eyes of the old men, their eagerness for some words of defiant success accomplished by the son of Macon Dead; and of the white men who strutted through the orchards and ate the Georgia peaches after they shot his grandfather's head off. Milkman took a deep breath and began to negotiate the rocks.

As soon as he put his foot on the first stone, he smelled money, although it was not a smell at all. It was like candy and sex and soft twinkling lights. Like piano music with a few strings in the background. He'd noticed it before when he waited under the pines near Pilate's house; more when the moon lit up the green sack that hung like a kept promise from her ceiling; and most when he tumbled lightly to the floor, sack in hand. Las Vegas and buried treasure; numbers dealers and Wells Fargo wagons; race track pay windows and spewing oil wells; craps, flushes, and sweepstakes tickets. Auctions, bank vaults, and heroin deals. It caused paralysis, trembling, dry throats, and sweaty palms. Urgency, and the feeling that "they" had been mastered or were on your side. Quiet men stood up and threw a queen down on the table hard enough to break her neck. Women sucked their bottom lips and put little red disks down in numbered squares. Lifeguards, A-students, eyed cash registers and speculated on how far away the door was. To win. There was nothing like it in the world.

Milkman became agile, pulling himself up the rock face, digging his knees into crevices, searching with his fingers for solid earth patches or ledges of stone. He left off thinking and let his body do the work. He stood up, finally, on level ground twenty feet to the right of the mouth of the cave. There he saw a crude footpath he might have found earlier if he had not been so hasty. That was the path the hunters used and that Pilate and his father had also used. None of them tore their clothes as he had, climbing twenty feet of steep rock.

He entered the cave and was blinded by the absence of light. He stepped back out and reentered, cupping his eyes. After a while, he could distinguish the ground from the wall of the cave. There was the ledge of rock where they'd slept, much larger than he had pictured. And worn places on the floor where fires had once burned, and several boulders standing around the entrance—one with a kind of V-shaped crown. But where were the bones? Circe said they dumped him in here. Farther back, probably, back where the shallow pit was. Milkman had no flashlight and his matches were certainly wet, but he tried to find a dry one anyway. Only one or two even sputtered. The rest were dead. Still, his eyes were getting used to the dark. He pulled a branch from a bush that grew near the entrance and bending forward, let it graze the ground before him as he walked. He had gone thirty or forty feet when he noticed the cave's walls were closer together. He could not see the roof at all. He stopped and began to move slowly sideways, the branch tip scratching a yard or so ahead. The side of his hand grazed rock and he flung the dry bat shit off it and moved to the left. The branch struck air. He stopped again, and lowered the tip until it touched ground again. Raising it up and down, and pressing it back and around, he could tell that he had found the pit. It was about two feet deep and maybe eight feet wide. Frantically he scraped the branch around the bottom. It hit something hard, again something else hard. Milkman swallowed and dropped to his knees. He squinted his eyes as hard as he could, but he couldn't see a thing. Suddenly he remembered a lighter in his vest pocket. He dropped the branch and fumbled for it, almost faint from the money smell—the twinkling lights, the piano music. He pulled it out, praying it would light. On the second try, it burst into flame and he peered down. The lighter went out. He snapped it back and held his hand over its fragile flame. At the bottom of the hole he saw rocks, boards, leaves, even a tin cup, but no gold. Stretched out on his stomach, holding the lighter in one hand, he swept the bottom with the other, clawing, pulling, fingering, poking. There were no fat little pigeon-breasted bags of gold. There was nothing. Nothing at all. And before he knew it, he was hollering a long, *awwww* sound into the pit. It triggered the bats, which swooped suddenly and dived in the darkness over his head. They startled him and he leaped to his feet, whereupon the sole of his right shoe split away from the soft cordovan leather. The bats drove him out in a lopsided run, lifting his foot high to accommodate the flopping sole.

In the sunlight once more, he stopped for breath. Dust, tears, and too bright light were in his eyes, but he was too angry and disgusted to rub them. He merely threw the lighter in a wide high arc into the trees at the foot of the hills and limped down the footpath, paying no attention to the direction he was going. He put his feet down wherever was most convenient. Quite suddenly, it seemed to him, he was at the creek again, but upstream where the crossing—about twelve feet here and so shallow he could see the stony bottom—was laid across with boards. He sat down and lashed the sole of his shoe to its top with his black string tie, then walked across the homemade bridge. The woods on the other side had a pathway.

Milkman began to shake with hunger. Real hunger, not the less than top-full feeling he was accustomed to, the nervous desire to taste something good. Real hunger. He believed if he didn't get something to eat that instant he would pass out. He examined the bushes, the branches, the ground for a berry, a nut, anything. But he didn't know what to look for, nor how they grew. Trembling, his stomach in a spasm, he tore off a few leaves and put them in his mouth. They were as bitter as gall, but he chewed them anyway, spit them out, and got others. He thought of the breakfast food Mrs. Cooper had put before him, which had disgusted him then. Fried eggs covered with grease, fresh-squeezed orange juice with seed and pulp floating in it, thick hand-cut bacon, a white-hot mound of grits and biscuits. It was her best effort, he knew, but perhaps because of the whiskey he'd drunk the night before, he could only bring himself to drink two cups of black coffee and eat two biscuits. The rest had nauseated him, and what he did eat he had left at Circe's door.

Some brush closed in on him and when he swept it angrily aside, he saw a stile and the road in front of him. Macadam, automobiles, fence posts, civilization. He looked at the sky to gauge the hour. The sun was a quarter of the way down from what even he knew was high noon. About one o'clock, he guessed. Nephew would have come and gone. He felt in his back pocket for his wallet. It was discolored at the edges from the water, but the contents were dry. Five hundred dollars, his driver's license, phone numbers on slips of paper, social security card, airline ticket stub, cleaners receipts. He looked up and down the road. He had to get food, and started walking south, where he believed Danville lay, hoping to hitch as soon as a car came by. He was not only ravenous; his feet hurt. The third car to pass stopped—a 1954 Chevrolet—and the driver, a black man, showed the same interest in Milkman's clothes that Nephew had shown. He seemed not to notice or care about the rip at the knee or under the arm, the tie-tied shoe, the leaves in Milkman's hair, or the dirt all over the suit.

"Where you headed, partner?"

"Danville. As close as I can get."

"Hop on in, then. Little out my way. I cut over to Buford, but I'll get you closer than you was."

"Preciate it," answered Milkman. He loved the car seat, loved it. And sank his weary back into its nylon and sighed.

"Good cut of suit," the man said. "I guess you ain't from here'bouts."

"No. Michigan."

"Sure' nough? Had a aunt move out there. Flint. You know Flint?"

"Yeah. I know Flint." Milkman's feet were singing, the tender skin of the ball louder than the heels. He dared not spread his toes, lest the singing never stop.

"What kinda place is it, Flint?"

"Jive. No place you'd want to go to."

"Thought so. Name sounds good, but I thought it'd be like that."

Milkman had noticed a six-bottle carton of Coca-Cola on the back seat when he got in the car. It was on his mind.

"Could I buy one of those Coca-Colas from you? I'm kinda thirsty."

"It's warm," said the man.

"Long as it's wet."

"Help yourself."

Milkman reached around and pulled a bottle out of its case.

"Got a bottle opener?"

The man took the bottle from him and put its head in his mouth and slowly pried the top off. Foam shot all over his chin and his lap before Milkman could take it from him.

"Hot." The man laughed and wiped himself with a navy- and-white handkerchief.

Milkman gulped the Coke, foam and all, in three or four seconds.

"Like another?"

He did but he said no. Just a cigarette.

"Don't smoke," said the man.

"Oh," said Milkman, and struggled against and lost to a long belch.

"Bus station's right around the bend there." They were just outside Danville. "You can make it easy."

"I really do thank you." Milkman opened the door. "What do I owe you? For the Coke and all?"

The man was smiling, but his face changed now. "My name's Garnett, Fred Garnett. I ain't got much, but I can afford a Coke and a lift now and then."

"I didn't mean ... I ..."

But Mr. Garnett had reached over and closed the door. Milkman could see him shaking his head as he drove off.

Milkman's feet hurt him so, he could have cried, but he made it to the diner/bus station and looked for the man behind the counter. He wasn't there, but a woman offered to help. There followed a long discussion in which he discovered that the bag was not there, the man was not there, she didn't know if a colored boy had picked it up or not, they didn't have a checkroom and she was mighty sorry but he could look at the station-master's if the boy didn't have it, and was there anything else she could do?

"Hamburgers," he said. "Give me some hamburgers and a cup of coffee."

"Yes, sir. How many?"

"Six," he said, but his stomach cramped on the fourth and bent him double with a pain that lasted off and on all the way to Roanoke. But before he left, he telephoned Reverend Cooper. His wife answered and told him that her husband was still at the freight yard and he could catch him there if he hurried. Milkman thanked her and hung up. Walking like a pimp in delicate shoes, he managed to get to the yard, which was fairly close to the bus station. He entered the gate and asked the first man he saw if Reverend Cooper was still there.

"Coop?" the man said. "I think he went on over to the station house. See it? Right over there."

Milkman followed his finger, and hobbled over the gravel and ties to the station house.

It was empty save for an old man dragging a crate.

"Excuse me," Milkman said. "Is Rev—is Coop still here?"

"Just left. If you run you can catch him," the man said. He wiped the sweat of exertion from his forehead.

Milkman thought about running anywhere on his tender feet and said, "Oh, well. I'll try to catch him another time." He turned to go.

"Say," said the man. "If you ain't gonna try to catch him, could you give me a hand with this?" He pointed down to the huge crate at his feet. Too tired to say no or explain, Milkman nodded. The two of them grunted and groaned over the box, and finally got it up on a dolly, where they could push it to the weighing platform. Milkman slumped over the crate and caught his breath, barely able to nod to the old man's thank yous. Then he went out of the station into the street.

He was tired now. Really tired. He didn't want to see Reverend Cooper and his success-starved friends again. And he certainly didn't want to explain anything to his father or Guitar just yet. So he hobbled back to the bus station and asked for the next bus leaving that was going south. It had to be south. And it had to be Virginia. Because now he thought he knew how to find out what had happened to the gold.

Full of hamburgers, sore of foot, sick to his stomach, but at least sitting down, he couldn't even feel the disappointment that lay in the pit in the cave. He slept heavily for several hours on the bus, woke and daydreamed, napped a little more, woke again at a rest stop and ate a bowl of pea soup. He went into a drugstore and replaced the shaving equipment and toilet articles he'd left at Reverend Cooper's, and decided to wait and get his shoe fixed (it was sealed with chewing gum now), his suit mended, and a new shirt in Virginia.

The Greyhound bus made a sound like the hum of the Weimaraners as it sped down the road, and Milkman shivered a little, the way he had when Circe glanced at them, sitting in the "last room," wondering if she would outlive them. But there were over thirty of them and reproducing all the time.

The low hills in the distance were no longer scenery to him. They were real places that could split your thirty-dollar shoes. More than anything in the world he'd wanted it to be there, for row upon row of those little bags to turn their fat pigeon chests up to his hands. He thought he wanted it in the name of Macon Dead's Georgia peaches, in the name of Circe and her golden-eyed dogs, and especially in the name of Reverend Cooper and his old-timey friends who began to die before their facial hair was out when they saw what happened to a black man like them—"ignorant as a hammer and broke as a convict"—who had made it anyway. He also thought he wanted it in the name of Guitar, to erase what looked like doubt in his face when Milkman left, the "I-know-you-gonna-fuck-up" look. There wasn't any gold, but now he knew that all the fine reasons for wanting it didn't mean a thing. The fact was he wanted the gold because it was gold and he wanted to own it. Free. As he had sat chomping the hamburgers in the bus station, imagining what going home would be like now—not only to have to say there was no gold, but also to know he was trapped there—his mind had begun to function clearly.

Circe said that Macon and Sing had boarded that wagon in Virginia, where they both came from. She also said Macon's body rose up from the ground at the first heavy rain, and that the Butlers, or somebody, dumped it in the hunters' cave one summer night. One summer night. And it was a body, a corpse, when they hauled it away, because they recognized him as a Negro. Yet Pilate said it was winter when she was there, and there were only bones. She said she went to see Circe and visited the cave four years later, in the snow, and took the white man's bones. Why didn't she see her father's bones? There should have been two skeletons. Did she step over one and collect the other? Surely Circe had told her the same thing she told him—that her father's body was in the cave. Did Pilate tell Circe that they had killed a man in there? Probably not, since Circe didn't mention it. Pilate said she took the white man's bones and didn't even look for the gold. But she lied. She had not mentioned the second skeleton because it wasn't there when she got to the cave. She didn't come back four years later—or if she did, it was her second trip. She came back *before* they dumped the Negro they found in the cave. She took the bones, all right; Milkman had seen them on the table in the jailhouse. But that's not all she took. She took the gold. To Virginia. And maybe somebody in Virginia would know.

Milkman followed in her tracks.

（选自 Morrison, Toni. *Song of Solomon*. New York: Vintage International, 2004: 156 – 201.）

Questions

1. What are the masterpieces of Toni Morrison?
2. Why is Toni Morrison so important?
3. What are the common themes of Toni Morrison's novels?
4. How does Toni Morrison deal with important phases of Black history?
5. What are the new approaches to interpret Morrison's works?

Unit 10
Amy Tan: *The Kitchen God's Wife*

Amy Tan is one of the most well-known contemporary Chinese American women writers; her first novel *The Joy Luck Club* (1989) won her a world-wide reputation, and her subsequent novels have met with critical acclaim. Born in 1952 in Oakland, California, Tan is the only daughter of Daisy and John Tan who had both emigrated from China. From childhood Tan struggled with the contradictions between her ethnic origins and the dominant western culture of the United States. At home, she encountered strange traditional Chinese customs and parents who had high expectations of her. At school, she was an outsider struggling in the predominantly white American world. Later, as an adult, she claimed that these bicultural tensions marked her childhood and adolescence. In a 1989 interview, Tan told Elaine Woo of the *Los Angeles Times*: "[Her parents] wanted us to have American circumstances and Chinese character." When she was fifteen, both her father and her older brother died of brain tumors. Their death had a profound effect on her family as her mother no longer believed in the Christian faith but reverted to Chinese customs and beliefs. Believing that a bad curse would fall on other family members, her mother decided to move. So, the Tan family embarked on a journey to Europe.

Caught in the conflicting pressure to conform to her mother's Chinese traditions and to follow the example of her Western peers, Amy Tan rebelled against whatever her mother said and expected. Without abiding by her mother's wish that she become a doctor or a pianist, Tan studied for a bachelor's and master's degree in English and linguistics. She dropped out of the doctoral program and worked her way through various jobs, such as a language consultant for disabled children and freelance writer. However, when her first story "Endgame" won her admission to the Squaw Valley Writers workshop directed by novelist, Oakley Hall, Tan began her career as a full-time writer.

With her mixed background of western Protestantism and Chinese tradition, her educational background in English and linguistics, her living experiences in Europe, and her extensive readings in contemporary works, Tan has accumulated varied and abundant materials for her novels. Her plural-cultural experience has taught her to consider multiple, conflicting points of view. In a 2013 interview with Joe Fassler, Tan states that "I question everything and yet I am open to everything. My values shift and grow with my experiences ... and as my content changes so does what I believe." As a result of her bi-cultural upbringing, Tan holds neither a Western nor a Chinese worldview but entertains the two in accordance with her experiences and her context. Her dual education has allowed her to form a syncretic philosophy that entertains Eastern and Western viewpoints.

At this point in time, Tan has written six bestselling novels. There are: *The Joy Luck Club* (1989), *The Kitchen God's Wife* (1991), *The Hundred Secret Senses* (1995), *The Bonesetter's Daughter* (2001), *The Saving Fish from Drowning* (2005), *The Valley of Amazement* (2013). And she has also published a collection of non-fiction essays entitled *The Opposite of Fate: Memories of a Writing Life* and a memoir entitled *Where the Past Begins: A Writer's Memoir*. In addition to these, she has published two children's books: *The Moon Lady* (1992) and *Sagwa, the Chinese Siamese Cat* (1994).

Published in 1991, Tan's subsequent novel *The Kitchen God's Wife* confirmed her reputation. It addresses the relationship between a Chinese immigrant mother (Winnie) and her American-born daughter (Pearl). "But the true focus of the novel is less on the mother-daughter dyad and more predominantly on the story of a woman who is born into wealth and position in pre-communist China, endures a degrading arranged marriage and the early deaths of three children, lives through World War II, emigrates to America, and successfully creates a relatively comfortable and stable life for herself in a new country and an alien culture."

Some critics think that it readdresses the mother-daughter relation so as to explore cultural acculturation and alienation. Others think "it is a retelling of the Kitchen God's story from a contemporary feminist point of view." In the traditional Chinese version of the tale, the wife disappears from the narrative after her husband becomes the Kitchen God. But in Tan's version, Weili, the wife who endures her husband's abuse is rewarded for her forbearance with another chance to experience happiness, and she becomes Winnie, the beloved wife of an American, the mother of her American-born daughter, Pearl, and the grandmother of two American children.

This novel has two narrators. In the first two chapters, the daughter Pearl narrates her difficult relationship with her mother Winnie, and her cultural confusion. Then, to bridge the gap between generations and cultures, the dominant narrator, the mother Winnie tells her daughter the stories of her miserable life in pre-communist China. At the end of the story, as both the mother and her daughter confide their secrets to each other, they reconcile with each other. By depicting the intricacies of the mother-daughter relationship, Tan further explores issues about cultural conflicts and reconciliation, the position of women in patriarchal society and the construction of identity.

Theme

In *The Kitchen God's Wife*, Amy Tan further explores the intricacies of the relationship between mother and daughter by situating them on opposite sides of a great cultural and linguistic divide. At the beginning of the novel, the daughter Pearl claims that she has a problematic relationship with her mother from whom she keeps her distance, both emotionally and geographically. And the mother Winnie is aware that the division between her and her daughter widened on the day of her husband Jimmy Louie's funeral when Winnie slapped Pearl because she was unable to weep. However, Pearl remembers her grief that was too deep for tears because she had lost the father for whom she had been "his 'perfect Pearl'… not the irritation I always seemed to be with my mother" (Tan, 45). Thus, Winnie and her daughter Pearl are separated by misunderstandings.

Besides, the cultural contradictions inherent in the relationship between Winnie and Pearl. As an immigrant and an ethnic minority, the protagonist, the mother Winnie, suffers exclusion and alienation from American society. The gap between the China she remembers and the America she inhabits creates a cultural barrier that separates her from subsequent generations. To bridge the gap between generations and cultures, Winnie has to tell her daughter the stories of her miserable life in pre-communist China. When Winnie narrates, her stories are filled with accounts of food shopping, preparation, cooking, and consumption. In Winnie's story-telling, items of food not only mark every turning point of her life, but also reveal the cultural conflicts between her and her decedents. Besides, she conjures up some hybrid food images serving to bridge the cultural gap between the character and her American-born daughter. Thus, food plays an essential role for the reconciliation between the mother Pearl and her daughter.

Cutting-edge Topic

As food narrative plays an essential role in Chinese American literature, the relevance of food and eating to issues of gender, identity, race and ethnicity has been widely addressed in Chinese American literary studies. Besides developing her preferred narrative technique of maternal story-telling, Tan embraces this Chinese American literary tradition of food writing. When Winnie narrates, her stories are filled with accounts of food shopping, preparation, cooking, and consumption. Do a close reading of depictions about food in detail, we can see how food constitutes major symbol that reinforce the novel's themes and functions as a narrative strategy.

Firstly, when recalling her girlhood in her uncle's family, where she lives after her mother's disappearance, Winnie employs a lot of food motifs. Her detailed description of the food for the New Year's meals indicates how important the New Year's meals are for Chinese people's celebration of the New Year. While Winnie narrates her transition from young girl to young wife, food outlines the cultural and geographical contexts of her life. Secondly, food is able to individualize the novel's characters through description of their food preferences and eating habits. Winnie mother's favorite food embodies her cultural confusion. She not only likes English biscuits but also craves a certain fish called wah-wah yu that she remembers as "so tender, so delicious ... [with] scales ... as soft and sweet as baby leaves" (Tan, 95). Thirdly, food motifs reveal patriarchal oppression upon women. After marrying Wen Fu, Winnie learns from her mother-in-law how to cook hot soup for her husband. She recalls that she had to "make him a proper hot soup, which was ready to serve only when I had scalded my little finger testing it" (Tan, 168). Whenever Winnie serves a hot soup, her little finger would be wounded for ensuring that he has a palatable dish. So, the cooking of this hot soup as taught by her mother-in-law symbolizes women's inferiority to men; they must undergo torture and misery from male-dominated society. Fourthly, food highlights the cultural differences between the immigrant generation and their American-born children. In the first chapter, at Bao-bao's engagement dinner, Pearl vividly depicts a scene that her daughter Cleo likes American fast food: McDonald hamburgers rather than jellyfish provided by her grandma, Winnie. The gap between generations is also seen in the daughter Pearl's attitude towards tofu. In Chinese cooking, soy products are as important as dairy products in western cooking. At the beginning of this novel, Winnie asks her daughter how much she pays for tofu. However, her daughter admits that she never buys tofu. She has no interest in tofu. And she doesn't even know its taste.

Last but not the least, while the daughter, Pearl's discourse on food reveals the cultural conflict between generations, her mother, Winnie's discourse on food attempts to bridge the cultural gap. Combining her memory of her past life in China and her life experience in America, the mother, Winnie conjures up some hybrid food images, such as Cho tofu, moon cake and magic spring so as to relocate her identity and to reconcile the mother-daughter's relations.

Excerpt

Chapter 1 The Shop of the Gods

Whenever my mother talks to me, she begins the conversation as if we were already in the middle of an argument.

"Pearl-ah, have to go, no choice," my mother said when she phoned last week. After several minutes I learned the reason for her call: Auntie

Helen was inviting the whole family to my cousin Bao-bao's engagement party.

"The whole family" means the Kwongs and the Louies. The Kwongs are Auntie Helen, Uncle Henry, Mary, Frank, and Bao-bao. And these days "the Louies" really refers only to my mother and me, since my father is dead and my brother, Samuel, lives in New Jersey. We've been known as "the whole family" for as long as I can remember, even though the Kwongs aren't related to us by blood, just by marriage; Auntie Helen's first husband was my mother's brother, who died long before I was born.

And then there's my cousin Bao-bao, whose real name is Roger. Everyone in the family has been calling him Bao-bao ever since he was a baby, which is what *bao-bao* means, "precious baby." Later, we kept calling him that because he was the crybaby who always wailed the minute my aunt and uncle walked in the door, claiming we other kids had been picking on him. And even though he's now thirty-one years old, we still think of him as Bao-bao—and we're still picking on him.

"Bao-bao? How can he have an engagement party?" I said. "This will be his third marriage."

"*Fourth* engagement!" my mother said. "Last one he didn't marry, broken off after we already sent a gift. Of course, Helen is not calling it engagement party. She is saying this is a big reunion for Mary."

"Mary is coming?" I asked. Mary and I have a history that goes beyond being cousins. She's married to Doug Cheu, who went to medical school with my husband, Phil Brandt, and in fact, she was the one who introduced us to each other sixteen years ago.

"Mary is coming, husband and children, too," my mother said. "Flying from Los Angeles next week. No time to get a special discount. *Full*-price tickets, can you imagine?"

"Next week?" I said, searching for excuses. "It's kind of late notice to change our plans. We're supposed to—"

"Auntie Helen already counted you in. Big banquet dinner at Water Dragon Restaurant—five tables. If you don't come she is one-half table short."

I pictured Auntie Helen, who is already quite short and round, shrinking to the size of a table leg. "Who else is coming?"

"Lots of big, *important* people," my mother answered, saying the word "important" as if to refer to people she didn't like. "Of course, she is also telling people Bao-bao will be there with his new fiancée. And then everybody asks, 'Fiancée? Bao-bao has a new fiancée?' Then Helen, she says, 'Oh, I forgot. This is supposed to be a big surprise announcement. Promise not to tell.' "

My mother sniffed. "She lets everyone know that way. So now you have to bring a gift, also a surprise. Last time what did you buy?"

"For Bao-bao and that college girl? I don't know, maybe a candy dish."

"After they broke up, did he send it back?"

"Probably not. I don't remember."

"You see! That's how the Kwongs are. This time don't spend so much."

Two days before the dinner I got another phone call from my mother.

"Now it is too late to do anything about it," she said, as if whatever it was were my fault. And then she told me Grand Auntie Du was dead at age ninety-seven. This news did come to me as a surprise; I thought she had already died years ago.

"She left you nice things," my mother said. "You can come get it this weekend."

Grand Auntie Du was actually Helen's blood relative, her father's half sister, or some such thing. I remember, however, it was my mother who had always helped take care of Grand Auntie. She carried out her garbage every week. She kept the old lady from subscribing to magazines every time she got a sweepstakes notice with her name printed next to the words "One Million Dollars." She petitioned Medi-Cal over and over again to pay for Grand Auntie's herbal medicines.

For years my mother used to complain to me how she did these things—not Helen. "Helen, *she* doesn't even offer," my mother would say. And then one day—this was maybe ten years ago—I cut my mother off. I said, "Why don't you just tell Auntie Helen what's bothering you and stop complaining?" This was what Phil had suggested I say, a perfectly reasonable way to get my mother to realize what was making her miserable so she could finally take positive action.

But when I said that, my mother looked at me with a blank face and absolute silence. And after that, she did stop complaining to me. In fact, she stopped talking to me for about two months. And when we did start talking again, there was no mention of Grand Auntie Du ever again. I guess that's why I came to think that Grand Auntie had already died long ago.

"What was it?" I asked when I heard the news, trying to sound quiet and shocked. "A stroke?"

"A bus," my mother said.

Apparently, Grand Auntie Du had been in vigorous health, right up to the end. She was riding the One California bus when it lurched to the side to avoid what my mother described as a "hotrod with crazy teenagers" running a stop sign. Grand Auntie pitched forward and fell in the aisle. My mother had gone right away to visit her at the hospital, of course. The doctors couldn't find anything wrong, besides the usual bumps and bruises. But Grand Auntie said she couldn't wait for the doctors to find out what she already knew. So she made my mother write down her will, who should get the thirty-year-old nubby sofa, her black-and-white TV set, that sort of thing. Late that night, she died of an undetected concussion. Helen had been planning to visit the next day, too late.

"Bao-bao Roger said we should sue, one million dollars," my mother reported. "Can you imagine? That kind of thinking. When we found out Grand Auntie died, he didn't cry, only wants to make money off her dead body! Hnh! Why should I tell him she left him two lamps? Maybe I will forget to tell him."

My mother paused. "She was a good lady. Fourteen wreaths already." And then she whispered: "Of course, we are giving everyone twenty-percent discount."

My mother and Auntie Helen co-own Ding Ho Flower Shop on Ross Alley in Chinatown. They got the idea of starting the business about twenty-five years ago, right after my father died and Auntie Helen was fired from her job. I suppose, in some way, the flower shop became the dream that would replace the disasters.

My mother had used the money donated by the First Chinese Baptist Church, where my father had served as an assistant pastor. And Auntie Helen used the money she had saved from her job at another flower shop, which was where she learned the business. That was also the place that had fired her. For being "too honest," is what Auntie Helen revealed to us as the reason. Although my mother suspected it was because Auntie Helen always urged her customers to buy the cheapest bouquets to save money.

"Sometimes I regret that I ever married into a Chinese family," Phil said when he heard we had to go to San Francisco, a hundred miles round-trip from our house in San Jose, made worse by weekend football traffic. Although he's become genuinely fond of my mother over the fifteen years we've been married, he's still exasperated by her demands. And a weekend with the extended family is definitely not his preferred way to spend his days off from the hospital.

"Are you sure we have to go?" he said absently. He was busy playing with a new software program he had just loaded onto his laptop computer. He pressed a key. "Hotcha!" he exclaimed to the screen, and clapped his hands. Phil is forty-three years old, and with his wiry gray hair he usually strikes most people as reserved and dignified. At that moment, however, he had the pure intensity of a little boy playing with a toy battleship.

I pretended to be equally busy, perusing the help-wanted section. Three months ago, I took a position as a speech and language clinician with the local school district. And while I was basically happy with the job, I secretly worried that I had missed a better opportunity. My mother had put those thoughts in my head. Right after I announced I had been chosen over two other candidates for the same position, she said, "Two? Only two people wanted that job?"

And now Phil looked up from his computer, concerned. And I knew what he was thinking, about my "medical condition," as we called it, the multiple sclerosis, which thus far had left me not debilitated but easily fatigued. "It'll be a stressful weekend," he said. "Besides, I thought you couldn't stand your cousin Bao-bao. Not to mention the fact that Mary will be there. God, what a dingbat."

"Um."

"So can't you get out of it?"

"Um-nh."

He sighed. And that was the end of the discussion. Over the years that we've been married, we've learned to sidestep the subject of my family, my duty. It was once the biggest source of our arguments. When we were first married, Phil used to say that I was driven by blind devotion to fear and guilt. I would counter that he was selfish, that the things one had to do in life sometimes had nothing to do with what was fun or convenient. And then he would say the only reason we had to go was that I had been manipulated into thinking I had no choice, and that I was doing the same thing to him. And then our first baby, Tessa, came along, and a year later my illness was diagnosed. The shape of our arguments changed. We no longer fought self-righteously over philosophical differences concerning individual choice, perhaps because

Phil developed a sense of duty toward the baby, as well as to me, or at least to my medical condition. So the whole issue of individual choice became tricky, a burden to keep up, until it fell away, along with smoking cigarettes, eating veal, and wearing ivory.

These days, we tend to argue about smaller, more specific issues—for example, my giving in to Tessa's demands to watch another half-hour of television, and not our different attitudes toward discipline as a whole. And in the end, we almost always agree—perhaps too readily, because we already know the outcome of most disagreements.

It's a smoother life, as easy as we can make it. Although it bothers me from time to time. In fact, sometimes I wish we could go back to the old days when Phil would argue and I would defend my position and convince at least myself that I was right. Whereas nowadays—today, for instance—I'm not really sure why I still give in to my family obligations. While I would never admit this to Phil, I've come to resent the duty. I'm not looking forward to seeing the Kwongs, especially Mary. And whenever I'm with my mother, I feel as though I have to spend the whole time avoiding land mines.

So maybe it was guilt toward Phil or anger toward myself that made me do this: I waited until the next day to tell Phil we'd have to stay overnight—to attend Grand Auntie Du's funeral as well.

For the dreaded weekend, Phil and I had decided to come into the city early to get settled and perhaps take the girls to the zoo. The day before, we had had a polite argument with my mother over where we would stay.

"That's very kind of you, Winnie," Phil reasoned with my mother over the phone. "But we've already made reservations at a hotel." I listened on the other line, glad that I had suggested he call and make the excuses.

"What hotel?" my mother asked.

"The Trave Lodge," Phil lied. We were actually booked at the Hyatt.

"Ai, too much money!" my mother concluded. "Why waste money that way? You can stay at my house, plenty of rooms."

And Phil had declined gracefully. "No, no, really. It's too much trouble. Really."

"Trouble for who?" my mother said.

So now Phil is getting the girls settled in the room that once belonged to my younger brother. This is where they always stay whenever Phil and

I go away for a medical convention. Actually, sometimes we just say it's a medical convention, and then we go back home and do all the household chores we aren't able to finish when the children are around.

Phil has decided that Tessa, who is eight, will sleep on the twin bed, and three-year-old Cleo will get the hideaway cot.

"It's my turn for the bed," says Cleo. "Ha-bu said."

"But Cleo," reasons Tessa, "you *like* the cot."

"Ha-bu!" Cleo calls for my mother to rescue her. "Ha-bu!"

Phil and I are staying in my old room, still crammed with its old-fashioned furniture. I haven't stayed here since I've been married. Except for the fact that everything is a bit too clean, the room looks the same as when I was a teenager: the double bed with its heavy legs and frame, the dressing table with the round mirror and inlay of ash, oak, burl, and mother-of-pearl. It's funny how I used to hate that table. Now it actually looks quite nice, art deco. I wonder if my mother would let me have it.

I notice that she has placed my old Chinese slippers under the bed, the ones with a hole at each of the big toes; nothing ever thrown away, in case it's needed again twenty years later. And Tessa and Cleo must have been rummaging around in the closet, scavenging through boxes of old toys and junk. Scattered near the slippers are doll clothes, a rhinestone tiara, and a pink plastic jewelry case with the words "My Secret Treasures" on top. They have even rehung the ridiculous Hollywood-style star on the door, the one I made in the sixth grade, spelling out my name, P-E-A-R-L, in pop-beads.

"Gosh," Phil says in a goofy voice. "This sure beats the hell out of staying at the TraveLodge." I slap his thigh. He pats the mismatched set of guest towels lying on the bed. The towels were a Christmas gift from the Kwongs right after our family moved from Chinatown to the Richmond district, which meant they had to be thirty years old.

And now Tessa and Cleo race into our room, clamoring that they're ready to go to the zoo. Phil is going to take them, while I go to Ding Ho Flower Shop to help out. My mother didn't exactly ask me to help, but she did say in a terse voice that Auntie Helen was leaving the shop early to get ready for the big dinner—in spite of the fact there was so much to do at the shop and Grand Auntie's funeral service was the very next day. And then she reminded me that Grand Auntie was always very proud of me—in our family "proud" is as close as we get to saying "love." And she suggested that maybe I should come by early to pick out a nice wreath.

"I should be back at five-thirty," I tell Phil.

"I wanna see African elephants," says Tessa, plopping down on our bed. And then she counts on her fingers: "And koala bears and a spiny anteater and a humpback whale." I have always wondered where she picked up this trait of listing things—from Phil? From me? From the television?

"Say 'Please,' " Phil reminds her, "and I don't think they have whales at the zoo."

I turn to Cleo. I sometimes worry she will become too passive in the shadow of her confident big sister. "And what do you want to see?" I ask her gently. She looks at her feet, searching for an answer.

"Dingbats," she finally says.

As I turn down Ross Alley, everything around me immediately becomes muted in tone. It is no longer the glaring afternoon sun and noisy Chinatown sidewalks filled with people doing their Saturday grocery shopping. The alley sounds are softer, quickly absorbed, and the light is hazy, almost greenish in cast.

On the right-hand side of the street is the same old barbershop, run by Al Fook, who I notice still uses electric clippers to shear his customers' sideburns. Across the street are the same trade and family associations, including a place that will send ancestor memorials back to China for a fee. And farther down the street is the shopfront of a fortune-teller. A hand-written sign taped to the window claims to have "the best lucky numbers, the best fortune advice," but the sign taped to the door says: "Out of Business."

As I walk past the door, a yellow pull-shade rustles. And suddenly a little girl appears, her hands pressed to the glass. She stares at me with a somber expression. I wave, but she does not wave back. She looks at me as if I don't belong here, which is how I feel.

And now I'm at Sam Fook Trading Company, a few doors down from the flower shop. It contains shelves full of good-luck charms and porcelain and wooden statues of lucky gods, hundreds of them. I've called this place the Shop of the Gods ever since I can remember. It also sells the kind of stuff people get for Buddhist funerals—spirit money, paper jewelry, incense, and the like.

"Hey, Pearl!" It's Mr. Hong, the owner, waving me to come in. When I first met him, I thought his name was Sam Fook, like the shop. I found out later that *sam fook* means "triple blessing" in old Cantonese, and according to my mother—or rather, her Hong Kong customers—*sam fook* sounds like a joke, like saying "the Three Stooges."

"I told him he should change the name," my mother had said. "Luckier that way. But he says he has too much business already."

"Hey, Pearl," Mr. Hong says when I walk in the door, "I got some things for your mother here, for the funeral tomorrow. You take it to her, okay?"

"Okay." He hands me a soft bundle.

I guess this means Grand Auntie's funeral will be Buddhist. Although she attended the FirstChinese Baptist Church for a number of years, both she and my mother stopped going right after my father died. In any case, I don't think Grand Auntie ever gave up her other beliefs, which weren't exactly Buddhist, just all the superstitious rituals concerning attracting good luck and avoiding bad. On those occasions when I did go up to her apartment, I used to play with her altar, a miniature red temple containing a framed picture of a Chinese god. In front of that was an imitation-brass urn filled with burnt incense sticks, and on the side were offerings of oranges, Lucky Strike cigarettes, and an airline mini-bottle of Johnnie Walker Red whiskey. It was like a Chinese version of a Christmas crèche.

And now I come to the flower shop itself. It is the bottom floor of a three-story brick building. The shop is about the size of a one-car garage and looks both sad and familiar. The front has a chipped red-bordered door covered with rusted burglarproof mesh. A plate-glass window says "Ding Ho Flower Shop" in English and Chinese. But it's easy to miss, because the place sits back slightly and always looks dark and closed, as it does today.

So the location my mother and Auntie Helen picked isn't exactly bustling. Yet they seem to have done all right. In a way, it's remarkable. After all these years, they've done almost nothing to keep up with the times or make the place more attractive. I open the door and bells jangle. I'm instantly engulfed in the pungent smell of gardenias, a scent I've always associated with funeral par-lors. The place is dimly lit, with only one fluorescent tube hanging over the cash register—and that's where my mother is, standing on a small footstool so she can see out over the counter, with dime-store reading glasses perched on her nose.

She is talking on the telephone in rapid Chinese and waves impatiently for me to come in and wait. Her hair is pulled straight back into a bun, not a strand ever out of place. The bun today has been made to look thicker with the addition of a false swatch of hair, a "horse's tail," she calls it, for wearing only on important occasions.

Actually, now I can tell—by the shrillness of her pitch and the predominance of negative "vuh-vuh-vuh" sounds—that she's arguing in Shanghainese, and not just plain Mandarin. This is serious. Most likely it's with a neighborhood supplier, to judge from the way she's punching in numbers on a portable calculator, then reading aloud the printed results in harsh tones, as if they were penal codes. She pushes the "No Sale" button on the cash register, and when the drawer pops forward, she pulls out a folded receipt, snaps it open with a jerk of her wrist, then reads numbers from that as well.

"Vuh! Vuh! Vuh!" she insists.

The cash register is used to store only odds and ends, or what my mother calls "ends and odds and evens." The register is broken. When my mother and Auntie Helen first bought the store and its fixtures, they found out soon enough that anytime the sales transaction added up to anything with a 9 in it, the whole register froze up. But they decided to keep the cash register anyway, "for stick-em-up," is how my mother explained it to me. If they were ever robbed, which has yet to happen, the robber would get only four dollars and a pile of pennies, all the money that is kept in the till. The real money is stashed underneath the counter, in a teapot with a spout that's been twice broken and glued back on. And the kettle sits on a hot plate that's missing a plug. I guess the idea is that no one would ever rob the store for a cup of cold tea.

I once told my mother and Auntie Helen that a robber would never believe that the shop had only four dollars to its name. I thought they should put at least twenty in the cash register to make the ruse seem more plausible. But my mother thought twenty dollars was too much to give a robber. And Auntie Helen said she would "worry sick" about losing that much money—so what good would the trick be then?

At the time, I considered giving them the twenty dollars myself to prove my point. But then I thought, What's the point? And as I look around the shop now, I realize maybe they were right. Who would ever consider robbing this place for more than getaway bus fare? No, this place is burglarproof just the way it is.

The shop has the same dull gray concrete floor of twenty-five years ago, now polished shiny with wear. The counter is covered with the same contact paper, green-and-white bamboo lattice on the sides and wood grain on the top. Even the phone my mother is using is the same old black model with a rotary dial and a fabric cord that doesn't coil or stretch. And over the years, the lime-colored walls have become faded and splotched, then cracked from the '89 earthquake. So now the place has the look of spidery decay and leaf mold.

"*Hau, hau,*" I now hear my mother saying. She seems to have reached some sort of agreement with the supplier. Finally she bangs the phone down. Although we have not seen each other since Christmas, almost a month ago, we do none of the casual hugs and kisses Phil and I exchange when we see his parents and friends. Instead, my mother walks out from around the counter, muttering, "Can you imagine? That man is cheating me! Tried to charge me for extra-rush delivery." She points to a box containing supplies of wire, clear cellophane, and sheets of green wax paper. "This is not my fault he forgot to come last week."

"How much extra?" I ask.

"Three dollars!" she exclaims. I never cease to be amazed by the amount of emotional turmoil my mother will go through for a few dollars.

"Why don't you just forget it? It's only three dollars—"

"I'm not concerned about money!" she fumes. "He's cheating me. This is not right. Last month, he tried to add another kind of extra charge too." I can tell she's about to launch into a blow-by-blow of last month's fight, when two well-dressed women with blond hair peer through the door.

"Are you open? Do any of you speak English?" one of them says in a Texas drawl.

My mother's face instantly cheers, and she nods, waving them in. "Come, come," she calls.

"Oh, we don't want to bother y'all," one of the ladies says. "If you might could just tell us where the fortune cookie factory is?"

Before I can answer, my mother tightens her face, shakes her head, and says, "Don't understand. Don't speak English."

"Why did you say that?" I ask when the two ladies retreat back into the alley. "I didn't know you hated tourists that much."

"Not tourists," she says. "That woman with the cookie factory, once she was mean to me. Why should I send her any good business?"

"How's business here?" I say, trying to steer the conversation away from what will surely become a tirade about the cookie woman down the street.

"Awful!" she says, and points to her inventory around the shop. "So busy—busy myself to death with this much business. You look, only this morning I had to make all these myself."

And I look. There are no modern arrangements of bent twigs or baskets of exotica with Latinate-drooping names. My mother opens the glass door to a refrigerator unit that once housed bottles of soda pop and beer.

"You see?" she says, and shows me a shelf with boutonnieres and corsages made out of carnations, neatly lined in rows according to color: white, pink, and red. No doubt we'll have to wear some of these tonight.

"And this," she continues. The second shelf is chock-full of milk-glass vases, each containing only a single rosebud, a fern frond, and a meager sprinkling of baby's breath. This is the type of floral arrangement you give to hospital patients who go in for exploratory surgery, when you don't know yet whether the person will be there for very long. My father received a lot of those when he first went into the hospital and later right before he died. "Very popular," my mother says.

"This, too, I had to make," she says, and points to the bottom shelf, which holds half a dozen small table sprays. "Some for tonight. Some for a retirement dinner," my mother explains, and perhaps because I don't look sufficiently impressed, she adds, "For assistant manager at Wells Fargo."

She walks me around to view her handiwork in other parts of the shop. Lining the walls are large funeral wreaths, propped on easels. "Ah?" my mother says, waiting for my opinion. I've always found wreaths hideously sad, like decorative lifesavers thrown out too late.

"Very pretty," I say.

And now she steers me toward her real pride and joy. At the front of the shop, the only place that gets filtered daylight for a few hours a day, are her "long-lasting bargains," as she calls them—philodendrons, rubber plants, chicken-feet bushes, and miniature tangerine trees. These are festooned with red banners, congratulating this business or that for its new store opening.

My mother has always been very proud of those red banners. She doesn't write the typical congratulatory sayings, like "Good Luck" or "Prosperity and Long Life." All the sayings, written in gold Chinese characters, are of her own inspiration, her thoughts about life and death, luck and hope: "First-Class Life for Your First Baby," "Double-Happiness Wedding Triples Family Fortunes," "Money Smells Good in Your New Restaurant Business," "Health Returns Fast, Always

Hoping."

My mother claims these banners are the reasons why Ding Ho Flower Shop has had success flowing through its door all these years. By success, I suppose she means that the same people over the last twenty-five years keep coming back. Only now it's less and less for shy brides and giddy grooms, and more and more for the sick, the old, and the dead.

She smiles mischievously, then tugs my elbow. "Now I show you the wreath I made for you."

I'm alarmed, and then I realize what she's talking about. She opens the door to the back of the shop. It's dark as a vault inside and I can't make out anything except the dense odor of funeral flowers. My mother is groping for the piece of string that snaps on the light. Finally the room is lit by the glare of a naked bulb that swings back and forth on a cord suspended from the high ceiling. And what I now see is horrifyingly beautiful—row after row of gleaming wreaths, all white gardenias and yellow chrysanthemums, red banners hanging down from their easels, looking like identically dressed heavenly attendants.

I am stunned by how much hard work this represents. I imagine my mother's small hands with their parchmentlike skin, furiously pulling out stray leaves, tucking in sharp ends of wire, inserting each flower into its proper place.

"This one." She points to a wreath in the middle of the first row. It looks the same as the others. "This one is yours. I wrote the wishes myself."

"What does it say?" I ask.

Her finger moves slowly down the red banner, as she reads in a formal Chinese I can't understand. And then she translates: "Farewell, Grand Auntie, heaven is lucky. From your favorite niece, Pearl Louie Brandt, and husband."

"Oh, I almost forgot." I hand her the bundle from Sam Fook's. "Mr. Hong said to give you this."

My mother snips the ribbon and opens the package. Inside are a dozen or so bundles of spirit money, money Grand Auntie can supposedly use to bribe her way along to Chinese heaven.

"I didn't know you believed in that stuff," I say.

"What's to believe," my mother says testily. "This is respect." And then she says softly, "I got one hundred million dollars. Ah! She was a good lady."

"Here we go," I say, and take a deep breath as we climb the stairs to the banquet room.

"Pearl! Phil! There you are." It's my cousin Mary. I haven't seen her in the two years since she and Doug moved to Los Angeles. We wait for Mary to move her way through the banquet crowd. She rushes toward us and gives me a kiss, then rubs my cheek and laughs over the extra blush she's added.

"You look terrific!" she tells me, and then she looks at Phil. "Really, both of you. Just sensational."

Mary must now be forty-one, about half a year older than I am. She's wearing heavy makeup and false eyelashes, and her hair is a confusing mass of curls and mousse. A silver-fox stole keeps slipping off her shoulders. As she pushes it up for the third time, she laughs and says, "Doug gave me this old thing for Christmas, what a bother." I wonder why she does bother, now that we're inside the restaurant. But that's Mary, the oldest child of the two families, so it's always seemed important to her to look the most successful.

"Jennifer and Michael," she calls, and snaps her fingers. "Come here and say hello to your auntie and uncle." She pulls her two teenage children over to her side, and gives them each a squeeze. "Come on, what do you say?" They stare at us with sullen faces, and each of them grunts and gives a small nod.

Jennifer has grown plump, while her eyes, lined in black, look small and hard. The top part of her hair is teased up in pointy spikes, with the rest falling limply down to the middle of her back. She looks as if she had been electrocuted. And Michael's face—it's starting to push out into sharp angles and his chin is covered with pimples. They're no longer cute, and I wonder if this will happen to Tessa and Cleo, if I will think this about them as well.

"You see how they are," Mary says apologetically. "Jennifer just got her first nylons and high heels for Christmas. She's so proud, no longer Mommy's little girl."

"Oh, Mother!" Jennifer wails, then struggles away from her mother's grasp and disappears into the crowd. Michael follows her.

"See how Michael's almost as tall as Doug?" Mary says, proudly watching her son as he ambles away. "He's on the junior varsity track team, and his coach says he's their best runner. I don't know where he got his height or his athletic ability—certainly not from me. Whenever I go for a jog, I come back a cripple," Mary says, laughing. And then, realizing what she's just said, she suddenly drops her smile, and searches the crowd: "Oh, there's Doug's parents. I better go say hello."

Phil squeezes my hand, and even though we say nothing, he knows I'm mad. "Just forget it," he says.

"I would," I shoot back, "if she could. She *always* does this."

When Phil and I married, it was Mary and Doug who were our matron of honor and best man, since they had introduced us. They were the first people we confided in when we found out I was pregnant with Tessa. And about seven years ago, Mary was the one who pushed me into aerobics when I complained I felt tired all the time. And later, when I had what seemed like a strange weakness in my right leg, Phil suggested I see Doug, who at the time was an orthopedist at a sports medicine clinic.

Months later, Doug told me the problem seemed to be something else, and right away I panicked and thought he meant bone cancer. He assured me he just meant he wasn't smart enough to figure it out himself. So he sent me to see his old college drinking buddy, the best neurologist at San Francisco Medical Center. After what seemed like a year of tests—after I persuaded myself the fatigue was caused by smoking and the weakness in my leg was sciatica left over from my pregnancy—the drinking buddy told me I had multiple sclerosis.

Mary had cried hysterically, then tried to console me, which made it all seem worse. For a while, she dropped by with casserole dishes from "terrific recipes" she "just happened to find," until I told her to stop. And later, she made a big show of telling me how Doug's friend had assured her that my case was really "quite mild," as if she were talking about the weather, that my life expectancy was not changed, that at age seventy I could be swinging a golf club and still hitting par, although I would have to be careful not to stress myself either physically or emotionally.

"So really, everything's normal," she said a bit too cheerfully, "except that Phil has to treat you nicer. And what could be wrong with that?"

"I don't play golf," was all I told her.

"I'll teach you," she said cheerily.

Of course, Mary was only trying to be kind. I admit that it was more my fault that our friendship became strained. I never told her directly how much her gestures of sympathy offended me. So of course she couldn't have known that I did not need someone to comfort me. I did not want to be coddled by casseroles. Kindness was compensation.

Kindness was a reminder that my life had changed, was always changing, that people thought I should just accept all this and become strong or brave, more enlightened, more peaceful. I wanted nothing to do with that. Instead, I wanted to live my life with the same focus as most people—to worry about my children's education, but not whether I would be around to see them graduate, to rejoice that I had lost five pounds, and not be fearful that my muscle mass was eroding away. I wanted what had become impossible: I wanted to forget.

I was furious that Doug and his drinking-buddy friend had discussed my medical condition with Mary. If they had told her that, then they must have also told her this: that with this disease, no prognosis could be made. I could be in remission for ten, twenty, thirty, or forty years. Or the disease could suddenly take off tomorrow and roll downhill, faster and faster, and at the bottom, I would be left sitting in a wheelchair, or worse.

I know Mary was aware of this, because I would often catch her looking at me from the corner of her eye whenever we passed someone who was disabled. One time she laughed nervously when she tried to park her car in a space that turned out to be a handicapped zone. "Oops!" she said, backing out fast. "We certainly don't need that."

In the beginning, Phil and I vowed to lead as normal a life together as possible. "As normal as possible"—it was like a meaningless chant. If I accidentally tripped over a toy left on the floor, I would spend ten minutes apologizing to Tessa for yelling at her, then another hour debating whether a "normal" person would have stumbled over the same thing. Once, when we went to the beach for the express purpose of forgetting about all of this, I was filled with morbid thoughts instead. I watched the waves eating away at the shore, and I wondered aloud to Phil whether I would one day be left as limp as seaweed, or stiff like a crab.

Meanwhile Phil would read his old textbooks and every medical article he could find on the subject. And then he would become depressed that his own medical training offered no better understanding of a disease that could be described only as "without known etiology," "extremely variable," "unpredictable," and "without specific treatment." He attended medical conferences on neurological disorders. He once took me to an MS support group, but we turned right around as soon as we saw the wheelchairs. He would perform what he called "weekly safety checks," testing my reflexes, monitoring the strength of my limbs. We even moved to a house with a swimming pool, so I could do daily muscle training. We did not mention to each other the fact that the house was one-story and had few steps and wide hallways that could someday be made wheelchair-accessible, if necessary.

We talked in code, as though we belonged to a secret cult, searching for a cure, or a pattern of symptoms we could watch for, some kind of salvation from constant worry. And eventually we learned not to talk about the future, either the grim possibilities or the vague hopes. We did not dwell on the past, whether it had been a virus or genetics that had caused this to happen. We concerned ourselves with the here and now, small victories over the mundane irritations of life—getting Tessa potty-trained, correcting a mistake on our charge-card bill, discovering why the car sputtered whenever we put it into third gear. Those became our constants, the things we could isolate and control in a life of unknown variables.

So I can't really blame Phil for pretending that everything is normal. I wanted that more than he did. And now I can't tell him what I really feel, what it's like. All I know is that I wake up each morning in a panic, terrified that something might have changed while I slept. And there are days when I become obsessed if I lose something, a button, thinking my life won't be normal until I find it again. There are days when I think Phil is the most inconsiderate man in the world, simply because he forgot to buy one item on the grocery list. There are days when I organize my underwear drawer by color, as if this might make some kind of difference. Those are the bad days.

On the good days, I remember that I am lucky—lucky by a new standard. In the last seven years, I have had only one major "flare-up," which now means I lose my balance easily, especially when I'm upset or in a hurry. But I can still walk. I still take out the garbage. And sometimes I actually can forget, for a few hours, or almost the entire day. Of course, the worst part is when I remember once again—often in unexpected ways—that I am living in a limbo land called remission.

That delicate balance always threatens to go out of kilter when I see my mother. Because that's when it hits me the hardest: I have this terrible disease and I've never told her.

I meant to tell her. There were several times when I planned to do exactly that. When I was first diagnosed, I said, "Ma, you know that slight problem with my leg I told you about. Well, thank God, it turned out *not* to be cancer, but—"

And right away, she told me about a customer of hers who had just died of cancer, how long he had suffered, how many wreaths the family had ordered. "Long time ago I saw that mole growing on his face," she said. "I told him, go see a doctor. No problem, he said, age spot—didn't do anything about it. By the time he died, his nose and cheek—all eaten away!" And then she warned me sternly, "That's why you have to be careful."

When Cleo was born, without complications on my part or hers, I again started to tell my mother. But she interrupted me, this time to lament how my father was not there to see his grandchildren. And then she went into her usual endless monologue about my father getting a fate he didn't deserve.

My father had died of stomach cancer when I was fourteen. And for years, my mother would search in her mind for the causes, as if she could still undo the disaster by finding the reason why it had occurred in the first place.

"He was such a good man," my mother would lament. "So why did he die?" And sometimes she cited God's will as the reason, only she gave it a different twist. She said it must have been because my father was a minister. "He listened to everyone else's troubles," she said. "He swallowed them until he made himself sick. Ah! *Ying-gai* find him another job."

Ying-gai was what my mother always said when she meant, I should have. *Ying-gai* meant she should have altered the direction of fate, she should have prevented disaster. To me, *ying-gai* meant my mother lived a life of regrets that never faded with time.

If anything, the regrets grew as she searched for more reasons underlying my father's death. One time she cited her own version of environmental causes—that the electrician had been sick at the time he rewired our kitchen. "He built that sickness right into our house," she declared. "It's true. I just found out the electrician died—of cancer, too. *Ying-gai* pick somebody else."

And there was also this superstition, what I came to think of as her theory of the Nine Bad Fates. She said she had once heard that a person is destined to die if eight bad things happen. If you don't recognize the eight ahead of time and prevent them, the ninth one is always fatal. And then she would ruminate over what the eight bad things might have been, how she should have been sharp enough to detect them in time.

To this day it drives me crazy, listening to her various hypotheses, the way religion, medicine, and superstition all merge with her own beliefs. She puts no faith in other people's logic—to her, logic is a sneaky excuse for tragedies, mistakes, and accidents. And according to my mother, *nothing* is an accident. She's like a Chinese version of Freud, or worse. Everything has a reason. Everything could have been prevented. The last time I was at her house, for example, I knocked over a framed picture of my father and broke the glass. My mother picked up the shards and moaned, "Why did this happen?" I thought it was a rhetorical question at first, but then she said to me, "Do you know?"

"It was an accident," I said. "My elbow bumped into it." And of course, her question had sent my mind racing, wondering if my clumsiness was a symptom of deterioration.

"Why this picture?" she muttered to herself.

So I never told my mother. At first I didn't want to hear her theories on my illness, what caused this to happen, how she should have done this or that to prevent it. I did not want her to remind me.

And now that so much time has gone by, the fact that I still haven't told her makes the illness seem ten times worse. I am always reminded, whenever I see her, whenever I hear her voice.

Mary knows that, and that's why I still get mad at her—not because she trips over herself to avoid talking about my medical condition. I'm mad because she told *her* mother, my Auntie Helen.

"I had to tell her," she explained to me in an offhand sort of way. "She was always saying to me, Tell Pearl to visit her mother more often, only a one-hour drive. Tell Pearl she should ask her mother to move in with her, less lonely for her mother that way. Finally, I told my mother I couldn't tell you those things. And she asked why not." Mary shrugged. "You know my mother. I couldn't lie to her. Of course, I made her *swear* not to tell your mother, that you were going to tell her yourself."

"I can drive," I told Mary. "And that's not the reason why I haven't asked my mother to live with me." And then I glared at her. "How could you do this?"

"She won't say anything," Mary said. "I made her promise." And then she added a bit defiantly, "Besides, you should have told your mother a long time ago."

Mary and I didn't exactly have a fight, but things definitely chilled between us after that. She already knew that was about the worst possible thing she could have done to me. Because she had done it once before, nine years ago, when I confided to her that I was pregnant. My first pregnancy had ended in a miscarriage early on, and my mother had gone on and on about how much coffee I drank, how it was my jogging that did it, how Phil should make sure I ate more. So when I became pregnant again, I decided to wait, to tell my mother when I was in my fourth month or so. But in the third month, I made the mistake of confiding in Mary. And Mary slipped this news to her mother. And Auntie Helen didn't exactly tell my mother. But when my mother proudly announced my pregnancy to the Kwongs, Auntie Helen immediately showed my mother the little yellow sweater she had already hand-knit for the baby.

I didn't stop hearing the laments from my mother, even after Tessa was born. "Why could you tell the Kwongs, not your own mother?" she'd complain. When she stewed over it and became really angry, she accused me of making her look like a fool: "Hnh! Auntie Helen was pretending to be so surprised, so innocent. 'Oh, I didn't knit the sweater for Pearl's baby,' she said, 'I made it just in case.'"

So far, Auntie Helen had kept the news about my medical condition to herself. But this didn't stop her from treating me like an invalid. When I used to go to her house, she would tell me to sit down right away, while she went to find me a pillow for my back. She would rub her palm up and down my arm, asking me how I was, telling me how she had always thought of me as a daughter. And then she would sigh and confess some bit of bad news, as if to balance out what she already knew about me.

"Your poor Uncle Henry, he almost got laid off last month," she would say. "So many budget cuts now. Who knows what's going to happen? Don't tell your mother. I don't want her to worry over us."

And then *I* would worry that Auntie Helen would think her little confessions were payment in kind, that she would take them as license to accidentally slip and tell my mother: "Oh, Winnie, I thought you knew about your daughter's tragedy."

And so I dreaded the day my mother would call and ask me a hundred different ways, "Why did Auntie Helen know? Why did you never tell me? Why didn't you let me prevent this from happening to you?"

And then what answer could I give?

At the dinner, we've been seated at the "kids' table," only now the "kids" are in their thirties and forties. The real kids—Tessa and Cleo—are seated with my mother.

Phil is the only non-Chinese tonight, although that wasn't the case at past family events. Bao-bao's two former wives were what Auntie Helen called "Americans," as if she were referring to a racial group. She must be thrilled that Bao-bao's bride-to-be is a girl named Mimi Wong, who is not only Chinese but from a well-to-do family that owns three travel agencies.

"She looks Japanese," my mother had said when we first arrived and had been introduced to Mimi. I don't know why she said that. To me, Mimi looks just plain weird, as well as awfully young. I guess that she is around twenty, although it may be her dyed orange hair and pierced nose that makes her seem so young. I heard that she was training to be a hairstylist at a trendy salon called Oliphant's. My mother heard that what Mimi did mostly was wash people's hair and sweep up loose clippings.

Bao-bao has changed his looks since the last time I saw him. His hair is slicked back with pomade. He has on a black T-shirt underneath an iridescent sharkskin suit. Each time he introduces Mimi to the guests, I allow myself to stare at her pierced nose. I wonder what happens when she has a cold.

"How's my favorite cuz?" Bao-bao says to me from across the table, then gives me a toast with his upraised champagne glass. "Lookin' good. I like the hair, short, nice. Mimi, what do you think of Pearl's haircut? Nice, huh?" He has a knack for handing out compliments like party favors, one for everybody. I wonder sometimes if I would have liked him better if I didn't already know so much about him.

"Hey, Phil, bro," Bao-bao calls, pouring more champagne. "You put on a few pounds, I see. The good life's been good. Maybe you're ready for that new system I told you about. A lot of decibels for the dollar." Bao-bao sells stereos and TVs at The Good Guys. He's very good at convincing people that their ears and eyes are refined enough to tell the difference between a standard model and its five-hundred-dollar upgrade. Phil once said that if Bao-bao were turnedloose, he could sell Bibles to the Shiites.

Behind us, at the "grownups' table," is a man named Loy Fong, "Uncle Loy." He turns around and offers a toast of ginger ale in a plastic glass. "So convenient for Mimi," he says. "All she has to do is add a *k* to her name to get a husband! 'Wong' to 'Kwong,' get it?" He laughs the loudest at his own joke, then turns back around to repeat the joke to the others at his table. Next to him is his wife, Edna. These people have been going to the same church for years, but they're not really that close to either the Kwongs or my family. I think they were invited because Edna Fong is in charge of ordering flowers for the sanctuary, and she's always bought them from Ding Ho, twenty percent off, of course.

Auntie Helen is sitting at the same table as Loy and Edna Fong. For this special occasion, she has on a baby-pink sateen Chinese dress, which is too tight for her plump body and already creased at her lap and above her round stomach. Every time she reaches over to pour more tea, her dress strains at the armpits, and I wonder which seam is going to rip first. Her thin hair has been newly permed, perhaps with the mistaken notion that it would look fuller. Instead her hair looks deep-fried, exposing her scalp underneath.

My mother is seated directly across from Auntie Helen. She is wearing a new blue dress she made herself—in fact, designed herself, she told me, "no pattern necessary." The dress is a simple A-line with pouffy princess sleeves. It makes my mother's thin body look waiflike.

"Such a pretty silk," Edna Fong says to her.

"Polyester," my mother proudly informs her. "Machine washable." Cleo slips off her chair and climbs up onto my mother's lap. "Ha-bu," she says, "I want to eat with chopsticks."

My mother spins the lazy Susan around and dips her chopsticks into the appetizer plate. "This is jellyfish," my mother explains, and dangles the quivering strand in front of Cleo's mouth. I watch my daughter open her mouth wide like a baby bird, and my mother drops the morsel in.

"See, you like it!" my mother proclaims as Cleo chomps and smiles. "When your mother was a little girl, she said it tasted just like rubber bands!"

"Don't tell me that!" Cleo suddenly shrieks and then wails, the half-eaten jellyfish dribbling out from her pouting lips.

"Don't cry, don't cry," Auntie Helen says soothingly from across the table. "Look, here's some fragrant beef, ah? Yum-yummy, tastes like McDonald hamburgers. Take it, you like."

And Cleo, still full of indignant sobs, reaches over for the slice of beef and gobbles it down. My mother's mouth is shut tight. She looks away.

And I feel so bad for her, that she's been betrayed by her memory and my childhood fondness for rubbery-tasting things. I think about a child's capacity to hurt her mother in ways she cannot ever imagine.

The evening turns out to be much worse than I expected.

Throughout the dinner I watch my mother and Auntie Helen getting on each other's nerves. They argue in Chinese over whether the pork is too salty, whether the chicken is overcooked, whether the Happy Family dish used too many water chestnuts to cut down on the ration of scallops. I see Phil trying to make polite conversation with my cousin Frank, who is chain-smoking, something Phil hates with a passion. I see old family friends who are not really friends making toasts to a bride-and-groom-to-be who will surely be divorced in two years' time. I smile woodenly and listen to Mary and Doug chatting to me as if we were still the best of friends.

Mostly I see my mother sitting one table away, and I feel as lonely as I imagine her to be. I think of the enormous distance that separates us and makes us unable to share the most important matters of our life. How did this happen?

And suddenly everything—the flower arrangements on the plastic-topped tables, my mother's memories of my childhood, the whole family—everything feels like a sham, and also sad and true. All these meaningless gestures, old misunderstandings, and painful secrets, why do we keep them up? I feel as if I were suffocating, and want to run away.

A hand taps my shoulder. It's Auntie Helen.

"Not too tired?" she whispers.

I shake my head.

"Then come help me cut the cake. Otherwise I have to pay the restaurant extra." And of course, I wonder what secret she's about to confess now.

In the kitchen, Auntie Helen cuts a white sheet cake into little squares and puts each piece on a paper plate. She licks whipped cream off her fingers, stuffs a falling strawberry back into its spongy center.

"Best cake in San Francisco," she says. "Mary got it from Sun Chee Bakery on Clement. You know the place?"

I shake my head and keep adding a plastic fork to each plate.

"Maybe you know something else, then," she says sternly. "About my own sickness?" She stops cutting, and looks at me, waiting for me to answer. I am surprised by her sudden change in tone, because I honestly don't know what she's talking about.

"Doesn't matter," she answers tartly, and goes back to cutting more cake. "I already know."

And standing in the kitchen like that, she tells me how she had to go to the doctor two months ago. She had fallen down her front steps on a rainy day and hit her head against the rail. And my mother, who was with her at the time, had taken her to the hospital. They took X rays: no broken bones, no concussion, not like Auntie Du, lucky for her. Instead they found a little dark spot on her skull, did more tests.

"And that's how I knew," she says, tapping her head, sounding triumphant. "God touched his finger there and told me, Time to go. I have a brain tumor."

I gasp, and Auntie Helen quickly adds, "Of course, the doctors did more tests later to make sure. Then they told me it is benign." She says this word as if she were calling out a bingo slot, B nine. "They said no problem, no need to operate."

I sigh, and she continues, "Your mother said, lucky you, nothing wrong. My children, your Uncle Henry, they all said, Now you will live forever. But what do you think they are really saying?"

I shake my head.

"You look. Why does Bao-bao suddenly say he is getting married? Why does Mary say she is flying home, bringing the whole family? Let's have a reunion, she says. And Frank, he got a haircut before I had to ask twice." She smiles. "Even your mother. Today she said at the shop, go, go, you are busy with your son's party. I can make the wreaths. Why are you shaking your head? This is true!"

Her face becomes more serious. "I said to myself, eh, why this big change, everyone so nice to me? Why so sudden? My children now respect me, why? They come to see me, why? Mary calls me Mommy again. Your mother wants to do all the work. You know why? They know. They all know I'm dying. They won't say, but I think it must be very fast."

I'm putting the plates on a tray. "Oh, Auntie Helen, I'm sure there's nothing wrong. If they said it's benign, it means it's—"

She holds up her hand. "No need to pretend with me. I'm not scared. I'm not a young woman anymore. Almost seventy-three."

"I'm not pretending," I insist. "You're not going to die."

"Everyone wants to keep this news from me, okay. They want to be nice before I die, okay. I can pretend too that I don't know."

I am starting to feel confused. I don't know whether Auntie Helen is really sick, or only imagining something bad out of her children's good intentions. It does strike me as strange, though, what she said about everyone's sudden change of character. It would be just like the Kwongs to pass around a secret and then pretend nobody knows a thing.

"Don't worry for me," she says, and pats my hand. "I am not telling you this so you have to worry. I only want to tell you so you understand why I can no longer keep your secret."

"What secret?"

She sighs deeply. "Pearl-ah, this is too much burden for me. It makes my heart and shoulders heavy that your mother does not know. How can I fly to heaven when this is weighing me down? No, you must tell your mother, Pearl. Tell her about your multiple neurosis."

I am too stunned to laugh or correct her mistake. "This is the right thing," Auntie Helen says with conviction. "If you cannot tell her, then I must tell her myself—before the Chinese New Year." She looks at me with a determined face.

And now I want to shake her, tell her to stop playing this game.

"Auntie Helen, you know I can't tell my mother that. You know how she is."

"Of course," she says. "For fifty years I've been knowing your mother. That's why I know this is the right time to tell her."

"Why should I tell her now? She'll only be angry that we kept it a secret."

She frowns. "You are only concerned your mother will be angry with you? Tst! Tst! So selfish."

"No, I mean, there's no reason to tell her now. I'm fine."

"You think you can hide this until she dies? Maybe she lives to be a hundred. Then what do you do, ah?"

"It's not that. I just don't want her to worry."

"This is her right to worry," says Auntie Helen. "She is your mother."

"But she shouldn't have to worry about something that isn't really a problem."

"That's why you should tell her now. No more problem after that."

"But then she'll wonder why we kept this a secret from her. She'll think it's worse than it is."

"Maybe she has secrets too." She smiles, then laughs at what must be a private joke. "Your mother, oh yes, plenty of secrets!"

I feel I am in a nightmare, arguing with someone who can't hear me. Maybe Auntie Helen is right and she does have a brain tumor. Maybe it's eaten away at her brain and she's gone crazy. "All right," I finally say. "But you can't be the one who tells her. I will."

Auntie Helen looks at me suspiciously. "This is a promise?"

"Promise," I whisper, and even I don't know if I'm lying.

She rubs my shoulder, plucks at the fabric of my green wool dress.

"This is a good color for you, Pearl. Anh! No more talking now. Let's go back." She hoists the tray of cakes.

"I can carry that," I say tersely. She hesitates, ready to argue. And then, perhaps in deference to her own illness, she lets me.

After the dinner, we are back at my mother's house. The girls have done their usual segue of giggling, then fighting, then wailing, and have finally fallen asleep. I had considered asking my mother about Auntie Helen's brain tumor but decided it was not the best time to have one subject lead into another. I'm exhausted. So after declining my mother's offers of tea, instant coffee, and orange juice, I stand up and yawn. "I'm going to bed," I say. Phil offers my mother a good-night kiss, which she cautiously accepts with a stiff upturned cheek. And at last we have escaped to our room.

"Did you bring your toothbrush?" my mother calls to us through our closed door. "Brush your teeth already?"

"Got 'em!" Phil calls back. "They're brushed."

"Enough blankets, enough towels?"

"Plenty," he says. He rolls his eyes at me. "Good night!" he calls, and turns off the light. It is quiet for about five seconds.

"Too cold? Heater can be turned up."

"Ma, we're fine," I say with a little too much irritation. And then I say, more gently this time, "Don't worry. Go to bed."

I hold my breath. There is only silence. And finally, I hear her slippers slowly padding down the hallway, each soft shuffle breaking my heart.

(选自 Tan, Amy. *The Kitchen God's Wife*. New York: Vintage Books, 1993: 11-37.)

Questions

1. What are the themes of this novel?
2. Summarize the miserable experiences that the protagonist, the mother Winnie suffered under the oppression of patriarchal system.
3. What are the main functions of food images in *The Kitchen God's Wife*?
4. How does discourse on food reveal every turning point of the protagonist, Winnie's lifetime and move the plot forward?
5. How does discourse on hybrid food relocate the mother, Winnie's identity and reconcile the mother-daughter relation?